CW00520273

Is

Time

For

Shariton

Park

Inside illustrations © Christine M. Walter.

© 2023 Christine M. Walter.

All rights reserved. No part of this book may be reproduced in any form or by any means without permission in writing from the author, Christine M. Walter: email qrissyw@gmail.com. The views expressed herein are the responsibility of the author. All characters in this book are fictitious, and any resemblance to actual persons, living or dead is purely coincidental.

Edited by Lynne Riffenburgh, Alexa Martineau, and Lauri Schoenfeld.

Book cover design by: Eschler Editing

A Time for

Shariton

Park

Christine M. Walter

Dedicated to

my dog, Chewbacca, for sitting by me through

thick and thin until this book was complete.

And to my own Mr. Darcy, Jared, who taught me what love is.

A note from the author...

I don't know about you, but I'm a music lover. I nearly always have a song in my head on repeat when I'm not actively listening to music. Music is a huge part of my life, so naturally it's going to be a part of my storytelling. With that in mind, I've created soundtracks to go along with my novels. Some songs are things she plays or sings, or simply songs that go along with the scenes. Enjoy!

Soundtrack

Paul de Senneville- Spring Waltz (Mariage d'Amour)

Enya - If I Could Be Where You Are

Enya- Orinoco Flow

Enya- Lothlórien

Supercalifragilisticexpialidocious-Disney

Toy Dolls- Spiders in the Dressing Room

Kiki's Delivery Service Theme song

Chopin- Nocturne in C sharp minor OP. posth B 49

Bach- prelude in C major

P.S. I've decided to rate my book using Michelle Penninton's rating system found at https://thewritinggals.com/michelles-clean-and-wholesome-category-content-diagram/

This book is rated at level one. :)

Chapter One

Present Day England, Celeste

Empty. An empty room meant a meaningless life. Right? At least the weight of that word pressed upon my chest with such force it seemed I could never live again. Never be normal. Every room of the four-bedroom flat held nothing but dust, much like how I felt inside. Dusty and alone. I stood at the entry with nothing but a rucksack and a carry-on suitcase. The memories shared between my father and me slapped me in the face. The smell of Papa's aftershave had long since drifted away, and it had only been a few months. How had it happened so fast? Poof. He's gone.

I needed to escape the hole he'd left in my life—a new start.

"A bit bleak, isn't it?" Mr. Moreau, Papa's coworker, stood in the doorway with me. He'd given me a moment to say goodbye, and now it was time to move on.

"Papa always used to say onward and upward. Keep moving," I said. Those words hung without much weight. *Empty.*

"He was the very best of men, Celeste. Best lawyer in all of London, in fact. I will miss working alongside him."

I nodded and turned to face him, away from the memories. "You've seen to all the legal rubbish, then?"

He smiled, "I have. I suppose the party's over downstairs?"

"As much of a farewell party as it could have been," I said, trying to keep my pain from showing.

"You didn't have any friends show up? Did they not get the invite?"

He would pity me if I admitted to him that my only friends were my father's friends. I couldn't let that happen. My only friends my whole life had been my books, art supplies, and piano. "I suspect there was a conflict of interest. No worries, though. I have a phone. They can call me if they want." I took hold of the carry-on and extended the handle.

Mr. Moreau bent to pick up the pack and grunted. "Heavens! What have you got in this pack of yours? Bricks?"

"Nearly. It's my father's coin collection. I couldn't part with it, nor trust it to the movers. So it will go with me until I figure out what to do with it all."

"What else is in here? It's breaking the seams." He lifted it a few times as if doing bicep curls.

"Piano sheet music and Jane Austen's *Sense and Sensibility*. And my sketchbook and tablet. I couldn't part with them, either or pack them in a box." I laughed at how he exaggerated lifting it to his shoulder.

"If nothing else, you'll get your exercise by lugging this around." He followed me out of the flat, stood beside me in the hall, and watched me lock the door for the last time. He held his hand out for the key, "I'll be sure to pass this on for you. The sale is complete, so nothing is tying you down now. You're free to run for a time, but don't forget to live. Find yourself, girl. And don't worry about your piano. I'll keep it tuned and in tip top shape for your return."

"Thank you," I said and kissed his cheek.

He smiled and rubbed a hand over his balding head. "Where are you going from here?"

"That is the question of the day, isn't it?" I turned and started for the lift to take us to the main floor. "I think I'll spend some time in a B and B where my parents once used to stay. After that, maybe Paris. I'd like to study some artwork there."

"Sounds like a plan. Remember your old and decaying friend back in boring ol' London when you become a famous painter."

I laughed. "That's not likely to happen."

His smiling eyes turned somber. "It's good to hear you can still laugh, my dear. His passing was sudden and far too soon for his age." The lift door opened, and we stepped inside. We descended, and the last conversation with my father returned to me, a memory of monumental proportions I'd never forget. He had called me while I meandered through the Basilica of Santa Croce in Florence, Italy. I remembered precisely where I was, standing among the carved tombs of those who were buried below the marble floors. He had asked me to attend a gala, which I fought against attending. I relented just before I heard a sound on his end of the line, a sound I later learned was his car crumbling into something almost unrecognizable. That event ended the study abroad trip I'd saved for and planned for more than two years.

I shook myself from the continuous recollection of that day and stepped out of the lift into the lobby.

"I took the liberty of calling you a cab to take you to the train station," Mr. Moreau said.

"I could have easily taken the Tube," I answered, but I felt grateful nonetheless.

"After carrying this pack for you, I'm glad I did." He grunted when he handed it over. "Heavens girl, how many coins did your father collect?"

"Dozens upon dozens. Some large. Some are no bigger than my thumbnail. Thank you for carrying them for me and for everything you've done. You were a good friend to my father, and I know he would say so if he were here." I gave him one last hug and stepped into the waiting cab. He waved goodbye until the taxi turned the corner. *He and his wife might be the only ones to miss me when I'm gone. What a sobering thought.*

I boarded the train at King's Cross station, settling into a seat and listening to my MP3 player. Bored of watching the familiar buildings fly by my window, I opened my rucksack and rifled through it restlessly. I dug past my piano sheet music, sketchbook, and personal toiletry bag. Under a lightweight cardigan, I found my father's boxes of coins, which had migrated to the bottom of the sack.

A few of the boxes contained new silver coins, while even more held solid gold coins, just one costing nearly a thousand pounds. These served as my father's backup plan in case the banks fell through. A little excessive, but that was Papa. He'd bought boxes containing dozens each, leaving me with thousands upon thousands of pounds' worth. The remaining coins he had collected painstakingly over the course of his lifetime. They held great value and were quite old, one even dating back to the end of the Roman Empire. Those I could never part with. I would entrust my father's collection to no one else, even if it meant stupidly traveling with them.

Once I figured out where I was going, they would be put into a lock box for safekeeping.

I pulled the cardigan out and put it on over my sleeveless dress, noticing the wrinkles and wishing I hadn't stuffed it into the bag. The train slowed, I pulled my cell out and called the familiar bed and breakfast near Thetford Forest Park to make a reservation. I left a message and hoped someone would return my call before I arrived at their doorstep.

Maybe I should have planned ahead.

The late afternoon sun shone through the clouds when the train pulled to the Cambridge station. I planned to take a bus from here to my parents' first vacation spot. To keep my mother's memory alive, my father took me there nearly every year before he passed. I knew how he felt. I wanted to keep *his* memory alive. The pull to return grew as I boarded the bus. I leaned against the window, watching trees and houses blur by. After a while, I grabbed the well-worn Jane Austen novel from my pack and read the familiar story.

Stories were what I could trust to lose myself in. Fictional men seemed much better than the boys I'd grown up with. Too many times, I'd been either ignored or bullied. As time passed I figured out what the universe had been trying to tell me: Men weren't interested in frizzy-haired book nerds. They wanted girls who could flirt and were posh. I couldn't manage to do any of those things. But I could read to get my romantic fix. So I did, almost constantly.

We weren't too far out of Ely when the bus driver announced a detour to bypass an accident ahead on the motorway. We exited and continued on a country lane.

Not but a few minutes went by when the bus jerked at the sound of a loud bang. My head knocked against the window while the driver tried to control the metal beast. The bus abruptly stopped taking up the entirety of the road. Everyone around me talked adamantly with one another. The driver hurried out of the bus and stepped back inside, grumbling a moment later.

A woman in front of me leaned over to her husband, "What did he say, dear?" her American accent pegged her as a tourist.

"I think we have a flat tire," the husband replied.

Chapter Two

1808 England, Charles

"Mr. Elsegood?"

My attention sharpened at the ignorant use of my name. I tried not to turn and scowl at the gossipmongers behind me.

The conversation continued. "Oh, no! He is a Lord. Charles Elsegood, Lord Shariton, Viscount of Shariton Park, Cambridgeshire, and Shariton Hall of London, in fact. Close your mouth, my dear. You look like a codfish. You should take more care. . ." The conversation drifted away and blended in with those around. Whoever it might have been, I was relieved that at least one of them had some sense.

A couple bumped into me, forcing me to step to the left, closer to the settee bordering the ballroom. A woman occupying the seat glanced up at me and gave a slight nod, then returned to her conversation with the lady beside her. My eyes moved with the lazy swish of her feathered fan, wishing I might pluck it from her hand and use it to relieve myself from the room's temperature. Even with the windows fully open to the night air, the lack of an early summer breeze did nothing for the mass of body heat that drifted around the room from the hundreds that mingled.

I despise dances.

My mind wandered to the country, my pleasantly cool library, and my favorite chair. From there, I couldn't help but ponder the prices I might fetch for the crops I would harvest this fall. My excellent herd of cattle would—

"Ah! Here you are, Lord Shariton. Dreaming up some scheme for a chance at a promenade with my daughter, no doubt." Mrs. Weston's presence gave me no satisfaction.

"Mrs. Weston," I said in acknowledgment.

Her large teeth protruded from her lips when she smiled. "Oh, you do look positively dull, Lord Shariton. You may wish to thank me once you hear what I have to tell, I daresay." She leaned in with a hand on my arm. "I hear the library has a nice breeze this time of day. I have seen several people enjoying the air from that side of the building, and I do believe Mr. Durand displays a new Vien painting above the mantle."

My brow rose with interest, "A Joseph Vien?"

"Yes, I believe so."

"Thank you, Mrs. Weston." I nodded and made my way to the opposite end of the room, glad for an excuse to step out of the ballroom. I glanced at my sister dancing the quadrille. *Ruth has friends to attend to her in my absence. I need not worry over her.*

I left the room and headed toward the library.

With luck I found the library to be vacant, and the windows were indeed open. The painting, however, did not resemble a Vien. That Mrs. Weston should think it a Joseph Vien proved her to be unfamiliar with the arts—or a storyteller. Considering the quiet, cool room far superior to the crowded ballroom, I made myself comfortable in the darkest

7

corner. The wingback chair felt well used. Perhaps it was Mr. Durand's favorite chair when he came to town for the Season. I found the chair to my liking, facing the open window, away from the door.

I had only a moment to take in the moonlit scenery outside before the door creaked open. The soft footsteps could only belong to a lady. The cloth from her gown rustled at her movement into the room.

"Lord Shariton?" the voice of Miss Weston, the very eligible and dimwitted daughter of Mrs. Weston, grated on my nerves.

I opened my mouth to respond but paused when she spoke again.

"I thought he would be here." Her whisper could only be perceived as disappointment.

She does not know I am here. Best not to clue her in otherwise. I moved not a muscle in the hope she might take her swift leave.

The door creaked again, "Mama, I thought you said he would be here."

Mrs. Weston's voice sounded from the other side of the opened door, growing louder as she entered the room. "He was here. I saw him come!" She clicked her tongue, "Oh, dear. Where could he have gone?"

"What do we do now, Mama?"

"Do not worry. I will search him out, and then you can have your little tête-à-tête. Be sure to be in his arms when I send Mrs. Durand inside."

My lips tightened, and my eyes narrowed. *So they planned to ensnare me into matrimony, did they?*

"By the time the night is over, you will surely be engaged, my dear," Mrs. Weston said in a whispered sing-song voice, then the click of the door behind her ended the conversation. Miss Weston paced about the room, reciting under her breath things she might say to me if I had fallen prey to their scheme.

My desire to stand and make known my outrage against this fiendish arrangement grew stronger by the minute. Knowing that if I did so,

8

I would step right into their ploy for title and wealth, I remained silent.

Of course, I must endure an itch on the nose while forced to hide as I did. I tried to ignore the urge to sneeze. To my great alleviation, Miss Weston was short on patience. Her troubled sigh and boisterous footsteps faded from the room.

My sigh mixed with the night air from the window. Never again would I trust a woman, especially one with a domineering and impertinent mother.

* * *

Present Day England, Celeste

"Listen up, you lot!" the driver called from the front of the bus, "this tin can has a puncture! Another bus has been dispatched and will arrive in a few hours."

Hours! Some of those around me protested indignantly, echoing my inward thoughts. A few gathered up their things and exited. I checked my surroundings and figured I could walk the rest of the way before the next bus arrived.

I began my walk, dragging my rolling carry-on behind me and keeping a tight hold of my rucksack. I glanced back at the group gathered around the bus, discussing whether to walk or wait. It appeared I was the only one choosing to walk.

I followed the road until I came to a narrow lane through the trees. A road closure sign was posted for motor cars, but not to those on foot, so I decided to press on. Several minutes later, I looked behind me again at the sound of a dove's coo. *Oh, dear.* Only one man followed. No one else was in sight.

His twitchy behavior made me nervous as his eyes fixed on me.

The man appeared as if he hadn't bathed in weeks and the hollow look in his eye gave me misgivings. His shabby hair stuck out from his cap, and the tattoos I'd noticed earlier depicted violent creatures writhing up his bare arms. He was exactly the kind of person you wouldn't want to be traveling alone with on a quiet road. I turned back and held tightly to the rucksack straps on my shoulders, thinking hard and fast.

I had taken kickboxing and self-defense classes several times—per Papa's request—but I was horrible at it. From the man's size, I doubted my ability to defend myself, and I didn't think I could remember what to do. His large arms looked the same size as my upper leg. I picked up my pace. His speed increased as well. He caught me watching him and darted forward in a full run.

He's after me! Sucking in the cool air jolted my body into action. My legs knew better than my frantic mind how to run, for which I was thankful. *Please, someone, drive by!* I plead, then remembered the road was closed. Peering at the forest next to me, I had an idea. *You can out-hike anyone.* The memory of my father's long-ago praise spurred my decision to head for the woods.

Leaving my carry-on behind, I darted sharply to the right and into the woods. The heavy coins and books slapped at my back. I gathered my long summer dress, hiking it to my knees, and leaped over fallen trees and rocks, praying I wouldn't fall. Feelings of gratitude rushed through my mind for my early-morning decision to wear ankle boots instead of sandals. The heavy pack slowed me, but I pressed on. The stranger's clumsy footfalls over the forest floor gave me the push I needed to outrun him. I didn't dare look back to see how close he was.

Noticing a large boulder up ahead, I dropped over the side and paused to listen. I could hear rustling through the brush faintly in the distance. *I'm losing him!* Cautiously, I raised my head over the top of the boulder. He wasn't in sight, but I could still hear him. The snaps of twigs were getting closer. My eyes darted about, searching for a hiding place, and I noticed a very large tree with the strangest roots I'd ever seen. One of the twisted roots made an arch big enough for someone to pass through. On the other side, it held a small hiding place. Without another thought, I hurried through the arch and into the tree's roots, ignoring the cobwebs and the rough bark that pricked at my clothes.

A few minutes passed, and the man came into view. Holding my breath, I watched him trample about. He disappeared. As in, he really disappeared. I blinked. *He's gone!* It reminded me of something I'd seen on TV when someone walks behind a lamppost or a tree and never appears on the other side. He was visible through that arch, and then not. *Poof. Gone. Impossible!* I bit my lip and tried not to make a sound while I waited. Holding my cries of fear inside had started a headache, and thinking about the strange way he had disappeared didn't help. It terrified me to have him chasing me, but seeing him vanish into thin air wasn't reassuring.

Am I in the Twilight Zone? My breath caught when he abruptly reappeared into view through the arch and trudged slowly back toward the road. I moved to the side of the arch and straightened to sit taller. He disappeared once again. I quickly lowered my head and saw him again through the archway, like a picture frame into another world. *What kind of trick is this?* Thoughts of ancient witches wandering the forest rushed into my mind, or was it possibly aliens creating a time warp? *This place is creepy.* I backed away from the tree and dared not go through it again, afraid of what might happen.

I knew there would be a road somewhere ahead of me at some point, so I continued onward, away from the direction the man headed. With each step or two, I looked back, to ensure he hadn't changed his direction. I soon figured he had given up and was long gone.

I slid my rucksack from my shoulders and rubbed where the straps pulled. I retrieved my phone from the side pocket. It turned on just fine, but I had no service. I dialed the number for the police, hoping the emergency number might allow me to make a call.

Nothing.

After I had walked for thirty minutes, trying every two minutes to get through on my cell, I noticed the air felt warmer than it should be for September. I pulled my cardigan off and tied it to my rucksack. The ground was fairly wet, as if it had just rained. As usual for this soggy country, the overcast sky threatened to rain again.

Onward I traveled until I came to a small hill, wondering why I hadn't come across a road. Completely out of ideas and seeing no other way around, I headed up. I had only climbed halfway when I realized my mistake. The mud was so deep and thick that it pulled my short boots and socks off my feet. When I tried to yank them free, I only managed to get myself muddier. Hot, angry tears fell down my cheeks, and I fought with my shoes.

"Fine. I'll go barefoot and buy another pair!" I shouted to no one.

Now barefoot, I continued up the short hill, breathing deeply at the top. The land below began at a gradual decline, then looked as if it might drop off, but only a few feet. I moved slower now that I had no shoes, careful not to hurt my feet. At the bottom, I found a small stream and washed my arms and hands.

My clothes were hopelessly caked in mud—ruined—so I sat beside the water and debated with myself. The only thing to do was continue. The sooner I arrived at any sort of habitation, the sooner I could get cleaned up.

Night came faster than expected, and my worry increased, for I'd not come across a road, a farm, or a house. Surely someone lived nearby. I checked my phone yet again. Still no service. My thoughts were consumed with longing for a warm room and a comfortable bed.

My stomach growled, and my shoulders ached with the bag's weight hanging on my back. I lifted my leg to step over a log, and my cardigan got caught, tipping me off balance. I turned to grab hold of the branch but fell backward instead. The ground didn't meet me when it should have. My panicked scream ended abruptly when my body hit. I rolled down a hill covered in vegetation. Stars flashed in my vision when my head hit something hard and cold. The impact jarred my neck and made my teeth chomp the inside of my cheek. Moaning, I sat up and looked back up the hill I'd rolled down then glanced around me. I'd fallen onto an unpaved road that stretched into the darkened trees.

My fingers touched my hairline and came away wet and sticky. I blinked at my fingers before my face. *Blood.* I held up four hands and twenty fingers, and they moved about as if waving to me. Tears pricked my eyes. This was not how I wished my day or life to end.

Chapter Three

1808 England, Charles

I listened to the trotting of my horse and rode through the moonlight, congratulating myself on being alone. I had left London in a hurry to get away from the hordes of debutantes and their overly enthusiastic mothers—Miss Weston and her mother, to be precise. As I was a young, eligible viscount, the women would jump at the chance of marriage with me. Thankfully I had become very good at dodging them.

My horse, Apollo, increased his speed, which drew my attention. I patted him and chuckled. "My, you are eager to return home. You may even hate London as much as I do, old boy."

A sound floated through the trees. I pulled on the reins to stop. For a moment, I thought I'd imagined the high-pitched scream. I leaned forward in my saddle, listening intently, and heard a moan come from up ahead. Instinctively, I reached for my musket and moved Apollo into motion.

As I continued ahead, I came across a young woman sitting at the side of the road. Her wild hair and dress were covered in mud. I glanced at her sodden, unstockinged legs and averted my eyes back to her head.

In the moonlight, her eyes were large with fear and surprise. For a moment, her mouth gaped before she shook her head and whispered something to herself. A dark bloodstain on her forehead glistened in the moonlight that shone down.

"You are in distress!" I called to her and dismounted. I knelt by her side and held out my hand. "Can I be of service to you?"

She furrowed her brow and regarded me, then reached for her head and said in a small voice, "I've only hit my head. No need to fuss."

From those few words and how she held her head high and her shoulders back, I gathered she was above the common ranks. Her words were too clear and perfect for her to be otherwise. "Where did you come from?" I searched the surroundings, hoping to discover how she came to be alone.

She studied me with narrowed eyes. "You wouldn't happen to have a mobile phone, would you? Mine's useless."

"My apologies, I do not understand you. I believe you have taken quite a blow to the head."

Her brow creased a bit more. "Why are you dressed like that? Did I interrupt a movie scene?" her eyes darted about anxiously.

"Movie scene? Forgive me, but you are talking nonsense. As for my attire, it is obviously suitable fashion for traveling." I waved at my overcoat, then adjusted my cravat, wanting to impress upon her that she was in the presence of a gentleman, so as to ease her fragile mind. Peculiarly, at my words, she seemed to panic.

Her eyes widened, and she leaned away. "Where am I?"

"You are near Shariton Park." I reached for her head to inspect her wound, but she pulled away.

"Oh, yes. That's the place that was bombed in World War II." Her voice was soft as if she spoke only to herself.

Now I knew she had hit her head hard. Raving about some world war that had never happened—she was definitely unwell. "I do not know which war you are referring to unless you mean the war with Napoleon."

The moonlight reflected in her wide eyes. "What do you mean?" She covered her mouth with both hands and shook her head. Her rapid breathing caused her shoulders to rise and fall. "Just my luck. He's delusional," she said under her breath, then asked more loudly, "What date do you *think* it is?"

The worry and confusion in her eyes concerned me. "You have taken quite a spill, miss. Please allow me to take you to Shariton, where I can have you looked after." I helped her to her feet. She swayed where she stood. I reached for the strange sack she carried on her back, and she moved away. "Please, allow me to take that—I can tie it to my horse if you wish."

She shook her head. "I'll carry it."

"You are not well. Please, allow me—" I leaned closer to help her.

"No!" she stepped away again and nearly fell, as though she were drunk.

Devil, take it, woman! Why is she being so difficult? I am a gentleman, not some ruffian. I reached out for her arm and held her up. Without giving her a chance to push away, I bent over, picked her up, and cradled her in my arms. "If you will not allow me to take your sack, then let me carry you to my horse. I fear you are not in your right mind."

"You don't need to carry me," she pushed against my chest. Fortunately, we reached my horse before she could topple out of my arms. I lifted her and breathed in her scent. She smelled like she was bathed in a sweet aroma mixed with the smell of dirt. No commoner smelled this good.

* * *

1808 England, Celeste

I tried to wrap my sore brain around what had happened. My head-ache increased with each bounce atop the horse. The trees moved to-and-fro as though the world danced. The man's arms held me in place while we moved down the dirt road. I held my rucksack in my lap and tried to keep in the saddle. Sitting sideways on a horse wasn't ideal, but it *was* a far cry better than straddling it in a dress. Although, I felt that at any moment I might slip off. I'd never ridden a horse before and knew I was going about it all wrong.

The image of the man disappearing in the forest through the tree's root kept repeating itself in my mind. Something odd had happened tonight. Something was strange about the whole thing, though I didn't know what. "Please, tell me . . . er . . . sir, what year is it?" I asked.

"We are in the eighteen hundred and eighth year of our Lord." He looked down at me with brows creased.

I had meant to laugh, but it came out more like a grunted snort. "This is absurd. I must have . . ." I groaned and rubbed my head. *Eighteen hundred and eight?* My mind raced. *Can I truly be in the past?* It might be possible—after all, I'd watched a man disappear before my eyes. And this man acted as though he'd never heard of World War II and he didn't know what I meant when I asked about movies and cell phones. *This is all impossible.*

"How did you come to be there, injured and without an escort?"

If I was really in the past, then I had better be careful how I acted and what I said, but then again, I would be playing into his joke. If it were a joke. I chose my words carefully, "We broke down and . . ." The thought came to me—act as though I have amnesia. "I don't remember.

17

I think someone was chasing me . . . I don't remember," I repeated. Part of it was true, at least.

"Do you remember your name?"

"Er . . . Celeste."

"Well, it would not be fitting to call you by your given name. What is your father's name?"

I swallowed hard. What would happen if he found out I was alone? I didn't answer right away. He must've thought I couldn't remember, for he interrupted my thoughts again.

"Well, if Celeste is all you can remember, then I will be forced to use your given name until your memory returns."

"I apologize. I don't remember." I turned my attention back to the road. I'd be forced to knock his block off if he was joking, because this wasn't a funny game to play on someone with a head injury.

We had yet to ride far when, in the moonlight, I could see the forest open up to one of the grandest estates around, one that reminded me of the Burghley House I'd once toured. The building before me greeted me with stone arches still intact. The windows, aglow with warm candlelight, were surrounded by carved stone. I remember coming here before when I was a child. Except the bombs had partially blown away the estate. It could be repaired, but the cost was too great for the family who owned it. It sat half abandoned as a reminder of what was. Only the caretaker remained, living at one end of the building. The Shariton Park that sat before me now was indeed beautiful and large and . . . in one piece—not a stone blackened, scarred, or out of place. It looked larger than I recalled.

This was all wrong. I knew for a fact that it hadn't been rebuilt—the ruined building had been in the news not long ago—but here it sat before me, whole and perfect. My breath caught as the realization hit me. *This place is real!* The corners of my vision darkened, and the trees around me spun and blurred until everything went black.

* * *

Charles

"Celeste?" I called to her and patted her cheeks softly. She moaned, and her head rolled back. I pulled her closer to my chest and hurried my horse through the front gates. When we arrived at the front door, my stable hand, John, arrived to help.

"My lord, what has happened?" John asked.

"I found this young lady in the woods nearby. She is injured." John took the girl's pack and dropped it to the ground, then helped her down from the horse. Once I dismounted, I took her from him and cradled her. Her weight was lighter without the strange shoulder bag. The estate doors flew open, and several of the servants appeared. I rushed to explain what had happened, and all I knew of this mysterious woman to those who came to assist. They followed me up the stairs, taking the orders I gave for fresh water, clean towels, and a doctor to be called.

"See to it that her sack is brought to her room." At my words, she awoke and looked about.

"What's happened? Where am I?" She tried to push herself out of my arms, creating great difficulty to keep us sure footed. She was a diminutive thing, so her strength took me by surprise. I rushed to set her on her feet.

"You fainted," I said.

She gazed about and stared at my servants who gathered around. "Candles?" Her eyes went wide, then rolled to the back of her head again.

I picked her back up and carried her to a room set aside for guests, far from my own. I feared having her too close to my sleeping chambers.

After all, she might be a lunatic.

* * *

Celeste

Heavy fabric rustling woke me, an unbearable light assaulted my eyes. I moved my limbs under the covers and stretched. The memory of last night rushed back to me. My run through the woods. A fall ending with a good thump on the head. A man on a horse, and a doctor at my side in this same bed. My breath quickened. *I'm in a manor house, of which should not exist in its entirety.*

Pale blue plastered walls and ceiling were beautifully decorated, and enormous gold filigree frames hung on each wall, displaying centuries-old paintings. The crown molding alone could belong in the grandest of palaces. Decorative plaster made an ornate design across a domed ceiling, and the painted window cast shadows across it all. A dark-stained wood vanity with intricately carved designs sat close to the window where a woman stood.

"Wow," I sat up quickly, then regretted my actions and reached for my bandaged head.

"Stay down, miss. I imagine your 'ead must be pounding something frightful." The young girl moved to the end of the bed. She wore a plain gray nineteenth-century dress with an apron around her waist.

"Where am I?" my voice sounded harsh.

"You are at Shariton Park, miss," she replied. "Lord Shariton has been asking about you. You have given us all a fright."

A dull ache pulsed through my head.

"'Twas only a scratch, miss. I am sure we can take the dressing off now." She stepped nearer and helped remove the bandage from my head. She smiled at me after looking at the wound. "It looks betta' now, miss. Your hair will hide any mark it might leave."

"What year is it?" *Oh, please let this all be a joke.*

"We are in the year of our Lord eighteen 'undred and eight, miss." She tilted her head with questions in her gaze. "Are you still needing rest, miss?"

I shook my head. If I were still in my own time, all of these people would have to be in on the joke. From what I'd observed last night, how everyone dressed and carried candlesticks around, I believed I must have traveled somehow to the past. I shook my head, and my heartbeat increased with every thought. *This is impossible. How am I ever to get back?*

My eyes dropped to a white nightgown I wore. I hugged myself and felt the heat rush to my ears and cheeks. "Where's my dress?"

Her smile fell. "'Tis gettin' cleaned." She glanced away, then back at me, as if trying to decide to say something. "I am sorry, miss . . . but where was your . . . underclothes?"

"My underclothes?"

"You were missing your short stays, waist slip . . . all of it." She gave me a strange look.

Is this really happening? This is happening! "They were wet and muddy." I didn't have a good explanation as to why I wasn't wearing traditional nineteenth-century undergarments. I wondered what they thought of my modern underwear.

"I have to ask . . . did something happen to you in the woods?"

I scrunched my nose and lifted one side of my upper lip, not sure what she could mean.

"Did a man . . ." she peered at the floor and shuffled her foot, "Ya know . . ."

My eyes widened when I realized what she was asking, "Goodness, no! I'd die if that ever happened."

21

She let out a heavy breath. "'Tis a relief. The doctor came to the same conclusion. Are you feeling well enough to bathe?"

The doctor came to the same conclusion . . . Yikes! I hugged my body.

I hesitated to answer, but nodded and followed her into an adjoining room where a large oak wardrobe with three panels of doors and two rows of drawers sat against one wall. An old metal bathtub with four curved legs stood in the middle of the room, filled with water. Before I could think about what would come next, the young woman started pulling my nightgown off and urging me into the water. It's sufficient to say I was completely embarrassed to be washed and waited on. Knowing it would lower my station to excuse her, I let her take care of me. I wouldn't want her to think me common, even if it meant a little discomfort on my end.

The flowery aroma of the oils she rubbed on my shoulders and the warmth of the water soothed my headache and relaxed me.

While I bathed, she informed me that her name was Annabeth. She also said that Miss Ruth Elsegood would be returning today, along with Sir Henry Garrison and his wife Lady Clair Garrison.

"Who's Miss Elsegood?"

"Lord Shariton's sister. She's a delight to be around. You will become fast friends, I am sure."

"Who's Lord Shariton?" I was full of stupid questions.

"Why, 'es the one that brought you here. 'Ave you never 'eard of 'im?"

I wondered momentarily at the difference in his last name compared to his sister's, then remembered that Shariton would be part of his title and Elsegood must be his surname.

"I've never heard of any of them," I responded. She helped me into some nineteenth-century undergarments and explained more about Miss Elsegood. I found the corset better than I expected. I was already self-conscious of the large size of my chest and didn't want to protrude from any dresses they might have me wear, so I squeezed as much as possible into the corset.

"I am surprised ya've not 'eard of my lord. Why Lord Shariton is a viscount and a respected gentleman. Also very eligible." She looked at me with a knowing grin.

I made a noise that was a mixture of a laugh and a snort, then closed my mouth to stop myself. She gaped at me as though she'd thought I'd be excited by the news rather than amused.

"If you're implying that I'd be interested in forming attachments with him, you're mistaken. I'm not ready to be tied down."

"I am sorry about the corset. I know it might be a bit out of fashion, as you are used to short stays, but Ruth had no short stays to spare. I retrieved the corset from the late Lady Elsegood's wardrobe." She motioned for me to sit, then began brushing my hair. "Ya have the most perfect 'ead of hair. It will be easy to do. I need not curl it."

Perfect head of hair? She must be joking. It curled and frizzed in the worst way. Even if I had a nice head of hair, I wasn't sure I'd have any left after her combing. Next time I bathed, I would have to sneak my hygiene bag in with me—conditioner was a must with my hair.

I touched the red scab along my hairline, glad it wasn't worse than it felt.

She pulled back pieces of my dark hair, pinning it into loops and leaving some ringlets to hang down. The front she left free, causing me to blow strands from my face. "The best way to do this is to cut some of this in front. The ringlets will naturally frame your face and give ya the most becoming look ya could 'ave," she said.

I raised an eyebrow at her, hesitating. "It will only go frizzy."

"Oh, we can use some oils to make it look soft and lovely. Oh, please let me cut it." She held her hands together and waited for my response.

I nodded, giving in. "Only a little." A haircut was the least of my worries at the moment. Right now, my mind was more preoccupied with how I could return to my own time, if I had traveled to the past. I still couldn't quite believe it.

Funny, here I sat in the time and place I'd always dreamed of, and all I could do was think about how to get back. I'd read every Jane Austen novel and watched each version of the movie based on her works. I knew how things worked in society. If they discovered I was a nobody, then I'd be expected to find my way financially. For the time being, I must act like a lady.

Annabeth clapped her hands and bounced before helping me into my muslin gown. "You truly are a beauty, miss. Have you had your chance for a Season in London?"

I decided to continue with the amnesia excuse. "I don't know."

Her face fell into a frown. "You do not know?" her hand went to her mouth, "Oh, our lordship did say you might not remember. Can you remember your name?"

I shook my head. "Only my first name, Celeste." When I saw myself in the mirror, I was surprised at the person peering back. My hair looked like it was meant to be pinned up and curled around my face. The corset caused me to stand even taller than usual and gave me the appearance of a confident lady for that brief moment—until I stared into my eyes and saw the uncertainty. My line of sight dropped, then caught the reflection of my rucksack by the side of the bed. My breath caught, and I went to it. "Did anyone look inside this?" I asked, trying not to look too frantic.

"No, miss. Lord Shariton did say ya were protective of your sack, so he had it brought 'ere last night."

I sighed and let my muscles relax.

"Are you ready to go down to breakfast? I believe Lord Shariton is still waitin' to see ya."

My heart raced. *What do I do? What do I say?* "Could you give me a minute alone first?"

She nodded and left the room.

I opened my rucksack and shuffled through it to ensure all its contents remained. The tension in my shoulders eased when I found everything was accounted for, but the uneasiness returned when the realization came upon me: what might these things look like to someone from the past? A plastic bag of shampoos, lotions, lip gloss, razors, feminine products—two piano books with photographs and dates—cash and coins inscribed with future dates. My MP3 player and tablet alone would indeed cause a commotion.

I dumped everything onto a small, folded blanket at the end of my bed, then pulled the smaller items out of the pockets. The only things I set aside were my small sketchbook with pencils and my lip gloss. Surely the leather-bound sketchbook would fit in. My lip gloss was small enough to hide. I put everything else back in the pack and wrapped the blanket around it, scouring the room in search of a hiding spot. A trunk sat at the end of the bed, but I thought it was too obvious a choice. Under the bed? No. Inside the wardrobe, I found an empty drawer; of course, this would be obvious, but I felt I had no other choice. I left my pencils and sketchbook on the end of the bed. My lip gloss went into my dress after I put a little on my lips.

My thoughts turned to breakfast where I would have to face the lord of this elaborate joke or, possibly, the lord of the far-off time of my dreams. I took another deep breath, thinking about all the stories from Jane Austen, trying to remember the rules of etiquette in her day. *Good gracious. Jane Austen is alive right now!* Knowing that fact caused me to giggle. *I'm actually living in the Regency era!* My heart quickened, and I hurried to the door.

Hold on.

Don't get carried away. This might all be a dream.

I had expected to see a hallway, but I found myself looking into a small sitting room. *Is this my own personal sitting room?* I studied the room while I crossed it. It appeared similar to my bedchamber.

When I opened the door, I stopped and examined the grand hallway, searching for any sign of electricity. The hall was beautifully decorated with crown molding at every corner and window. It was better than I had imagined it could be. Paintings lined the walls, from the ceiling to just above the floor, with no signs of modern living anywhere—no switch or plug, only paintings. I heard footsteps just before Annabeth hurrying toward me.

"Oh, you are ready, miss. Come along and I will show you to the breakfast room."

I followed her down a flight of stairs to a room with a table, chairs, and sofas. The room was charming, but I didn't have time to enjoy the decor, for Lord Shariton sat at the table. My stomach turned, and my legs felt weak as the importance of the moment fell upon me. All the excitement of being here vanished, and anxiety flooded in.

Lord Shariton sat reading a newspaper. I stepped forward hesitantly, not knowing if I should make my presence known or wait for him to notice me. *Should I walk in?*

I watched him for a moment, wondering what to do. From what I could see of his face, partially hidden behind the paper, he appeared to be about ten years older than me, and handsome, to boot. His brown, short hair was combed to sit long on top, and it swept toward his high cheekbones. His cravat and collar tucked under his chin, almost hiding it completely. He looked important, the kind of person you wouldn't want to disturb. I started to back out of the room, when I heard the paper rustle.

Chapter Four

Charles

I caught movement from the corner of my eye and moved the paper from my view. A young woman stood in the doorway with her back to me. Her shoulders were raised to her ears, as if she'd been caught. *I must speak with the servants once again. They should have announced the young lady at the door.*

"Good morning, Celeste." I stood, waited until she turned, and then greeted her with a slight bow. Her green eyes caught me off guard. I had considered her to be mildly attractive last night, but upon seeing her looking presentable and no longer covered in earth, I was startled into silence. She was a natural beauty. Her young skin, clean and clear . . . and her eyes! They were big and full of lashes. Her beauty unnerved me.

It took me a moment to gather my wits and gesture toward the chair across from me. "Please, have a seat and I shall gather food for you from the sideboard."

She moved without a sound or a rustle to her seat. "Thank you . . . sir," said in a whisper.

My ears perked. My lord or your lordship, I was used to, never sir. After I gathered her a plate of food and set it before her, I sat and tried to keep my gaze from her, for she was staring at me intently. She blinked, shook her head as though dislodging a thought, and turned toward the window. I watched her for a moment while she gingerly ate the food. How she held herself again told me she was no commoner—but who could she be?

"How is your head?"

She turned and peered straight at me, "Better, thank you."

My heart hammered in my chest. *Why do I feel so nervous?* "Do you remember what happened to you last night?"

She shook her head. "Not all . . . at least, not before you found me."

"You remember nothing before?" I asked, pressing for more answers.

"Only that our bus—carriage—broke down and . . . I was running for quite some time from someone . . . I don't remember who." She glanced away, not meeting my eye.

"Do you remember your father's name?"

She looked down, and her voice became so soft that I barely caught her reply as she murmured that she had not. I followed her eyes to her hands and noticed they were small, soft, and delicate. On her right hand, she twisted a rather intricate ring full of diamonds. Another sign she was born of more noble blood.

"What about any relations?"

"No."

"Do you remember where you came from?" Irritation was beginning to prick at my thoughts, and I tried not to narrow my brow and frown at her.

"No, sir," she said, looking out the window. I caught the light glisten of tears pooling in her lashes. A sudden urge to make them disappear overtook me. I resisted. I wanted answers more than I wanted to please her.

"Well, I am at a loss to know what to do for you. You do not know your full name, where you came from, or whose care you are under." I breathed out a gush of air. She turned her dark eyes back to me and blinked. A tear fell, and she wiped it away.

"I'm sorry. I don't wish to be a burden to you."

I was relieved by her reaction. This might be an encouraging sign. "You will not be a burden, so you must not think on it," I said, hoping she could see that I meant what I said. "We will wait and hope that in time, your memories will return. In the meantime, you are welcome to stay. How do you like Annabeth?"

"She's very kind," she replied, with only a hint of a smile.

"Good, she is at your disposal for the duration of your stay. My sister, Miss Elsegood, will be joining us. I trust Annabeth has already told you?"

She nodded without taking her eyes off me.

"I hope you will find a friend in her. If you will excuse me, I have business to attend to. Enjoy the grounds if you like, or you can wait for someone to show you the house."

I breathed heavily when I left the room, relieved to be away from her gaze. One thing was certain if she had come here with plans to woo me into matrimony, she did not let on that this was her intention. It seemed—for now—that she was safe.

At least, I hope so.

* * *

29

Celeste

My breath rushed from my lungs when Lord Shariton left. *I can't believe I cried in front of him. Ugh! Why did my emotions have to surface at that moment?* I was glad, though, that he didn't force me into saying more than I had. I wanted to ask if there was any way I could get back to the road where he found me, but that would've been foolish. What kind of gentleman would escort a young lady out into the woods and leave her to wander, not knowing where she was going? It wouldn't be logical.

I let a smile slip at the thought of the slight cleft in his chin and his broad shoulders. *No. He's too old. More than two hundred years older than me!*

I sat, waiting to see if my appetite would return. When it didn't, I stood and walked around the grand room to admire the paintings on the walls. I shifted and wiggle in my corset. There was an itch right underneath; no matter how I tried, I couldn't satisfy it. *This will drive me bonkers!*

I fidgeted out of the room, and made my way past the grand staircase and down a hall. When a servant came out of a room, I asked her where I could find the garden door. She directed me to a door at the back of the estate beyond a greenhouse.

My breath caught when I stood atop the stone steps, entranced by my surroundings. Great groupings of trees were scattered about the grounds. Neatly trimmed hedges made a perfect labyrinth with a gravel path leading into it. Beyond the hedges sat a green field that gradually rose to a small hill, and a breeze moved through a thick forest, causing the branches to sway to and fro. A sweet, flowery scent tickled my senses, causing me to take deep breaths through my nose. I was in love.

A giggle rose inside me, and I hurried down the gravel path. Tipping my head back toward the sun, I breathed deeply while I walked, happily strolling through the maze of hedges. I had always dreamed of doing exactly this—even in regency clothes.

* * *

Charles

Upon returning to the house, I found that Henry, Lady Garrison, and Ruth had arrived.

"Charles, my dear brother," Ruth held her hand out for me and I took it and kissed her cheek.

"Ruth, I am glad you have returned in good order." I nodded at Lady Garrison, then at her husband, Henry. "I have something of importance to say to you all. I hope I will not delay your time of rest before dinner."

"What is it, Charles?" Henry asked.

"On my way home last night, I came across a young woman. She was abandoned and injured."

"Upon my soul!" Lady Garrison's shocked expression matched those around her.

"Was she seriously injured?" Ruth asked.

"No, she merely received a bump on the head, but she does not remember anything about her life before now."

Lady Garrison gasped.

"You are jesting, brother." Ruth's blue eyes were large with worry.

"I am afraid not, Ruth. I am looking to you to befriend her. Perhaps, you can help her stimulate her memory."

She straightened and nodded.

"Do you not know anything about her?" Henry asked.

"I do not know much, but I believe her to be a noblewoman by how she speaks and presents herself." I paused and watched Ruth rub her head and yawn. "Forgive me. You must be spent after your long journey. Ladies, rest well." I turned, nodding in the direction of the drawing room. "Henry, may I speak to you for a moment?"

"Of course." Henry followed me into the drawing-room, and the ladies went to their rooms, whispering with their heads bent toward each other.

"Henry, I must impose on you a bit longer and ask you to stay. I am not unsure how long it will take for her memories to return, so I may need your assistance. Also, it would be more convenient to have more people around."

"Of course, we will stay as long as you need us."

"Much obliged."

"Was she. . . did any rogue of a man have his way with her in the woods?"

"No. Annabeth has reassured me on that account." I felt my ears warm. I dared not mention what Annabeth relayed of the state of her underthings.

"That is a relief, I must say. Does she know her name?"

"Celeste. She does not know her surname nor any relations she might have." I watched Henry's reaction of bewilderment, his eyes nearly popping from his head.

"How can one remember their given name and not their surname?" he asked.

"My sentiments exactly."

Henry took hold of a chess piece from the table and moved it in his hands. "Do you believe she is holding back information on purpose so she can enjoy the luxury of your hospitality?"

"That is something I would like to know."

"Only time will tell," he replied.

Chapter Five

Celeste

"This gown is lovely, is it not?" Annabeth asked, holding the gown out in front of me.

I felt a giggle well within me when my eyes took in the fine, nineteenth-century gown. I pushed down my excitement by clearing my throat and biting both my lips. *I feel like a princess!* I nodded.

"Miss Ruth has given it to ya for your use. She said she is able to buy more gowns in town, so she no longer needs it."

"She's so kind." I forced the words out, not knowing what to think. Was Ruth the kind of person to wave her charity in my face? *I sure hope not.*

Annabeth helped me into the gown and made some touch-ups to my hair. I pulled on the top of the dress, trying to position it a little higher. I wasn't used to wearing my clothing low in front. I was more the type to wear sweaters and bulky clothes to hide my figure. This gown accentuated it.

Annabeth noticed my discomfort, "Is there somethin' wrong?"

"Do you think it's . . ." I tugged it down again.

"You will be fine, miss."

I watched her work her magic to make my curls bunch together so they didn't frizz. "Do you like being a lady's maid?" Curiosity filled my mind about what a servant's life was like. I'd seen quite a few working and hurrying about the estate. Each time I caught sight of one, they would scurry away before I could voice a greeting. Earlier, I had to chase after one young servant and ask the way back to my room.

"I am not a lady's maid, I am a 'ousemaid, and I am very fortunate to be working 'ere at Shariton. It is me 'ome," she said.

"Doesn't it bother you to wait on everyone else? Wouldn't you like to live a different life?"

"What otha' kind of life is there to live for someone like me?" she asked, as though she already knew the answer. "Most people do not get a chance like I 'ave. I am the lucky one."

"I would get tired of waiting on others all my life."

Her body stiffened, and her natural smile turned to a frown. "Lord Shariton is kind 'n I would not want to work anywhere else. I am 'appy. We all are."

"I apologize. I didn't mean to offend." *I'm an idiot.*

Her smile returned. "No offense taken, miss," she said and then turned to pick up my day dress. While she wasn't looking, I pulled the lotion out of my wardrobe, squeezed a dollop in my hand, and replaced the bottle. The scent of coconuts filled the air around me. The soap I'd used earlier caused my skin to dry out and drove me bonkers all day.

Annabeth escorted me downstairs to show me to the drawing room. At the door, she bid me to enter before leaving. *Breathe in, one, two, three* . . . I turned my mother's wedding ring around my finger once and tried to clear my nervousness away. I cleared my throat, knowing it wouldn't help the heartburn building inside me, but wishing it would. Anxiety always caused my digestive system to go haywire. Here I was, having my first dining experience in a grand mansion in the time of Jane Austen. I should be thrilled, but all I wanted to do was run from this place and these people. How could I continue to lie and pretend like I belonged? Maybe I could make an excuse and skip tonight's dinner. But then I'd have to endure it another night.

Best to get it done and over with.

I breathed in the air around me and held onto my hands to prevent them from shaking. I entered, and let my shoulders drop, resolved to at least appear to be relaxed. The room was empty of people.

A smile built upon my lips when I noticed the piano in the corner. I hadn't seen one in months, not since my father's piano was sold for charity. The familiar warmth I once had at the sight of the instrument faded as memories of the last time I had played for my father tugged at my heart, wearing it thin. That day, side by side before the piano, was one of my last memories with Papa. He asked me to play one last song before we left for the airport, and we chose a jazzy duet we had composed ourselves. Each time we played the tune, it evolved into something new. I would never play that song again. I couldn't.

I walked to the piano, touching the carved wood, and my fingers ached to move up and down the cool ivory keys. Tears pooled in my lashes, and I hurried to wipe them away. I couldn't be found crying when everyone showed up for dinner. *Get a hold of yourself.*

Just then, the door opened, and a young woman about my age stepped in. She had light brown hair with tints of strawberry red framing a round face and bright blue eyes. She smiled at me and curtsied. I almost didn't know what to do before remembering that people curtsied when they met.

I curtsied in return.

"You must be the young woman my brother saved in the woods." She came to me and hugged me, but I could only stand there, stiff as a board. "I am deeply sorry for what happened to you. You must have been terrified."

I half smiled and nodded, not knowing what to say.

"My name is Ruth, and I want you to call me Ruth—no Miss Elsegood or any of that nonsense. We are friends now." She hugged me again.

"Er . . . Thank you, Ruth. My name is Celeste." *So far, so good. I can do introductions.*

Her smile broadened. "You have such a sweet voice. For a moment, I thought you would sound more common. My brother is right in saying you must be from a nobleman's family."

They think I'm the daughter of a nobleman? I didn't get a chance to respond, for two more people arrived. Ruth introduced them as Sir and Lady Garrison, friends of the family. Sir Garrison appeared to be in his thirties, and Lady Garrison in her mid-twenties. Both were shorter than expected. I kept my answers brief, and said as little as possible while the Garrisons peppered me with questions. As the introductions and small talk were ending, Lord Shariton entered.

"My apologies for my tardiness. It could not be helped." He almost let his last word drop when he caught sight of me. There was a look of surprise in his eyes, and his footsteps faltered.

I dropped my head to check my dress and wondered if Annabeth could have been wrong about the low front. My face burned. My attention drifted toward the piano, and I avoided eye contact. *Oh, please let the candlelight be dim enough to hide my blush.* The silence didn't last long, as someone announced dinner was ready.

"Charles, my dear brother, as this is not a fashionable dinner party and we are among friends, I hope you will escort our guest into dinner, so that she may feel more welcome," Ruth said beside me.

So, his name is Charles. I hadn't dared to ask anyone his first name. Watching Lord Shariton caused a foreign reaction within me at every glance, and it took great effort to will the heat in my face to stop. He nodded at Ruth. He came to me and held out his arm.

I walked with him into the dining room, keeping my eyes ahead. He helped me to a seat, then took his seat at the head of the table directly to my left. From reading Regency books, I knew that one of the seats next to the head of the house was a position of great honor, but for the life of me I couldn't remember if it was on the left or right side that held the importance. Ruth sat directly across from me at his left, and the Garrisons took the seats on our other side, across from each other.

Seconds later, the first course was laid before us containing a variety of meats with several side dishes to choose from. Their savory aroma filled the room around us and caused my stomach to growl. The footmen passed gravies and sauces around the room in their white wigs and tailcoats. I caught myself before thanking them when I remembered that it wasn't part of a protocol to speak with the help.

Lady Garrison started the conversation. "Celeste, do you like to read?"

To keep with my amnesia story, I answered, "I believe so. I don't remember." In truth, books were my only friends.

"You do know how to read?" Sir Garrison asked.

I wanted to roll my eyes at such a question. "I believe so, sir."

"We may have to test you later." He acted much too eager to find me out.

"I imagine not having any memories to fall back on can be daunting." Ruth smiled at me and then took a bite of her food.

"I don't seem to know much about myself, other than what I came here with."

"Pray, and what was that?" Lady Garrison asked.

"Only my pencils and sketchbook, with a few personal belongings."

"Well, there is something," Sir Garrison said. He had a rather soft and warm look about him. I could see why Lady Garrison had chosen him for a husband. They were a good match. Both were beautiful and kind. An overwhelming feeling of self-consciousness overcame me being in this room with beautiful and important people.

"I would love to see your work," Ruth said.

"We all would, after dinner," Lady Garrison agreed.

My face grew hot once again. Lord Shariton's eyes were on me. I could feel it. I ate with caution, trying to steady my hand, hoping the food wouldn't fall off my fork.

Does he wish to make me more uncomfortable?

It took some courage to glance up to see him watching my face. I was relieved he wasn't looking elsewhere. When I turned my head, I caught Ruth staring at me, then at her brother. She smirked as though she had a secret.

"I cannot wait to unravel the secrets inside your mind. I hope you will indulge me over the next few days while I plague you with questions," Ruth said.

Everyone seemed as eager as Ruth. *It seems I am to become their lab rat.* Listening to the conversations throughout dinner, I noticed their form of language was different than I was used to. I began to panic that they might catch on and I wondered about my choice of words. *Speak as little as possible.*

When dinner finished, I joined Ruth and Lady Garrison in the drawing room and listened to them talk about London and all its adventures. While they spoke, I watched the candles flicker in the room. It felt weird not to see modern lights in the room.

"Have you been to London?" Lady Garrison asked.

I shrugged. "I don't know. Possibly, at least, I remember a big city." *Curses! That wasn't the right thing to say!*

"Of course, how silly of me." She laid her hand on my arm. "It really is a shame you cannot recall even the simplest memories. It must be maddening."

I nodded.

They talked more about London and the entertainment they enjoyed most. I remained quiet and listened. I found it strange to be thinking of the modern London I knew while they only knew the old London.

"Celeste, why not retrieve your sketchbook and show us some of your work? The men should be done with their drink by the time you return." Lady Garrison gave me a gentle smile.

I left the room, feeling relieved to have a chance to scratch an itch under my corset. Hurrying to my chamber—as they called it—I opened my sketchbook and flipped through its pages. Knowing I couldn't show them pictures of the modern world, I had to do something. The clothes of the people in my drawings would be shocking to those downstairs. I tore out five drawings and hid them in my wardrobe. In doing so, I felt like I had cut open my own flesh. I had never damaged my artwork, and it felt wrong. Each piece was a part of me, and seeing it torn felt brutal. My heart slowed when I flipped through the book one last time. Most of my drawings were of statues from Italy and could pass for something I'd drawn in this time. A few were faces, one of them Papa. I paused at the drawing of him and thought of how much I missed him. I wished he were here and could tell me what to do.

Do I look for a way back? Where would I even begin? How could I find my way back without help or hours upon hours of searching?

I'm hopeless.

Chapter Six

Charles

"Have you made any inquiries about Celeste?" Henry asked me whilst we drank our port.

"I have sent some letters out to several of my acquaintances. Too soon for any reply." I was not in the mood to drink. I rarely was, and tonight I felt more eager to be in the drawing room with the ladies. I wanted to know what they might be discussing and discovering about Celeste.

I turned and watched Henry take a drink. "How is Clair getting on without her children?" I asked. Both Henry and Clair had been away from their children for the last two months, and I knew it was difficult for them.

"She misses them terribly."

"She must not have been too thrilled with the idea of staying longer.

I apologize."

"It could not be helped," he replied.

I took a sip of my drink and set the glass down. "Why not send for them? They could stay here as easily as there."

He chuckled. "Surely you cannot be serious. You are not used to children."

"If it would make your wife happy, then a little discomfort, if any, on my end will not be a bother." I hated to be the one to cause a lengthy separation from their children.

"We would not want to trouble you."

"No trouble, no trouble." I waved and sat forward.

"You may end up regretting this," he laughed. "It will make Clair positively happy. Thank you, Charles."

"Always a pleasure," I said. "Now, are you finished with your port? I am anxious to hear the conversations happening in the drawing room."

"I can see you are," he chuckled. He gave me a pointed glance that I knew well, with one brow higher than the other and a smirk on his face.

"What is going on in that head of yours, Henry? I hope you are not reading too much into this."

"Well, it is easy to read. I saw your face when you walked into the drawing room and beheld the lovely eyes of young Celeste," he continued to grin at me.

The image of that moment when she took my arm and walked with me into the dining room, flashed through my mind. The sweet unidentifiable smell of her lingered. I blinked hard and pushed the thought of her to the side, glaring at him. "Do pray, hold your tongue. Any man would be a fool not to be taken back by her beauty. It could not be helped—but it does not mean that I have any deep regard for her."

"Then tell me why you could not take your eyes off her during dinner?"

"I was trying to read her. Find some flaw in her story. Or perhaps more story than she is letting on. Nothing more." I paused and gave him a firm look so he knew I meant what I said, "I do not want you thinking otherwise or discussing it with anyone. I do not need rumors causing trouble."

"Understood. I daresay your foresight in asking me and Clair to stay was spot on. Someone most definitely needs to keep an eye or two on you."

I glared sideways at him. "Why is that?"

"We would not want you to make a cake of yourself, now would we?" He chuckled at my hard glare, then set his drink down and followed me into the drawing room. I scanned the room and noticed Celeste was missing from the group. Before I could ask where she had gone, Henry spoke, "Where is Celeste?"

"She went to get her sketchbook." Clair patted the spot next to her on the sofa for Henry to sit with her.

"Has she been gone long?" I asked.

"Long enough," Ruth replied.

I went to the window to watch the sun lower in the sky and wondered, not for the first time, how in the devil she had found herself alone in the woods. The door to the drawing room opened, and I watched Celeste enter and my heart beat faster. I willed it to calm itself. I was not going to react like this every time I saw her. It would go away in time.

"Oh. Come here and sit by me," Ruth said excitedly, patting the spot beside her.

Celeste glanced at me before taking her place. "I'm afraid I don't have very many drawings in here. I suppose it's a newer sketchbook."

I moved to the back of the sofa, trying to get a better view when Celeste opened it. Ruth leaned in as well. I had never seen work so life-like in a simple sketchbook, and I had not expected to see such detail.

Ruth gasped. She must have been equally surprised. "Oh, how beautiful. I have never seen such glorious work." She touched Celeste's arm and sighed, "You truly are gifted."

"Come now. Let us see. 'Tis not fair to keep it from us," Henry chuckled. Celeste turned the book to show Henry and Clair.

Clair also gasped, and Henry stood, bending forward to see clearer. "Upon my word! You are gifted. I confess I assumed Miss Elsegood to be exaggerating, but I see she was spot on."

I walked around the sofa and sat beside Celeste, studying her drawing. Her sweet scent flooded my lungs and filled me with euphoria. *What could that scent be?* I glanced up at her face. Her cheeks were a nice rosy color. She flipped to another page, and I reached out for it. "May I?"

She nodded and passed the sketchbook to me.

"I know this. I have seen this statue somewhere in Italy." I studied it and turned to look directly at her. Our eyes met. She seemed pleased. I cleared my throat. "You have been to Italy before?"

Her facial expression changed, and her brow creased. "I suppose."

"You did draw this, did you not?" I asked, now worried she was withholding something from me.

"Yes, sir. I remember where I sat while I drew it . . . nothing more."

Celeste held her hand out for me to return the book, but I ignored it.

I flipped the page and found another drawing of architecture I knew from somewhere in Italy. I studied it intently, trying to unlock the memory of where I had seen this. Then it came to me, "Santé Croce. This is Santé Croce."

"Yes, sir." She smiled at me. It was the first time she had done so, and it stopped my heart. Her eyes lit up, and her teeth were so white and straight. I had never seen teeth like hers before. Her dimples appeared and deepened. She looked away, blushing. Clearing my throat, I studied the sketchbook again.

"So, now we know you are very gifted at drawing. Let us see if you can play the piano," Ruth said. She stood and pulled Celeste to her feet.

"Oh, I don't know if I could," Celeste's voice was tight, her eyes large.

"You will not know until you try." Ruth led her across the room. Celeste sat at the piano, and all the happiness she revealed over her drawings had flittered away.

"Let's start with something everyone knows." Ruth placed some music sheets in front of Celeste. "There, this should do it."

"Ah, no. I don't know that one," Celeste's cheeks reddened.

"Too difficult?" Ruth asked.

Celeste shook her head. Her lips pressed together and her fingers gently stroked a few notes. She played something unfamiliar, something far different than I heard before. She played the notes, smooth and sweet, without flaws. It seemed the piece Ruth suggested had been too simple for her. She had her eyes closed through the last part of the song. I fell, lost in the sweet sounds that drifted through the room. At her last soft note, I woke from my reverie and focused on shaking the daze that had consumed me. When she opened her eyes tears fell down her cheeks.

She stood, almost stumbling as she did. "I—I'm so sorry. Please forgive me." Celeste lowered her head and said quietly, "I think I'll go. . ." She headed to the door. "Goodnight, everyone. Dinner was . . . stupendous."

I stood, not knowing what to do to help her. I reacted too late, and she was gone.

"What do you suppose that was about?" Ruth asked with brows raised.

Chapter Seven

Celeste

I was able to smother my crying long enough for Annabeth to help me out of my gown and unpin my hair. The moment she left, I threw myself on my bed and cried. *Why did I play that song?* That song held a wonderful memory of Papa. At the age of twelve, I learned to play *Fur Elise*. When I could at last play it through without flaws, I was so happy and proud of myself that I pulled my father into the piano room and made him sit and listen to me. Of course I never had to make him. He always enjoyed listening to me. After I played, he patted my hand, telling me how proud he was of me, and then kissed my cheek.

At the time my heart soared, but now, I ached. It felt as though it had been wrung through a pasta machine. To add to my pain, I had cried in front of everyone. How could I be such a fool thinking I could play a song and not be affected by it? Well, it wasn't going to happen again.

A knock sounded at the door. I stopped mid-cry, wiped away my tears, and pulled a blanket around my shoulders before moving to the door.

"Sorry to disturb you, Celeste. May I come in?" Ruth peeked around the door. In her hands, she held my sketchbook. I opened the door wider to let her in. She sat on my bed with me and took my hand, "Are you well?"

"I'm fine."

Ruth gave me a puzzled look. I mentally kicked myself for using such modern words as "I'm fine".

"What happened?"

What should I say? How can I explain? I took a deep breath, "I discovered a memory that's very dear to me." I lowered my head so she couldn't see in my eyes that there was more to it.

"And it was brought on by you playing the piano?" she asked.

I nodded.

"Well, this is good news then." She hugged me. "You have a memory. Tell me who was in your memory. Could it be a relative or a man you once were deeply in love with?" she asked, giggling.

"No . . . not . . . I've never been in love."

"How do you know if you cannot recall anything?"

"I'd remember love." I wanted to laugh at the absurdity of my situation. I'd never even been kissed, let alone loved by any young man—unless I count Rey Harwood, the boy down the street. I never counted him. Sharing a peck on the lips with someone at the tender age of nine didn't qualify.

"So, a relative, then?"

"An image . . . he's my father."

She clapped her hands and gasped with delight. "And his name?"

I shook my head. "No name. Only a memory."

Her face fell. "Do not worry. We will figure it out in time," she said, standing. "Oh, I really should tell you. You probably already know this and let it slip, but you should address my brother as My Lord, Lord Shariton, or the like, not sir."

I covered my warm cheeks. "Oh, I . . . how ignorant of me."

"I wish you did not have to use such frivolous titles, but I cannot rightly permit you to use anything otherwise. I hope you understand."

"Oh, yes. Thank you for correcting me, but I hope you'll excuse me. I may slip up here and there."

"Please, do not lose any sleep over it. He does not mind too terribly." She glided to the door in her thin slippers. "I wish you a peaceful slumber in hopes your memory will return." She waved and shut the door.

* * *

Celeste

The next morning I woke early and dressed in something I could button on my own. I pulled my hair up and pinned it as best I could. The front of my hair frizzed terribly, but it couldn't be helped until Annabeth could work her magic. The house sat silent, all but the soft footfalls of housemaids beginning their daily chores. The moment I passed the gardens, I held my dress to my knees and ran, but only a short distance. Since coming here my lungs felt great, as though all the pollution from London had cleared from them. I could breathe well and run without wheezing. The only thing that could improve it would be some running clothes and shoes. Running in a dress and boots wasn't ideal. I guess beggars can't be choosers. I should be grateful I wear the same size shoe as Ruth, and her dresses fit reasonably well.

I jogged for quite some time while I watched the sun burn away the mist in the trees around me. I couldn't stop myself from falling in love with the scenery around me. The morning dew gathering at the tips of the leaves dripped upon my shoulders, and a mother duck and her ducklings hurried into the trees on their way to the closest pond. Their quacking grew distant and less frequent the farther away I traveled from them.

I stopped, bent over, and rested my hands on my knees. I kicked one leg back and stretched my legs the best I could in the dress. The movement was healing.

A red-breasted robin landed on a tree nearby and whistled a tune in greeting. I whistled a tune back. Papa had taught me how to whistle, and I became extremely good at it. The bird fluttered away, and I giggled. I hadn't been this lighthearted when I first woke up, so it had to be the running that created my good mood.

My head lowered, watching where I walked, and I noticed a rock of peculiar shape. I bent, picked it up, and brushed the damp dirt away for a better look. Gold and green speckles caught the sun and glittered. Being a rock collector, my father would've loved this one.

I breathed deeply, then turned to look at the view behind me. My breath caught, and a smile fell from my face. Lord Shariton sat atop his horse nearby and stared at me. Instantly I thought of my frizzy hair. I dropped the rock and brushed my hair away from my eyes, trying to flatten the frizz as best I could.

"I'm sorry. I didn't know . . ." *What do I say?* "I didn't know I was being watched."

"I beg your pardon. I suppose I should have made myself known, but I have learned a few things about you by being silent."

I fidgeted. "You have?"

"Yes, I have." He continued to watch me.

Is he going to make me ask? "What did you learn?" *Oops. Maybe I should have added the word 'pray' in front of that sentence, like they do when they ask things.*

He led his horse closer and dismounted, standing before me. "First, I have discovered that you are faster than you look. Second, you can whistle—which I have never heard a woman do. Third, you can, indeed, laugh."

Oops. I guess I shouldn't have done all that.

I lowered my head and caught sight of my hands. "Holy mud!" I began to brush the dirt off my hands before I remembered that I had just used my hands to graze at my face and hair. Heat rose in my cheeks when he pulled a handkerchief from his pocket.

"I do not think this mud is from holy ground." He struggled not to smirk, possibly amused with my oddity, which only caused me to get warmer in the ears.

I avoided his gaze and took the outstretched handkerchief, wiping frantically at my face. Each time I glanced at him, I found his gaze too intense, and I didn't know what to think of it. It seemed he didn't want to laugh or offend me, but he peered at me as though he was pondering something important.

He broke the silence. "Do you always run like that?"

"Y—yes."

"You should take more care—and wear a bonnet next time you go out." He gestured toward my head. A little pink touched his cheeks as though embarrassed.

I've got no bonnet. No. That won't do. "But I have no bonnet," I said, flinching that I'd used the word *but* in my sentence.

"You do not?" He cleared his throat. "Of course, you have not. You came with nothing, to begin with." He said with an accusing tone.

"I apologize, sir—my lord." I looked at my hands again and tried to clear the rest of the dirt.

"It could not be helped." He glanced into the woods at the path I had come through. "Did you run the whole way?"

I nodded slowly.

His eyes widened. "You must be near faint. Let me give you a ride back." He pulled his horse closer to me.

I took several steps back. I had only ridden a horse once when Lord Shariton found me in the woods. At the time, my thoughts were preoccupied by things other than horses.

He noticed my hesitation and asked, "Do not tell me you would enjoy walking back all that way?"

I didn't answer. Truth be told, I had come a long way and was feeling a bit tired now that I had stopped. Walking back would take me until well after breakfast.

"Come, I will help you up."

"No thanks. I'm fine—er, I'm good—well." *Stupid mouth!*

"I insist. This horse may not be as gentle as some of the others I keep, but he does well enough." He patted the horse's neck.

I bit back a retort to his demand, lowering my head, and I whispered, "I don't know how to ride."

He furrowed his brow. "Did your father not keep horses?"

Wait. What have I gotten myself into? If I answered no, he would think me poor and much lower in station. I felt it important to keep him believing I came from a higher rank. My father did own a few cars. In this day and age, a car would equal a horse in value, so in retrospect, yes, he did keep horses. "I suppose he did. . ." Now for the excuse. "But, I don't remember . . . I'm not sure he allowed me to ride." *Ugh! Pretending to have memory loss is difficult, and it's getting me into trouble.*

His one brow rose, then he paused. "I will teach you, then." He stepped to me, took me by the elbow, and placed me before the horse, "Celeste, meet Apollo."

I stood and stared at the large animal in front of me.

"Come . . . " he took my hand and placed it against Apollo's cheek, "feel his softness."

My heart whirled at his lovely hand touching mine. *Yes, he might be handsome, but he's still too old!* The horse was warm and soft—softer than satin. Growing up, I had been too afraid to pet a horse. Then, as I grew older, I never had the chance to be close to one again. Other than when I sat upon Apollo a few nights ago, of course. A smile spread across my face. I reached up with my other hand and felt the warmth of his sleek neck.

"He's beautiful."

Lord Shariton lowered his head, then cleared his throat. "Now that you've met let's get you on." He paused. "I know it is not becoming for a lady to ride upon a saddle such as this, but I promise to be a gentleman and look away." His cheeks were as scarlet as the favorite holiday sweater I wore when I was twelve.

Seeing how embarrassed he became by simply mentioning something of that nature made me want to laugh out loud. I tilted my head to hide my grin. He pulled me by the elbow and instructed me how to mount, then knelt and held out his linked hands for me.

My amusement vanished and worry overcame me, partially about riding the stallion and partly due to simply getting *on. Does he think it will be so simple with a dress on?*

He peered up at me. "Well?"

I lifted my foot.

"Other foot," he said.

I raised the other foot and placed it in his hands. I did as he instructed and attempted to swing my leg over the horse. Unfortunately, my leg stopped at the top when my dress restricted me. I clung to the saddle, afraid of falling back. Just when I thought myself doomed to fall, I felt Lord Shariton's hands at my hips, and he heaved me up into the saddle. My eyebrows rose at his strength and ability to get me up high enough and easily set me there. I leaned forward and held onto the saddle, afraid the horse would bolt.

Lord Shariton laughed before averting his eyes, "You look like a frightened child up there."

"I am."

"You cannot lie on the horse. Sit tall. Your legs must hang over the sides."

I sat up and my dress moved to my knees, revealing my stockings. This must not look very ladylike. Lord Shariton glanced away.

"Sit tall. I will lead him." He took the reins and held them while he walked us forward, keeping his head forward. "Let yourself move with him. Not against him," he said over his shoulder.

Apollo carried me slowly back down the path toward the house. The gentle sway of the horse's steps lulled me into a state of contentment, and my fears melted away. I watched the trees inch by, realizing at this pace, it would take ages to get back.

"Can't we move any faster?"

He glanced up at me before turning his head forward again. "If you do not mind me riding with you—though propriety would demand that I not." He cleared his throat. "You would not think me ungentlemanly, would you?"

I wanted to laugh. If he only knew what went on during my time. Riding a horse together with someone wasn't a big deal compared to the life most people led. "I won't think any less of you."

"Excellent. Walking slowly was making me irritable. And besides, I am famished and do not wish to miss my morning meal."

I laughed briefly, then moved forward to make room for him. He gave me the reins to hold, mounted, reached around me, and claimed the reins once again. He gave the command, and we started forward at a very fast pace.

Though I initially felt nervous, I soon realized Lord Shariton was in control of the animal, and my nerves settled. The wind in my hair caused a rush of joy to course through me. I may have even laughed again.

* * *

Charles

Sheer joy was what I felt when I heard her laughing while we rode back toward the house. When she turned her head to the side, I could see her smile light up her cheeks. I wanted to laugh with her, but I forced it away as quickly as the emotion came. Realizing the danger in letting those feelings overcome me, I willed myself to turn my thoughts elsewhere. *I will not lose my head over someone about whom I know nothing.*

It was difficult to ride with her. Not because she sat in the way but because she was close. The desire to wrap my arms around her and hold her tight grew stronger at every moment. I shook my head slightly and pushed the feelings aside. *I will not lose my head over someone I do not know.* I repeated the thought over in my mind. My shoulders relaxed when we came to the edge of the gardens and stopped.

"You do not mind walking from here, do you? I need to take Apollo back to the stables."

"Not at all," she answered.

When I dismounted, my feet hit the ground heavily, and then I held my hand out for hers. She took it and leaned her body to the side. Discovering I had neglected to instruct her on how to dismount successfully, I caught her around the waist and set her feet on the ground.

"Sorry," she breathed with wide eyes—those big, beautiful eyes.

It took a moment to clear my mind and remember to release her waist. "Perhaps next time I can teach you to dismount," I said, clearing my throat.

53

"Yes. Maybe you should." The rosiness in her cheeks deepened in color. "Thank you, my lord, for the ride back. It was thrilling."

She turned on her heel and hurried away. I watched her curls bounce with each step she took until she was hidden behind a hedge.

Chapter Eight

Celeste

I sat at breakfast with Ruth before any of the others joined us. I found myself opening up to her. She was easy to like. I learned that she was only six months younger than me. Like myself, she was fond of reading and singing. She told me of all she loved to do and spoke of the men she met in London.

"You would love London, although I find that most of the men there are a bit dimwitted and only looking for a fortune. Charles had to save me from a few of those fortune hunters." She paused. "I am fortunate to have a brother as caring as Charles."

"Yes. He seems like the kind of man to care well for his sister. So . . . were there no men that caught your eye?"

She smiled and blushed. "There was one gentleman I liked, but he has not shown much interest in me. I have been hoping he would follow me here, but I am not so sure he will."

"It's only been a couple of days. I'm sure you will hear from him soon," I said, taking a bite of a strawberry.

"Well, perhaps you are right, but we only met toward the end of our stay, and it was not long enough to get attached. I do not know if he has any feelings for me." She appeared worried.

Forget him! You're too young anyway. Those are the words I wished I could say, but I wasn't in the twenty-first century. "Even if nothing happens, you're still very young. You'll find someone, I'm sure." It was strange talking about her getting married. No one I knew would be discussing matrimony at such a young age. There would only be talk of universities and careers. An overwhelming sorrow for her and all young girls fell upon me. What chance did she have of marrying someone she loved? I only knew the stories from Austen, and I hadn't yet experienced the real life of the Regency era—at least not to its fullest extent.

She gave me a crooked smile and asked, "Do you wish to be married soon?"

I tried to scoff, but it came out more of a snort. "Heavens, no."

"Well, of course, you do. Every young girl dreams of it."

"I am too young."

"Too young?" she huffed. "Why, you can't be much older than I. You are not too young."

I smiled nervously, reached for another strawberry, and knocked my plate off the table. Its contents fell onto the floor and scattered. *"Oh caro! Come sciocco di me!"* I cried and dropped to my hands and knees to pick up the food.

"Goodness. Was that Italian?" Ruth laughed.

"Oh . . ." I hadn't realized I'd spoken in a different language. "Yes."

"Do you speak it fluently?" she asked.

Once I'd picked up the last piece, I sat down with my plate of food. "Almost."

"Well, now we know one more thing about you. How exciting!" She bounced in her seat. "Uncovering this mystery about you will be the most fun I will have all summer."

I wasn't so sure.

"Good morning," Lady and Sir Garrison said together at their entry.

"Forgive us. We are a little late in waking. I was writing to my children. We have been permitted to invite them here," Lady Garrison said with delight.

"How glorious! I have good news as well," Ruth cried. "I have discovered that our dearest Celeste speaks Italian."

Sir Garrison's eyebrow rose. "Indeed? How much time did you spend there?" he asked in Italian. It was difficult to understand him, as he didn't pronounce the words the way I was used to.

"I'm not sure," I answered back in Italian.

"You are not from there?" His pronunciation made it challenging to interpret.

"No. I don't speak fluently enough, nor do I think in Italian," I answered.

"This is delightful news," Lady Garrison said.

"Pray, what is delightful?" Lord Shariton inquired, entering the room.

"Celeste speaks Italian, dear brother," Ruth said happily.

"Ah, that is one language I have not become fluent in, and I have always regretted it," he responded without looking at me. "Do you speak Latin as well?"

"Not unless pig Latin counts!" Heat rose in my cheeks at everyone's bewildered stares.

"She says she does not speak Italian fluently, but her pronunciation is far better than my own, I daresay," Sir Garrison stated while he buttered his bread. "Charles, did you say the vicar has left for Essex?"

Thank you, Sir Garrison, for changing the subject. Soon the topic of conversations drifted to the activities of the day. We all chatted while we ate. I was becoming more comfortable in their company, though I still worried about what I said, hoping not to say something uncivil. Manners were a bit different in their day and age. I ran conversations through my mind and thought about ways of saying the same thing, hoping it would help.

When everyone finished, Ruth suggested giving me a tour of the house.

"I would love that, thank you," I replied.

"May I join you?" Lord Shariton asked.

My muscles stiffened, and my stomach flip-flopped at the idea.

"Of course. We would be delighted, would we not, Celeste?" Ruth asked me.

"Delighted," I said, though not loud enough.

* * *

Charles

I do not know what possessed me to ask to join them on the tour. Surely they would have a more enjoyable time without me, and I had business to attend to, but I felt a great need to be near Celeste. We made our way around the rooms and down the corridors. Ruth showed her the paintings of our family line, and I watched Celeste admire them. She smiled more in that short time than she had the entire first day after her arrival. Her smiles were breathtaking.

Watching her study the artwork, conversing softly with Ruth and their heads bent together, I began to recognize a reserve I felt about her. She did not give information freely. When praised for her own artwork, she turned the attention around, making it a point to identify something wonderful in everyone and everything around her. It was not that she did not take the praise graciously, but rather chose to put something else above her.

Celeste was perfectly at ease with Ruth, but when I drew closer or asked her a question, she grew quiet and fidgeted. I wondered if she was that way around all men or if it was I alone who made her uncomfortable.

* * *

Celeste

I had never seen so many paintings, statues, and busts in one place outside of the Vatican Museum. Ruth stopped before each one, explaining who it was and where it came from. I enjoyed every piece, feeling the desire to return and study each one in its entirety. A sitting room at one side of the estate had walls covered in elaborate paintings of gardens populated by half-naked people. Almost every inch of ceiling in the rooms and each hall was decorated with plastered vines and swirled designs. The extravagant furniture comfortably filled the rooms, making them picture-perfect. It was beyond what I could dream up.

"Here is the ballroom," Ruth said happily, breaking my concentration from studying a bust near the ballroom doors.

"How lovely." I entered the room, my shoes echoing off the high golden walls. I felt the sudden urge to whistle, but refrained due to Lord Shariton's earlier comments.

"Charles, look at the eagerness in Celeste's eyes! We should throw her a ball to satisfy that."

"Oh! No, no, no, really. You don't need to do that." My heartbeat quickened.

"Ruth, we do not know of what family she hails from. I would not want to overstep my bounds," Lord Shariton smoothly replied.

I wanted to hug him, feeling relieved.

"Then throw *me* a ball. Please, Charles! How I long to dance and see my friends." She stared at him with what I would call puppy dog eyes.

"How can I say no to you, Ruth?" He chuckled and shook his head.

She clapped her hands and kissed her brother's cheek. "Oh, thank you, dear brother!"

The blood drained from my face. *A ball?* I didn't know the first thing about dancing the way they did. I only knew the steps for the more modern waltz my father had taught me. The only time I'd been to a dance was when I attended fancy functions with my father. Even then, I needed coaching to get through the steps.

"Whatever is the matter, Celeste?" Ruth exclaimed when she turned back to me. My discomfort must have been evident in my demeanor.

"I don't know if I can dance." I hid my hands behind my back and wiped the sweat on my dress. *I can see it now . . . everyone standing over me, laughing while I lay sprawled out on the floor.*

"That is because you do not remember. Your memory of the dances will return once they have begun." Ruth took my arm and led me from the room.

Fiddlesticks. "No. Really. I don't dance." My voice cracked when a lump formed in my throat. *Oh, please forget about the ball!*

"Charles and I can help you practice. Never fear." She directed me from the room into the hall once more.

We walked down the grand hall and into another room. The smell of old books drifted toward me and woke my senses. All my discomfort and nervousness ceased once I entered. In this room, I was home.

"This, of course, is the library." Ruth led me in and let go of my arm at our entry. Instinctively, I headed toward the opposite wall full of books, like a moth to a flame. Every surface was covered with books, save the fireplace and the tall windows opposite. I nearly bumped into the sofa in my distraction. *Ah, serenity.*

"Excuse my interruption, Miss Elsegood, but Mrs. Cromwell and Miss Cromwell are here to see you," a servant announced from the doorway. "They are waiting in the blue room."

"Thank you, Albert. I will be right there," Ruth answered. "Would you like to join us, Celeste? The Cromwells are our neighbors, you see. I am sure they would love to meet you."

My shoulders rose, and I shifted my weight, trying to find an excuse not to join them. Meeting with people outside my comfort zone might be the end of me. I had only begun to feel comfortable with Ruth. "I am not ready for the questions they might have." Again I hid my hands behind my back and twisted my ring around my finger.

"A wise choice," Lord Shariton said to me.

Ruth nodded, then left the room, seeming a little disappointed.

I breathed deeply, took a book from the shelf, and opened it to smell its familiar scent. I slid it back into place, then ran my fingers along the many beautiful spines. When I turned, I found Lord Shariton watching me. Our eyes met from across the room. I waited for him to speak, for I didn't know what to say. He stood there looking at me.

He cleared his throat. "If you will excuse me," he said, leaving.

That was strange. My shoulders relaxed, and I returned to the books. I grabbed one from the shelf, and sat down in a large, soft chair. I pulled my feet up under me and began a new life in the world of pages.

Chapter Nine

Charles

"Have you seen Celeste?" Ruth asked as soon as I entered through the back door.

"No, I have not seen her since last with you."

She scrunched her nose for a moment. "Can you go find her, Charles? I need to get to my room to dress for dinner."

"Of course," I turned my steps toward the library. Judging by how happy and comfortable she appeared earlier, I would most likely find her tucked among the books. She had looked at home in that room. When I approached, I quietly walked, to avoid disturbing her reading. I found her asleep on a chaise lounge with a book lying across her chest.

I tip-toed across the room toward her. She looked like an angel lying there—a perfect angel. I covered my mouth, trying not to laugh, when I noticed a bit of drool glistening on her cheek. Perhaps not quite so perfect. My eyes fell on the book she had been reading. It was a collection of French poems my father found in Paris on his travels when I was younger. *So, she knows how to read French?*

My eyes paused on her hand resting next to her head, and I felt the urge to touch it. I reached out and brushed the tip of her pinky down past her wrist. She did not move, nor did her breathing change. Again I moved my fingers up to the tip of her pinky and back down again. Her skin was soft, warm, and delicate. Her eyelids fluttered open at the same time a snort sounded from her throat. She blinked, then jerked back. Her face turned into a frown, and her cheeks reddened.

"Rest well?" I asked in French, moving my hand away. She sat up abruptly, and the book nearly hit the floor. I caught it and held it out to her. She noticed the drool and wiped at her cheek with her head down. Her eyes darted about the room as if she did not want to meet my gaze. "I will not tell," I spoke again in French and winked at her.

She turned her head from me and fussed with the pillow behind her. "I apologize for falling asleep. I hope I didn't inconvenience you in any way." Her voice was rough and just above a whisper. She spoke French so beautifully that I could not help but admire her.

"So, are you French?"

She cleared her throat. "No. Again, I'm not fluent enough. I couldn't understand half of what was in that book. I do enjoy learning it, though." She still kept her head down.

The memory of Mrs. Weston and Miss Weston's plans of forced engagement entered my mind, and I stiffened. "I wonder how you can remember how to speak Italian and French, yet you cannot remember your relative's names." I tried not to sound accusing, but it seemed I saw something hiding in her eyes any time it was mentioned.

"I . . ." She did not finish her sentence.

I held my hand out for her. "My apologies. Celeste, dinner is drawing nigh. Perhaps you should make yourself ready."

She slowly placed her hand in mine, and I helped her to her feet. I resisted the urge to hold her hand longer and let it drop. I held my arm out for her, leading her out of the room and down the hall, where we parted ways without another word.

I had hoped to speak with her more, but she seemed to want to avoid making conversation. I believed I might have inadvertently caused her discomfort. With this realization, I spun around. My speed down the corridor increased, moving toward her door. My hand balled, ready to knock, when I paused. *What am I doing? What do I need to apologize for? I have done nothing wrong. I am acting the fool. This is not me.* My hand dropped to my side, and I huffed at her door, turned, and proceeded to my room to change.

She'd had me like a vice from the moment I met her. That fact irritated me beyond belief. I despised that I felt attracted to her for her beauty. Why her? Why did I have to be drawn to someone I knew nothing about? Could I trust her? I'd be dashed if I lost my head over someone who might wish to ensnare me. There were too many unknowns.

With a loud bang, I forced my door closed and paced the room, feeling uneasy over my attraction. *I am better than this. I am a wealthy man who does not rely on women who make fools and lay traps. She will not bat her eyes at me and try to win me over. She will be thrown out at the first sign of any affection that is formed on her part.*

* * *

Celeste

After my embarrassing moment with the drool and Lord Shariton's beautiful eyes boring into my soul as if he knew all my secrets, it was difficult to look him in the eye again. During dinner, I continually found

64

him studying me. I felt myself unraveling at the seams with anxiety—especially because he looked displeased when I caught him looking. There had been a moment earlier in the day when I thought we could be good friends, but seeing his facial reactions at dinner, I supposed I was wrong.

During the meal, I learned we had been invited by the Cromwells to a ball at their estate in just a few days. *How am I to learn to dance in only a few days?*

Before the women entered the drawing room, I noticed Ruth nudging Charles, whispering to him, and glancing at me. He nodded before she stood, took my arm, and walked me into the room. Heat rose in my cheeks. I hated when I knew people were talking about me.

The tension in my shoulders lessened when no one asked me to play the piano again. Instead, Lady Garrison and Ruth played, giving me the chance to sit with my eyes closed, wishing I could record its sounds. I pictured myself by my father's side. I knew if he were here, he'd be tapping his foot to the beat, and his eyebrows would rise and lower with each dramatic crescendo.

After they played a few songs, Ruth stood. "Did Charles tell you he is to throw me a ball?" she asked Lady and Sir Garrison.

"No. He did not," Lady Garrison answered with a pleased expression.

"He has agreed to it this very day."

"When is this ball to be held?" Sir Garrison asked Lord Shariton.

"That was what I wanted to ask you, Lady Garrison. I wondered if you could help Ruth in the preparations," Lord Shariton said.

"Nothing would please me more," she replied.

"When is the next full moon?" Lord Shariton asked.

"I believe over a week from now," Sir Garrison said.

"Could you have a ball planned by then?" Lord Shariton asked the two women.

"Of course. We must plan it quickly, but we will manage," Lady Garrison replied.

Ruth held her hand out for me, and I took it. She pulled me to my feet. "Speaking of the ball, Celeste needs to practice her dances. Would you be so kind, Sir and Lady Garrison, to help us teach her?" She motioned for her brother to stand. "I will play the song. Lady Garrison, could you help coach her?"

"I would be delighted." Lady and Sir Garrison stood, as did Lord Shariton.

I'm sure my face was bright red, for I felt the heat in my cheeks. Lord Shariton must have noticed, for he had a slight smile and a twinkle in his eye. *Does he think I'm amusing?*

"Charles, you be her partner." Ruth led me to stand across from her brother.

"Perhaps I could watch Sir and Lady Garrison dance first, for I don't know if I can remember the steps," I said.

"Yes, of course," Ruth agreed. "Stand aside then," she instructed and went to the piano to begin her piece.

I watched the movements of the two dancers and tried to catch the patterns. It looked simple enough.

"Now you try," Ruth said to me from the piano.

I moved to the spot next to Lady Garrison and across from Lord Shariton. He smiled at me, and I blushed back. *Why am I always doing that? I can't possibly like him. He's got to be at least five years older than me.* While I waited for the music to begin, a different dance came into my mind. *Put your right hand in. Put your right hand out. Put your right hand in and shake it all about.* I bit my lips to hold my laughter in.

The music began. Charles stepped forward, and I met him, took his hand, and he led me around once, then let go. Lady Garrison instructed me to move back, then across, curtsy at her husband, and take his hand. I did as she instructed and moved back. They were all kind and

66

patient while they helped me with the movements. My embarrassment deepened as I bumped into Lord Shariton. He merely smiled and helped me remember the next part of the dance. We went through it again, and it was a little easier than I expected. Far easier than trying to learn any hip-hop dances from my time. When we ended, I withheld the urge to pat myself on the back because I hadn't stepped on anyone's feet. Lord Shariton sat beside me, and Ruth joined us on my other side.

"It seems your memory of dancing has not fully returned," Lord Shariton grinned at me.

"Charles. Pray, hold your tongue—she tried her best," Ruth reprimanded him.

I guess it didn't go as well as I thought.

"We will practice again tomorrow." Ruth took my hand in one of hers, patting it with the other.

"She will learn, and then she will be the belle of the ball," Lord Shariton softly murmured in French, watching me closely.

"Whatever did you say to make her blush?" Ruth asked her brother. I kept my head down. I could hear Sir Garrison trying to hold back his laughter. Lady Garrison glanced back and forth between Lord Shariton and her husband, then at me.

"Apparently, she speaks French, as well," Sir Garrison stated, then added in French, "Did you spend time there?"

I answered in French. "Only a short visit. My father spent most of his time there." The instant I finished speaking, my hand flew to my lips.

Lord Shariton's posture stiffened, and his brow lowered. "You speak of your father as if you remember him well enough. What is his name?"

I had been caught. He knew that I knew my father's name. I thought for a moment, trying to create a story for him. "Damian . . . Sir Damian Roberts." I added the Sir in hopes of elevating my situation.

"*Sir* Damian Roberts?" Lord Shariton asked. "I have never heard of him. What is his title?"

If I gave my father a title that was too high in rank, then I could be causing myself more trouble. "He has been knighted." Hopefully knighthood wouldn't be too high.

"Do you know where he is?"

I thought for a moment. "I . . . perhaps . . . he may be in the south of France."

"Where?" He was very forceful about getting answers.

"I remember Frejus. There, on the southern coast." It was the first place I thought of. "I remember spending time there. He may be there . . . or—"

"And what of your mother?"

"I have a memory of her funeral . . . when I was young," I whispered, then turned my head to hide the tears that threatened to come. With the Garrisons across from me, Ruth and Lord Shariton on either side, I had nowhere to hide. At any moment, tears would burst from my eyes, so I stood. "Please excuse me. I think I'll turn—retire early."

* * *

Charles

After Celeste—or rather, Miss Roberts—left the room, I received a glare from my sister. She had warned me just after dinner to be kind toward Celeste. Ruth knew me well enough to notice my unease. I feared she knew me too well. Her expression suddenly relaxed as she stood and announced that she also would be retiring, as did Clair.

"I will be up momentarily," Henry said to his wife.

"Good night, Lord Shariton."

"Good night," I said to both women. When the door closed behind them, Henry grinned at me.

"You said last night that you did not have feelings for her, but I have to disagree, dear friend. You have been charmed."

"Preposterous," I waved my hand as if batting his words away.

"You cannot see your face, Charles. You certainly admire her." He laughed and watched me squirm.

He had me. I groaned, bent over, placed my head in my hands, then rubbed them down my face, raising my head to look at his grin.

"You cannot trick me, my friend. I have known you for too long," Henry chuckled.

"What am I to do? As her caretaker, I cannot seek her hand." I lowered my head into my hands again.

"Now that we know her father's name, we can contact him to retrieve her. Once she is in her father's care, you will be free to chase her across the world if you wish."

"*If* he can get through the blockade," I paused. What reason could her father have to travel to France? Was he a ranking officer . . . or a traitor serving Napoleon? "Where was she traveling? In whose care was she supposed to be?" I sighed and sat back. "There is a lot she is not disclosing."

"All in due time, Charles." He stood and went to the door. "Try to get some sleep, my friend, though I know it might be difficult." His laughter echoed down the hall with his footsteps.

I sighed. I had all but admitted to my oldest friend that I had fallen in love; therefore, I must admit it to myself. *This is absurd.* It had been but a few days . . . and yet, now, I indeed admired Celeste, but I could not act on it. How could this happen in such a short time?

Chapter Ten

Celeste

The bed felt soft enough, but I couldn't sleep, most likely due to my nap earlier. I couldn't get Lord Shariton's stern gaze out of my mind. His ability to see right through me caused unease. It was useless trying to sleep. I stood and pulled Ruth's old robe over my nightgown. Since listening to Ruth play the piano, I felt a great need to play it myself. Alone. Carefully, I opened the bedroom door and wondered if I dared chance going to the drawing room to play. Would the sound carry upstairs?

With the silence of a ninja, I stepped into the corridor and gently closed the door behind me. The scenes from horror movies I'd watched as a kid—against my father's wishes—played over in my thoughts as I passed the large oil paintings on the walls. Films of haunted mansions were my favorite—not because I enjoyed the horror, but because I was fascinated by the grandeur of the large houses. Call me crazy, but I would have loved to be locked inside an old house, free to wander about. At the moment, however, I felt differently. It was a wee bit too spooky in real life.

The hair at the end of my braid caught around my finger in my nervous twisting. I went down the stairs and into the drawing room, all the while with the feeling of something creeping up my back. The dimming blaze in the fireplace gave me enough light to make my way across the empty room to the piano. The seat creaked when I sat, letting my fingers rest on the keys. Now I could play and cry without an audience to witness my tears.

The tinkling of notes rang through the room, breaking the silence and causing my shoulders to rise and my eyes to close. Surely the house was large, and the bedrooms far enough away that I'd not wake anyone. If I touched the keys gently, the sound wouldn't carry much farther than this room.

Taking a deep breath, I began a piece from one of Papa's favorite movies—*The Man from Snowy River*.

The song's last note faded like the dimming of the fire's embers. "That was for you, Papa." Tears blurred my vision. I wiped them away and began another song I'd been dying to play—well, one of them. I wanted to play several, but I chose one mellower to avoid waking anyone. My vision blurred with tears to the point I couldn't see which keys my fingers were touching, but I played on. My heart bled for my father as the memories faded in and out.

When I finished, I stood and moved to admire the sliver of the moon outside the window, but from the corner of my eye, I saw shadows move, and my heart leaped with fear. I turned to see who might be in the room, but found no one there.

Feeling a little frightened at the thought of someone—or something—roaming the large mansion at night, I hurried from the room and made it to my bed safe and sound. I curled up under the covers and searched my mind for the unclear image I had seen from the corner of my eye. *Did I truly see someone in the hall by the door? Or was it my imagination?*

* * *

Charles

My fingertips brushed my door handle when I saw movement down the hall. Without much thought, I pressed against the wall and froze. Celeste walked to the stairs and did not see me. Her feet did not make a sound on the stairway at her descent, and I wondered how she could step so silently. Staying against the wall, I hurried to the top of the stairs and peered down. It was surprising how fast she moved, for she had already entered the drawing room. I made haste without making a sound down the stairs to follow her.

Before I reached the door, I heard the piano. The sweet sound, sweeter than I had ever heard, floated to me. The melody was unfamiliar, but she played full of emotion and conveyed a sense of peace. I leaned my head inside the doorway and saw her long dark braid shining in the moonlight that reached her through the window. Over the unfamiliar melody, I caught the sound of her softly weeping. In that moment, I wanted to go to her, clear her tears away, and hold her until she was right again.

The song ended and she paused, saying something softly as she wiped her tears away. *Play on, gentle lady.* I nearly sighed when she began another song, as tender and beautiful as the first. This time she smiled, and my heartbeat quickened in my chest.

I scowled, closed my eyes, and willed my heart to calm. This was a pretty fix I found myself in. Standing here making a cake of myself was not helping in the least. When Celeste finished her songs, she stood. Not wanting her to know I had intruded on her private moment, I quickly returned to the stairs. Once I got back to my room, I opened the door and peeked out and down the hall. She twirled her hair around her fingers, and made her way back to her room.

I sat on my bed and tried to remember the sound of the music she had played. It was unlike any I had ever heard. Remembering earlier this evening the color of her blushing cheeks, I realized I must have been an overbearing simpleton for causing her discomfort and pain. My heart fell. Someone who could play with such emotion and tenderness and had such a gentle demeanor deserved to be treated better. I would not cause her discomfort again.

* * *

Celeste

The tapping of the rain woke me. I sighed. Walking today was a no-go. Gradually, I dressed and brushed through my hair. Knowing Annabeth would want to help me with my hair, I waited for as long as I could stand. My mood matched the dreary skies. From the way Lord Shariton sounded last night, it seemed he couldn't wait to find my father and have me gone. *Maybe I can go back? There's a chance I could find my way back to the tree . . . if I look long enough, possibly.* With my hair still undone, I headed to the library.

As I walked the halls, I could hear servants hurrying about their morning duties—though I rarely saw them. *How many servants does it take to run a place like this?* None I'd encountered looked at me directly when I did spot them.

The smell of books settled my mood somewhat. I found the book I'd started earlier and helped myself to a settee. I tucked my bare feet under me and soothed my troubled thoughts with the book. There was so much of it that I didn't comprehend. After several minutes of understanding very little, I stood and went to the shelf to find a book of translations from French to English. My back faced the door, so I didn't see anyone enter the room. It wasn't until I heard someone's shoe creak behind me that I turned.

I gasped, then let my shoulders drop with a sigh of relief.

"Forgive me for startling you. I thought you had heard me enter," Lord Shariton paused, his eyes scanning the books beyond me. "I was curious about what you were searching for."

I lowered my gaze to the book in my hand. "I was looking for a book to help me translate from French to English."

He glanced at the book in my hand, and then peered at the rows of books. "I believe I might have one in here, Miss Roberts." He gazed at me and I tried to look away, but found it difficult. "If you wish, I could help you translate."

He had used my formal name, and I felt oddly hurt by it. My face warmed. I didn't answer him, so he stepped to my side and took the book from me.

"What passages confuse you?"

I took a deep breath and pointed at a few words on the page. "Here and here. I'm unfamiliar with those."

He tried to hold back a smile. "So, you know this word here is 'sweetheart.'"

I nodded, not wanting him to know I hadn't.

"'My love, embrace me, kiss me. Let our breath—'"

My hands lashed out, and took the book from his hands. "I understand now."

"So, those words were kiss . . . and embrace. You will remember them next time?" he said, then chuckled.

My face burned with embarrassment. "You can make fun of me, Lord Shariton, but I wasn't taught those words in French."

He stopped laughing but continued to smile. "I apologize, Miss Roberts. I suppose your tutor had no reason to teach you such words."

"No, she didn't. Why are you grinning at me like that? Had I known what this book said, I wouldn't have let you read it to me." I paused and watched his shoulders shaking in silent laughter. My own laughter pushed from my lips. "Oh, stop!" I freely released, putting the book down on the small table, and I moved toward the door.

"Oh, please do not take offense," Lord Shariton protested, taking my arm to stop me from leaving.

My crooked smile couldn't be helped. "No offense taken. I'm just . . ."

He let go of my arm and held his hand behind his back. "I have embarrassed you. My apologies. My mother taught me better conduct than I have just shown."

"No," I tilted my head toward him. "You're a perfect gentleman."

"Come now . . . I see it in your eyes. There is more you wish to say."

"It's . . . nice to see that you can laugh, tease, and act a bit more . . . normal than I first thought."

"Normal?" His head cocked to the side, and his lips pulled together. "Sometimes you say such odd . . . never mind." He lowered his head and rocked on his heels. "There I go again. It seems I have a talent for making you blush."

I open my mouth and it seems rubbish is all that comes out. "Yes, well . . . I should go."

He nodded and bowed ever so slightly.

I grinned and blushed the entire walk to my room. Despite my embarrassment, I felt more at ease with him after that small exchange of . . . whatever one might call it. It couldn't have been flirtation. He didn't seem the sort of man to flirt with a girl.

After getting my hair done and eating breakfast, I joined Ruth and Lady Garrison in planning the ball. They were happy to have someone with an artistic hand to add some flare to the invitations. I enjoyed the work and their company, and I realized how truly starved I was for friendship. I hadn't had true friends my whole life. Ruth and I had so much in common. She was a little more talkative than I, but I enjoyed it. She still allowed me a chance to speak.

While we were gathered together, happily chatting away, one of the servants came to the door. "There is a delivery for Miss Roberts."

My mouth hung open for a moment. Ruth noticed my bewilderment. *Who would be sending me packages here? I don't know anyone.*

"Bring them in here, Herbert," Ruth said to the older man. Herbert opened the door to allow a man carrying several large boxes into the room.

"Holy boxes, Batman!" I said with wide eyes. Everyone turned to me with puzzled faces. When I realized what I'd said, heat burst into my ears. It used to be a habit of mine to call out 'Holy—whatever it was—Batman' when I was amazed at something. I'd have to be more careful from now on. *Oops.* The others directed their attention to the boxes, and I followed them across the room. The men left the room and closed the door.

Not knowing what to think or do, I let Ruth and Lady Garrison have the honor of opening them.

"There is no name on them—but that does not matter. I know they must be from Charles," Ruth stated.

My heart fluttered like a bird trapped in a cage when she opened the first box. A beautiful gown lay neatly wrapped inside, and the following two large boxes contained day dresses. In all, I received three gowns, three day dresses, two bonnets along with some gloves, a short coat called a Spencer, shoes, and other accessories. I also was given a short stays which was to replace my corset.

The women oohed and ahhed over the new clothing while I stood horrified. I didn't need him to buy me clothing. I had money—though not money from this time—but still, I had some. Now I felt like I owed him something, and I didn't like that feeling. From what I'd read online while researching the Regency era for an essay in school, I knew that a dress cost a huge amount of money. Most people during this time were lucky to have two. Of course, from what I knew of Lord Shariton, he had plenty of money—but still, it didn't sit well with me to owe him so much.

Besides, I couldn't stay here or carry these items back with me. Could I trust him not to hang this over my head?

"What do you think, Celeste?" Ruth held out a bonnet for me. "Isn't my brother the most thoughtful man around?"

I opened my mouth and found that my voice was hushed. "Very thoughtful."

"You are a bashful thing." Lady Garrison took my arm and pulled me closer. "He did you a great honor in getting these for you. You should be happy."

I forced a smile. "Please don't think me ungrateful—I'm merely . . . shocked."

Ruth hugged me and laughed. "I cannot wait to see you in the ball gown. You will look breathtaking."

A bit later, I followed Herbert up the stairs to my room, where he left the boxes on my bed. Annabeth came to help me put things away, but I dismissed her and did it myself. When Annabeth came in to help me prepare for dinner, she went on and on about how beautiful the dresses were. She pulled one of them out and readied it for me to put on. Her face fell when she noticed my expression.

"Do you not wish to wear it, miss?"

I didn't answer.

"You do not wish to offend Lord Shariton by not wearing his gift!" She held it up for me to slip into. I couldn't explain the emotion I felt. Not only did I feel guilty and as if I owed Lord Shariton, but I also felt like accepting these gifts made my being here more final. *Do I belong here? Should I stay?*

With a gulp, I moved hesitantly to her and let her fasten the dress.

She fixed my hair and clapped her hands when she had finished. "May I be so bold, miss, as to say you are the most beautiful woman I 'ave 'ad the honor of serving!"

I lowered my head. "Thank you." I didn't agree with her, but I didn't want to be rude. She smiled at me in the mirror, while I considered how I could repay Lord Shariton. "Annabeth, I need to . . . take care of some business, and I wondered who Lord Shariton uses to handle his financial matters?"

"Well, I do not know for certain, but you can always talk to Mr. Evens. 'E's the estate manager and a very trustworthy and kind man. 'E could help you. Or there is 'erbert. I don't know the solicitor."

"Could you send for Mr. Evens?"

"Right now?" she asked.

"Yes, please. I'll meet with him in the library."

"Of course, miss. Right away, then." She hurried from the room. I opened the wardrobe, quietly emptied a box of the newer gold coins into a small drawstring bag, and made my way down to the library.

When Mr. Evens arrived, I was surprised to see how old he was. His skin almost hung off his bones, though when he moved his arms, I could see some strength left in them. "You needed me, Miss Roberts?"

"Yes. I'm sorry to bother you, but I need someone's help. Can I trust you with a most secret and important assignment?" My hands shook, and I clasped the bag tighter for fear of dropping it. *Can I really go through with this?* Here I was, ready to trade some of my father's collection of coins, never to see them again. At least they weren't the older most prized ones.

"O' course, Miss Roberts."

"I have some money. It was mis-cast . . . or some such thing," I waved my arm nervously. "The wrong date is on the coins, and I wondered if you could help me trade them in for the right kind and amount. I suppose they tally them by weight anyway. Could you please help?"

He smiled warmly. "O' course, miss."

I relaxed a little and held the coins out to him. "Please keep this a secret, even from Lord Shariton. No one must know."

He cleared his throat and stood a little taller. "I will take care of it right away." He studied me as if trying to figure me out, then left the room.

My heart thumped. Had I done the right thing, trusting him with my money? I'd just handed him a few thousand pounds' worth of coins. My father would be furious. It was too late now. Worry weighed on my shoulders as I walked back to the drawing room.

Chapter Eleven

Charles

Miss Roberts was the last to enter the drawing room for dinner. Everyone in the room lit up, exclaiming how beautiful she looked in her new gown. All I could do was stare. She blushed and made her way to me.

"Lord Shariton, I want to thank you for my new clothing. The dresses are wonderful, and you were so thoughtful to give them to me, but I'd like to repay you for them."

I waved my hand. "There is no need to repay me, Miss Roberts. You came with nothing, and you were in need of something that fit you. My only regret is that I did not have the foresight to order you a riding habit until I had already ordered this for you." *Lud, I hope I have not made a mistake in purchasing her clothing.*

She breathed out in a rush. "Please, my lord, I would like to repay you."

I touched her chin and returned my hand back quickly, trying to keep my eyes locked on hers and not her lips. "No. It is my gift to you," I said, then cleared my throat, hoping she did not see my urge to kiss her. Her eyes dropped, and a crease formed between her brow. I wondered what thought could have caused such a look.

We made our way into the dining room, and her expression troubled me. I squared my shoulders and sat down, making up my mind to erase that look of worry from her face. Despite my best efforts over dinner, she only smiled slightly in conversation, but would not truly give herself over to enjoyment the entire evening.

After everyone had retired for the evening, I went to the library to see if I could find the book Miss Roberts had searched for. I could tell the moment she walked into the library that books were what moved her. Perhaps I could entice a smile to pull at her pink, full lips by simply giving her something to study, and thus, I might get to sleep tonight. The book should have been in a specified spot, but it was missing. I looked for some time, but it grew late, so I quietly headed out into the hall. The sound of the piano caused me to pause. *What luck! She is playing again!*

I stepped to the door and listened to her play another unknown song. It was strange and had an odd rhythm, but was no less enchanting. The clouds outside made it too dark to see anything of her face, but I watched her nonetheless. After she played three musical numbers, she stood and moved toward the door. I did not react fast enough, so I hauled myself into the hall and around the corner. The soft rustle of her nightgown flowed to the stairs. She paused, then moved in a different direction. When I peered around the corner, I saw her heading toward the ballroom. I knew it was not very gentlemanly of me to follow a young lady around at night, but curiosity got the best of me.

* * *

Celeste

I stepped into the ballroom, pushing aside my fears that something might jump out at me at any moment. Instead, I focused on the steps of the new dance I had practiced earlier with Lord Shariton. I closed my eyes and danced until I felt comfortable with them. Thinking of him near me, pressing his fingers at the small of my back while he moved me through the steps of the dance, caused me to sigh.

I filled my lungs and glanced up at the ceiling far above me. This room had a great echo, and I wanted to try it out. With another deep breath, I started to sing one of Enya's most somber songs, one that spoke directly to me. The words to the song, *If I Could Be Where You Are*, echoed my thoughts deep within. I dared not wake the house, so I sang softly. I sat on the cold floor and thought of my father while I sang and let the emotion fill my soul.

I paused after the chorus and let the tears fall. I knew I didn't sing as well as Enya, but I enjoyed doing so. It made me feel more connected to Papa, who once loved to hear me sing.

I wiped my tears, ready to begin the second verse, when the sound of something hitting the floor echoed around the bare room. Thoughts of zombies and ghouls flashed in my mind, and panic surged through me. The sound came from the door I had entered. I stood and ran to the opposite side of the room, pulling open one of the large doors. In my haste, I hadn't realized the door led outside until I felt the cold wind hit me hard in the face. The smell of rain still hung in the air from hours before.

The wind slammed the door behind me at the exact moment I heard a man's voice call out. I didn't know who it was—perhaps one of the servants. Sticking around to find out who it might be filled me with panic, so I ran, knowing it was foolish to run out into the darkness alone.

When the immediate fear dissipated, the familiar feeling of humiliation took its place. Unless that noise came from a resident ghost, someone had witnessed a sacred moment.

Angry tears fell at each quickened step through the gardens. My name echoed into the night, called by multiple voices. Blindly, I ran up the grass field that led along the side of the forest. *I'm such an idiot! What am I doing?*

The wet ground made my bare feet ache, and the hems of both nightgown and robe were soaked through. I pulled them higher to prevent them from sticking to my legs and tripping me, not caring about propriety. A moment later, the sky opened and the rain beat down on me. Water dripped down my back, chilling me to the bone.

Something sharp pierced my foot, causing me to stumble to the ground. The water soaked me from top to bottom. The object in my foot sliced into my flesh even further when I fell, and pain shot through my foot and leg. I rolled to a sitting position, pulling my foot to my face to investigate.

"Blast these stupid thorns!" I cried out, taking the thorn from my foot. I rubbed my foot and whimpered in the dark rain. A great chasm in my heart tore wider still, and my father's absence was the cause. Blinking at the rain, I glared at the darkness above and screamed at the top of my lungs, "You weren't supposed to leave me! Not you! How dare you! I *hate* you!" I dropped my head and sobbed, wiping my nose with my gown.

"Celeste!" I jumped at the sound of Lord Shariton's voice over my shoulder. He came running up and knelt beside me. "Are you hurt? You are getting soaked!"

He helped me to my feet. Wincing with each step, I walked beside him toward the house. He wanted to assist me, but I held up my hand and stubbornly told him I could manage. When we reached the end of the garden nearest the house, I spoke my thoughts. "Was it you . . . in the ballroom?"

He slowly nodded. "Yes. Please forgive me, Miss Roberts."

Heat washed through me. *He was spying on me?* Increasing my speed, I headed up the stairs.

"Celeste! *Please!*" he called after me. *He witnessed me blubbering all over myself! Where's a shovel so I may bury myself six feet under?*

The fact that my feet were wet and a little muddy didn't occur to me as I crossed the smooth marble floor of the ballroom once again. My feet flew up and my head fell backward, hitting the hard stone. The breath gushed from my body, and I tried desperately to get it back. My lungs shrunk in size, and refused to function.

Seconds later, Lord Shariton was beside me, speaking quickly to someone behind him. "Go get Annabeth out of bed and send her to Miss Roberts' room."

The air again filled my lungs, and I worked to steady my breathing. I blinked up at him and whispered, "Charles."

With a frown, he pulled me into his arms and carried me from the room. I didn't resist his help this time, but leaned into him instead. The pain in my head caused the walls and floor to spin, driving the fight out of me.

Gently he placed me on the trunk in my room and turned to Annabeth. "Hold a candle here." He took my head in his wet hands, "Look at me, Celeste. Do you remember what happened?"

It was difficult to focus on him with the tears that blurred my vision, but I managed. "I'm okay," I whispered and hiccupped.

"What do you mean by okay?"

Oh. Okay must be modern. "I'm well."

His thumb rubbed against my cheek, and he stared at me a moment longer. "Get her out of these wet clothes and into dry ones. Call me when you are finished." He let go of me and left the room.

"Yes, my lord." Annabeth curtsied and closed the door behind him. She didn't say a word while she helped me change clothes. Being back in my room, and my bed seemed to clear my head. *What have I done? I acted like a child—worse than a child—I acted like a sniveling fool. What must he think of me?*

* * *

Charles

Sleep abandoned me through the night. Pacing my room was all I could do. Miss Roberts seemed to be doing better, but I could not help but feel worried. Guilt tore at me for sneaking about and scaring her near to death. I should not have listened in on her. She obviously sang about someone she loved dearly, most likely a young man, judging by her behavior. The idea of her pining for some unknown man caused a surge of jealousy to course through me. It was an unfamiliar feeling—at least to this degree.

When I woke in the morning after a short stint of restless sleep, I hurried to find Annabeth and learn how Miss Roberts was faring.

"She was still sleeping, my lord, only a moment ago," Annabeth replied.

"Let me know when she wakes. I will be conversing with Mr. Evens."

"Yes, my lord," she curtsied and hurried away.

Keeping to my usual morning routine seemed my only option, except for the ride on Apollo that I took every morning. I wanted to stay close in case there was any change in Miss Roberts. To my dismay, Mr. Evens had disappeared, and no one seemed to know where he had gone. Feeling discouraged and agitated, I headed back into the house before breakfast. Annabeth found me in my library.

"She's awake, but keeps to 'er room, my lord."

"How is she?"

"She seems well, only a bit sad."

"Annabeth," I picked up the book of French poetry and gave it to her, "please give her this to read. Tell her I am still looking for a translation book."

"Yes, my lord."

Celeste stayed in her room all that day and through the night. I did not get a chance to tell her how sorry I was.

Chapter Twelve

Celeste

    The window felt cool against my skin and the sketched pad's familiar feel gave me comfort. Drawing had a way of healing. All the crying I had done last night helped, although now I felt foolish. Ashamed by my behavior, I couldn't bring myself to dress and join the others.

    I had no one's shoulder to cry on during my father's death and funeral. Once that horrible week ended, my father's friends went about their lives. The only person I'd had for company was my old nanny, who had a habit of drinking away her sorrows. I shook the memories from my mind and tried to let go of the sadness trapped inside. It was time to let it pass.

    Ruth came in a couple of times. She tried to get me to open up, but I changed the subject and let her talk about other things. She begged me to come and speak with her brother. She said he was moping about the house and needed to see me. I didn't understand why he'd care to see me—especially after all the grief I'd caused him.

The servants brought my meals to my room, though I ate little. I was tired of this bland food which I wasn't accustomed to. I craved chocolate and Indian curry with naan to scoop it. Though they occasionally served chocolate, there certainly weren't any candy bars lying about.

The book of poetry Lord Shariton had delivered to me lay on the desk, but it held no interest. The piano called to me, but I stayed in my room, wishing to mourn alone. Having cried most of the day, I went to sleep immediately and woke early the next day. The warmth of my bed held me captive until I eventually talked myself into getting up. I'd have to face everyone soon enough.

Annabeth helped me with my hair, and I wore my new day dress, hoping to please Lord Shariton. I wondered if he might be angry with me after what I'd done. Perhaps my behavior had made him aware that I'm not of the social class he believes. It was highly unlikely that dignified ladies went about with their dresses pulled to their knees, yelling at the sky and cursing at every turn.

I should go home.

It was too early for breakfast. I headed into the gardens, hoping the fresh air would brighten my thoughts. A bush of roses tempted me to stop and smell them.

A galloping horse drew my attention, and beyond the hedge, I spotted Lord Shariton atop his horse. He pulled to a stop at the stables and dismounted. The sight of him caused a mixture of emotions, most of them indecipherable. I brushed my hands down my dress, took a steady breath, and walked toward the stables. It would be easier to apologize to him now than in front of everyone at breakfast. When I reached the stables, he was heading out.

He stopped short when he saw me. "Miss Roberts."

"Good morning, Lord Shariton. I want to apolog—"

He held his hand up to cut me off. "It is I who should be apologizing. Please forgive me for disturbing a sacred moment." His voice was smooth and calm, bringing a warm intensity to his words.

"You're forgiven." I stared at my feet and added, "I hope you can forgive me for running, then refusing your help—and calling you by your given name. Reflecting on all I did, I realize it was unladylike, and I'm completely humiliated by my behavior."

He stepped to me and lifted my chin. I felt that he could see into my soul. "You have no need to apologize." His eyes darted back and forth between my own.

His scent encircled me, and I had to fight the sudden urge to kiss him. Immediately, I stepped back and dropped my head, ashamed of my thoughts. He was a Lord, and I was nothing but an accidental time traveler who didn't belong. There were so many reasons not to be overcome by infatuation for him, most of which had everything to do with the time gap in our lives. Momentarily, my eyes lowered to study his boots, not daring to look back at him. He began to say something, then turned abruptly away. I lifted my head to see Mr. Evens waving at me.

"Miss Roberts!" he called and walked toward me.

Lord Shariton stared back and forth from Mr. Evens to me with his eyebrows squished together.

"Please excuse me, Lord Shariton. I'll be just a moment," I said, giving him a quick smile and stepping away.

I ignored Lord Shariton's questioning glance and walked to Mr. Evens, feeling a little upset that Mr. Evens would call me in front of Lord Shariton, undoubtedly causing more suspicion. When I reached Mr. Evens, I continued walking away from Lord Shariton to prevent him from overhearing. Mr. Evens followed. I noticed he carried a wooden box.

"Do you have something for me, Mr. Evens?"

"Yes, Miss Roberts. I have your coins. Ya now have a collection of silver, copper coins, and some notes to replace what you gave me."

With a glance over my shoulder, I saw Lord Shariton heading into the house's side door. I turned to Mr. Evens and held my hand out for the box. "Thank you for doing this for me, Mr. Evens. It was very kind of you." I opened the box and found several coins and paper notes. Not knowing how much things cost in this time period, I hadn't a clue what to give him. "Can I pay you with some of this?"

He held up his hands. "No. I will not take one quid. If Lord Shariton found out I took any of it from ya, he'd 'ave me horsewhipped."

"You're joking."

"Perhaps I am. I will not be taking any of it from ya, miss; ya can be sure every last piece is there. Paid a hefty price, he did. Ya had pure gold, ya did. Well, I best be getting on." He began backing away.

"Someday, I'll repay you. Thanks for being a friend."

His smile softened his weathered face. "My pleasure to serve ya, miss." He bowed, turned around, and whistled as he walked away.

My shoulders relaxed. I entered through the side door and hurried up to my room. After taking a few paper notes and coins from the box, I hid the rest in my wardrobe. The coins clanged together in my reticule as I cinched it shut before making my way to breakfast.

When I entered the room, Ruth stood and came to me with open arms. "It is good to see you out and walking around again, my sweet friend." She kissed my cheek and rested her hand on my arm.

I glanced at Lord Shariton who had a strange look on his face. He was watching me very intently. *What's new?*

"We, too, are happy to see you up and smiling again," Sir Garrison said, biting into a roll.

Lady Garrison hugged me. "Are you well now, dear?"

I nodded and gave a wan smile, then sat to eat. Ruth and Lady Garrison immediately started updating me on the ball preparations. As I listened to them recite innumerable details, I glanced at Lord Shariton, who still watched me. He was good at making me uncomfortable.

Lady Garrison practically bounced in her seat when she announced her children would be arriving today—which was odd for an elegant lady to do. I liked her all the more for it. Her excitement made me think of those days when Papa would come home from a long trip, and I couldn't physically contain my joy.

When I had nearly finished eating my breakfast, Lord Shariton stood and excused himself. I leaned toward the group of women and whispered, "If you'll excuse me, I need to take care of something."

I hurried from the room and called after Lord Shariton, "Please, sir—your lordship!"

He stopped and waited for me to catch up.

"I wanted to give you something," I said and cleared my throat. "It didn't sit well, not giving this to you. I don't know if it's enough, for I don't know much about such things, but here." I carefully placed the weighty reticule into his hand.

Raising an eyebrow, he tugged it open, and his head jerked back. "Where did you get this?"

"From my father."

"How much more do you have?" he asked.

I shrugged, which probably wasn't a very ladylike thing to do.

"Show me," he said forcefully.

Concern rose in my throat. He didn't look happy.

He stepped closer. "Show me now."

My voice caught, then squeaked out, "It's in my room."

To my surprise, he took me by the arm, and marched me up the stairs. His grip was firm but not enough to cause discomfort. I felt like a child who had done something terribly wrong. My heart hammered against my ribs, and I wondered how to calm him as we swept along the hall. When we reached my room, he opened the door and impatiently

91

waved me in, staying outside.

"Show me," he demanded again.

My hands shook. I went to the wardrobe, opened it, and carefully uncovered the box with the money. I pulled it out and took it into the hall to show him. He fingered a few coins and inspected the notes.

His brow rose again. "Is this what you were given by Mr. Evens?"

I nodded.

"Miss Roberts, how much do you have here?"

I hesitated, but seeing the determination in his eyes, I answered truthfully. *I'm so tired of lying.* Assuming he meant everything and I wasn't exactly sure how much inflation would affect what I had, so I replied, "I'm not certain, but in total, I have around five million."

His eyes bugged. "F—five million pounds?"

He sat down on the nearest chair in the corridor as if his legs couldn't hold him. "You must not know the seriousness of your situation, Miss Roberts. Your money must be the largest amount I have seen in a woman's dowry. Knowing as much . . ." He paused and came to me. He placed the coins on the chair, took me by both hands while looking into my eyes, and asked in a soft tone, "Has your father passed?"

"I . . ." My heart went wild. I blinked as though he had slapped me in the face. *How could he know?*

"The only reason for a young woman to be in possession of her dowry before marriage is if her father has already passed away."

I lowered my head and nodded, trying in vain to hold back tears.

He dropped his hands and rubbed at his face. "Did you indeed have memory loss?"

"No," I whispered. I couldn't lie to him any longer. The lies were becoming overwhelming.

He huffed and took a few steps away. "You lied this whole time? To all of us?"

Choked by emotion, I attempted an explanation, "I'm sorry. I should've told you the truth, but I was afraid." I covered my mouth to muffle my cries.

He turned and looked at me with a hard gaze. His eyes hurt to look into, so I lowered my head. His footsteps came closer and his sigh tickled the top of my head. Gently he rested his hands on my shoulders, and I kept my head down, wiping at my eyes.

He held out a handkerchief and I took it. "That is why you've been so sad these last few days. You've been mourning your father? That song you sang . . . it was for him?"

"Yes," I hiccupped, then began to cry harder. "You must think me foolish."

"You are not foolish, and I can understand why you did what you did."

I relaxed a bit.

"Who were you traveling with, and where were you heading?" he asked.

"No one. I traveled alone." It was a true statement, but not in the same sense that he understood it. To travel alone in my own time wasn't a big deal, but here—now—it wasn't done.

He stepped away from me. "You were alone? Where were you heading?"

I shrugged. "I don't know. Away from where I was, I suppose."

"And where was that?"

"London. I had no one to turn to whom I could trust. I had to leave."

"No friends or relatives?"

"No one." It was the truth. I had no one—until now. Now I had Ruth and the Garrisons, and hopefully . . .

"Were you running away from someone?"

I slowly nodded. "Just a man."

"What is his name?" he asked.

"I don't know him. It was just a man on the road, but he won't be a bother now. He won't know where to find me."

He cleared his throat. "Miss Roberts, I needn't have any scruples in speaking the truth with you. You are mature enough to understand the danger you are in now. If word got out that you had a sizable dowry, every fortune hunter around would knock down my door and try anything to get your money. Do you understand what I mean?"

I thought of the stories I'd read of men talking women into running away with them for the sole purpose of getting their money. Some would try kidnapping if it came down to it. "What do I do?"

"First, we need to find a better hiding place than your wardrobe. You can leave that up to me—"

"I'll find one," I said quickly.

"Very well. Second, I will need to act as your protector—your guardian—to keep you safe and help you choose the right man to . . . marry." His Adam's apple moved up and down. More than likely, he regretted taking me in with the strain I most definitely had caused him.

I'm not old enough to marry. Thoughts of returning to my own time filled my mind with confusion. Because I'd repaid him for the gowns he'd bought, I felt free to leave. I'd have to leave.

If I did go back, I would be alone again. If I stayed, I might have the chance to cultivate these new friendships and experience a period I had always exalted, but I could end up married—as someone's property.

"Have you spoken to anyone about this money?" he asked.

"No. Only Mr. Evens knows I have it," I replied.

"Good. Keep it that way." He dropped the gold coins and notes I had given him into the wooden box and closed it.

"But that's for you!" I protested.

He picked up the box and held it out to me. I took it, and he rested his hand on my arm. "Please, let me take care of you, Celeste."

I smiled at the sound of my name. His voice was so soothing and warm. The touch of his hand made me ache to be held in his arms. My

94

ears and cheeks grew hot. *Didn't he say he is to be my matchmaker? He isn't interested in me.*

He began to walk down the corridor, then stopped and looked back. "If you are in need of *anything*, let me know."

I nodded. "Thank you, my lord." At that moment, I wished I could call him by his given name. "My lord" seemed so distant and formal. He was my friend now, and I'd hoped that he would ask me to call him Charles. I would wait for him to do that. I wouldn't want to be disrespectful to my friend.

Chapter Thirteen

Charles

After discussing matters with Celeste, I went to find Mr. Evens. He was in with the hens, repairing a fence.

"Mr. Evens!" I called.

"Yes, my lord," he dropped his tools and hurried to my side.

"I spoke with Miss Roberts. I understand that you helped her with her money."

His face fell. "Yes, I did, and she made me promise not to tell."

"Well, the secret is out, and now I know why you were missing for the last day and a half. Pray, how exactly did you receive the money?"

"She gave it to me, my lord."

I narrowed my eyes in confusion. "Why would she give you money simply for you to return it to her?"

"The money she gave me was cast wrong. The dates on it read two thousand and something. So I traded it in for her."

How very odd. "Did you give her every last coin?"

"Of course. She tried to give me some in payment, but I refused." His shoulders lifted, and his chest rose with pride.

I nodded. "Thank you, Mr. Evens. You're a good man. I am pleased she could trust you with this."

"I am happy to serve, my lord."

"Tell me, did you speak to anyone else about this matter?"

He paused, and a look of consternation crossed his face. "Well, my lord, whilst I was talking with the man at the bank, a gentleman waiting there did—that is to say—he was real friendly-like and began asking questions. I was careful and never told him where the money came from, but . . ."

Anger boiled inside me. "Who was he?"

"I do not know, my lord."

Not wishing Mr. Evens to feel the brunt of my anger, I left without another word. He was a good man, and I liked him, even if he occasionally acted a little dimwitted.

* * *

Celeste

That afternoon Sir and Lady Garrison's children arrived along with their maid, Susan. The Garrisons had three children—Thomas was nine, Mary was six, and George was three. After their long journey, they were eager to run about and play. The maid appeared exhausted, so I offered to watch the children while she unpacked their trunks. The kids followed me into the garden, and we played with Lord Shariton's dogs in the warm breeze. The dogs were so large I had to pick little George up many times after he was knocked over. Each time, I brushed him off and told him he was a strong, sturdy little man who could handle a little fall without any fuss, and he smiled and ran off to play again.

I enjoyed my time with them and found them perfectly behaved. I taught them a few games I had played as a child until we were told it was time to dress for dinner. The children moaned in protest—as did I.

Once dressed, I hurried to the drawing room, anxious to see the children again. They weren't there when I arrived, and dinner was announced the moment I entered. Lord Shariton stood ready with his arm out for me, then directed me to my seat at his right. I still expected to see the children arrive at any moment, but I didn't want to ask about them. Reflecting on things I'd learned while reading Jane Austen, I tried to remember if children were invited to dine with the adults. In the end, I was glad I held my tongue. Papa once told me, "Better to remain silent and be thought a fool than to speak and remove all doubt."

* * *

Charles

In the time between dinner and dessert, I gave permission for the children to join us. As I did so, I glanced at Miss Roberts, noticing with pleasure the way her smile lit up her eyes. When the children entered, the two youngest made their way to their mother for kisses, then hurried promptly to Miss Roberts' side. I was surprised to see how eager they were to be with her. She seemed equally as happy to have them.

Miss Roberts pushed her chair back and pulled little Mary onto her lap. George leaned against her as if he wanted to join his sister.

"It seems the children are drawn to you, Miss Roberts," Henry said.

"I hope you don't mind," Miss Roberts blushed and gazed at Clair.

"I am happy they have found friendship with you, my dear. It is only natural. After all, you radiate kindness and love in everything you do," Clair said.

Miss Roberts' blush deepened. "They're the dearest things. Though I'm not surprised. They simply mimic their parents in their sweetness." She returned her attention to the children, helping them with their fruit and nuts.

I could not help but admire her ease with the children. When I'd observed her playing with them earlier, I thought perhaps she was doing a good deed in helping their maid, but now I saw she truly enjoyed having them near.

After a few minutes, the women and children made their way into the drawing-room, and I stayed behind with Henry.

"Can I tell you something in confidence, Henry?"

"Of course. Need you ask?"

I peered at him hard. "You cannot breathe a word of this to anyone. I am only telling you so you can help me."

"Charles, you've known me for years. You can trust me."

I cleared my throat and nodded. "It has come to my attention that Miss Roberts' father has passed away."

His jaw fell slack, and his eyes widened. "She remembers?"

I nodded. "Her memories have returned." I did not tell him she had them all along. I did not want to cause her any more discomfort. "I have also learned she has her dowry with her."

"Oh?" his eyebrow rose.

"It is the largest sum I have seen a woman—" I shook my head. I had nearly called her out as a liar when she shared the amount with me earlier, but her eyes showed no deceit, only regret, and remorse. "Millions."

"Oh." Now both eyebrows rose. "Does anyone else know?"

"Possibly."

His surprise turned to solemnity. "I see. Every fortune hunter will be after her."

I nodded again. "When we attend the Cromwell's ball tomorrow, I need you on the alert. She must not be left alone." The thought of Celeste at the mercy of a brute of a man caused my grip to tighten on my glass of port. I hastened to set it down lest I should break it.

"Of course. Does she understand the gravity of her situation?"

I nodded. "I have informed her."

"Does she have a relative she can go to? Or perhaps a friend?" Henry asked.

"No. She was abandoned for reasons I cannot understand," I rubbed my chin.

"So, the task of guardianship has fallen to you," he tipped his glass at me, then swallowed the contents with relish.

"Though I do not want it," I sighed.

"Then marry the girl!" he laughed.

"Do not be daft. You know I cannot. Firstly, I am in the delicate position of hosting her as my guest, now even my ward. And secondly, we cannot be sure there is no family out there expecting her, who might frown upon the match. Besides, I do not know how she feels about me, and I would not wish her to think I am set to marry her for her money."

"I see," he set his empty glass down. "Then you will have to suffer through several social events over the months to come and perhaps watch as she is swept off her feet by some other man who no doubt does not deserve her."

I glared at him. "Let us join the ladies."

In the drawing-room, the children gathered around Miss Roberts once again. Even the eldest, Thomas, was sitting beside her, trying not to show his interest. She sang a playful tune in Italian, punctuated by animal sounds. At the end of the song, she reached for George and growled, and he giggled with delight.

Susan seemed pleased to have someone else keeping the children entertained.

"Where did you learn a song like that?" I asked.

A slight smile pulled at her lips. "My grandmother sang it to me when I was a child."

"Your grandmother?" I sat down across from her.

"She was from Rome."

"Ah, that would explain the slight olive tone of your skin," I said, admiring how her soft cheeks turned rosy at my words.

Ruth must have noticed Miss Roberts' discomfort, swiftly changing the subject to that of the upcoming dances. We had been invited to yet another ball taking place a few days before our own. Miss Roberts played with the children, only occasionally joining in the conversation.

"Would you like to see a magic trick?" she asked them.

They clapped their hands and nodded with enthusiasm. She held her hands together, one fingertip covering the joint of another, then slowly moved one hand away. The tip of one finger moved away with it, as though it had been cut off. The children gasped in horror, giggled, and moved closer.

"Your finger's off!" Mary cried with delight.

I chuckled, knowing the secret.

"How clever," Ruth giggled.

"You certainly have a way with children," Clair said admiringly.

"If you found yourself unmarried and needing an income, you would make a wonderful governess, Miss Roberts," Susan swayed as she spoke as if she rocked a child to sleep.

Henry laughed a deep, boisterous laugh. "I do not believe she will need to worry about that!"

I gave him a look only he could understand, then watched his smile fade slightly. "I believe what Sir Garrison means is that a lady of Miss Roberts' beauty and accomplishments is sure to be admired wherever she goes," I said smoothly, hoping to deflect any question that might come of Henry's lapse. Her face fell instead of the blush blooming on her check that I expected to see. She glanced up at me, and our eyes met. Quickly, she turned her attention back to the children, teasing and chatting with them.

She truly was one of a kind. Leaning forward, I caught the attention of little Mary and waved her over to me. She came with a bounce in her curls. Cupping my hand around her tiny ear, I whispered, "Did you know that Miss Roberts plays the pianoforte?" She shook her head. "Yes, but she is a bit shy about playing. Could you persuade her to play for us?"

She smiled brightly and nodded, then hurried to Miss Roberts' side. "Play a song for me . . . please."

Miss Roberts' eyes grew large, narrowed briefly, and then she smiled kindly at Mary. "Do you like the piano?"

"Oh, very much. Yes, miss." The little girl looked so hopeful that I knew Miss Roberts could not say no.

"Very well," she stood and gave me another sharp glance. I chuckled—my plan had worked.

Ruth laughed, "Oh, I am so glad you will play for us again, Celeste."

Miss Roberts sat at the piano, and by memory, she played a well-known piece by Bach. As she neared the end, I stood and moved closer to her side. Her fingers moved across the keys so easily, playing with more passion and emotion than I had ever witnessed. When she finished, she folded her hands in her lap, but did not look up at me.

I leaned in and whispered, "Play something . . . something *different.* Like what you play at night."

Her head snapped, "You've heard me play, also?" She blushed so often I wanted to laugh.

I nodded. "You play beautifully."

She turned back to the piano, her hands hesitating over the keys. Then her fingers pressed against the notes and moved up and down, playing a piece that filled me with wonder. It was enchanting. When she had finished, the room fell into stunned silence for a moment, and then everyone erupted in delighted applause.

"I have never heard a piece such as that. Simply breathtaking!" Clair held her hand over her heart.

"Can you play one you can sing along with?" Ruth asked from across the room.

Miss Roberts nodded, then paused in thought. Her fingers flowed over the keys again and her voice was clear as she sang. It was how I imagined an angel would sound. The song flowed like a gentle breeze across a sun-kissed field of honey wheat. She sang about a lost love. It was as though I could see a piece of her heart opening up and letting us peek at what lay inside.

When she stopped, she stood, and everyone applauded.

"I have never heard that music, dear. Did you write those songs yourself?" Clair asked, and Miss Roberts sat beside her on the sofa.

Miss Roberts glanced at me. I still stood next to the piano, awestruck by her playing and the words she had sung. She shook her head. "I didn't write them. I'm not lucky enough to have a talent for writing music."

"Where are they from, then? Who wrote them?" Ruth persisted.

Miss Roberts' face flushed. "I can't say. My father gave me the music and I'm afraid I don't remember the composer's name."

She looked away, toying with a tassel that hung from the pillow beside her. In her demeanor, I read a lie. *What is she hiding, and why?*

Chapter Fourteen

Celeste

My embarrassment seemed never to cease. After playing the piano, I couldn't help but shy away from the compliments of my companions. I took comfort in the knowledge that they didn't know the songs I played and, therefore, couldn't tell where I'd messed up. When Ruth asked who'd written the music, I'd frozen with panic. I wasn't prepared to answer. Musicians from my time wrote both songs, and of course, I couldn't tell them the truth. I didn't want to take credit for something that wasn't my own, so I gave them the best answer I could think of. In an effort to avoid more questions, I excused myself, pleading the need for rest.

Glancing at Lord Shariton, I stood. He studied me once again. I shifted from foot to foot, looked away and said goodnight.

After preparing for bed, I went to see Ruth. She had finished changing into her nightgown when I knocked and was let in.

"Just in time. I need someone to help me take my hair out," she said, sitting in the chair in front of her vanity.

"I would be happy to help." I moved behind her and began to pull the pins from her hair, letting it fall in a sheet down her back. "You have such thick hair."

"Yes. It can be bothersome at times," she replied, then grew quiet while she watched me in the mirror. "What do you wish for in a husband?"

Caught off guard, I shifted from one foot to the other and avoided her gaze. "I . . . I don't know."

"Do not tell me you have never thought of it. It is the only future we women have been allotted."

I tried to come up with an answer. All I could think of was Lord Shariton. A smirk grew on her face as if she could read my thoughts. Before she could start prodding and speculating, I started talking. "I guess I would want someone strong, wise, loves to read, likes to laugh, is open-minded, and most of all . . . he would have to be kind."

"Very good. I believe he has *all* of those qualities," she smirked.

"Who?" I pretended not to know what she meant.

"Who do you think?" she grinned, undeterred.

"You know I haven't been out yet, so I couldn't possibly have met anyone—and I don't know who you're referring to," I finished in a rush, avoiding her eyes. I directed the question back at her, "What qualities do *you* wish for in a husband?"

She smiled knowingly, but answered nonetheless, "Someone dashing and clever. A man who loves travel and adventure . . . and riding. I do not want a dull, dimwitted husband."

"Then I hope you get your wish," I laughed and finished braiding her hair. We were both silent for a few moments. I decided to ask the question that had been on my mind. "Ruth, what happened to your parents?"

She took a deep breath and met my gaze in the mirror with such sad eyes that I began to regret my prying. "My father died when I was thirteen, then my mother two years later."

"I'm so sorry." I knew how hard it was for her.

"Both of them fell ill before passing on," she sighed. "It was difficult to see them suffer."

"My mother died when I was very young. My father died . . . recently," I sighed as well. I couldn't tell her how they had died. She wouldn't understand what cars were.

"It is difficult at times, is it not?"

I nodded. "I'm happy you have a brother to keep you company and look after you." I tried to smile but felt it fall flat. *Oh, how I wish for a brother.*

"You have no siblings?"

I shook my head.

We were quiet for a time when she abruptly shrieked, jumped up, and ran into her sitting room.

I jumped, too. "What is it?" I peered around in alarm and hurried to her.

"A spider! There!" She pointed through the doorway and toward her bed.

Relieved, I laughed and removed my hand from my heart. "Is that all?"

She screamed again when the spider darted across the floor toward us. She scrambled onto a chair, holding her nightgown up to her knees.

"It's only a spider," I laughed again and knelt on the floor.

At that moment, Lord Shariton burst into the room. "I heard a scre—" He stopped, staring at me on the floor. Ruth and I must look utterly ridiculous. He straightened, his shirt unbuttoned at the top and his cravat hanging from his hand. *Wow! Who knew a neck could look so hot?*

"It's only a spider," I repeated. I laid my hand before the spider and it climbed on me. I was reminded of a song by a punk rock band about spiders in the dressing room. The song played in my mind, and I watched their reactions.

Both of their jaws hung slack, shocked at what I had done. I stepped past Lord Shariton, breathing in his scent as I did so. I set the spider down in the open window across the hall. "Good night, Ruth. I hope you sleep better, knowing the scary spider is out here for the night. Good night, Lord Shariton," I curtsied. With a bounce in my step, I sang the spider song, remembering when Papa and I used to dance around the kitchen, singing. I was eight when he introduced me to the *Toy Dolls* and their crazy, fun music—although he didn't let me listen to *all* of their music. Papa was also the one to teach me not to fear spiders. He would be proud.

That night, I wished I could remember the part of the song I'd messed up earlier on the piano. I spent a long time thinking about it until I gave up on sleep, slipped out of bed, went to the wardrobe, and pulled out my piano books. The covers were printed with the artists' photographs. The pictures alone would immediately give them away as being entirely out of place. I took the covers off the books and threw them into the dim fire, watching the flames light up the room around me. Its warmth increased and touched my cheeks. Now if someone glanced at the pages, they might seem similar as long as no one noticed that the sheet music was perfectly printed, not handwritten.

I waited a little while, then tucked the music under my arm and went to the door. Surely everyone was in bed by now. The stairs creaked a bit when I tiptoed down them. The drawing-room doors were open and I hurried in to sit at the window. The overcast sky outside hid the moon. Searching in the dark, I found a candle, lit it from the dwindling embers of the fire, and set it next to the piano where I placed my books.

As I flipped through the pages, I came to the one I had played earlier. I fumbled through the beginning, but my fingers found the rhythm and finished the song. Flipping through the pages again, I discovered one I hadn't played in ages. It was much later when fatigue hit me enough to sleep. With a deep breath, I blew out the candle and returned it to the mantle; then, with books in hand, I left the room. I peered at the floor, careful not to slip in the dark, but when I raised my head, I froze, my shoulders high and stiff.

There, at the bottom of the stairs, stood Lord Shariton. With a gasp, I hid the books behind my back.

"Why is it that you feel the need to hide your talent from us, Miss Roberts?" He sounded calm, but almost accusing.

I lowered my head, "I . . . I don't . . ." *Think, blockhead!* "I don't know," I finished lamely.

He stepped to me and lifted my chin. It was too dark to read his expression. Was he angry? I couldn't tell.

"You do not need to hide, Miss Roberts. You may play as often as you wish." He glanced over my shoulder. "May I?" he reached for the books, and I jerked away. My heart gave one hard thump in my chest. If he were to look at them, I would be doomed. I couldn't explain well enough for him to understand. He would think me mad—or possibly burn me at the stake for being a witch or something of the like.

"May I see your music?" he asked again, holding out his hand.

I shook my head.

His shoulders rose. "Very well, Miss Roberts. I bid you goodnight." With that, he headed up the stairs and disappeared around the corner.

Back in my room, I came to the conclusion that it wasn't safe for me to keep the books any longer, so, with great reluctance, I threw them into the dwindling embers of the fireplace.

The light danced across my nightgown, and tears filled my eyes. Covering my mouth, I watched the black, curled pages glowing in the night. From Lord Shariton's point of view, I could see how my behavior might have seemed absurd, but the consequences of him seeing the perfectly printed pages could've been beyond dreadful.

Chapter Fifteen

Celeste

I woke early the next morning and made my way downstairs. When I approached the front entry, Herbert, one of the servants, stopped me.

"Miss Roberts, some packages came for you." He pointed at a group of boxes sitting near the door.

I froze, wondering if they were again from Lord Shariton.

"Would you like to take a look at them, miss?" he asked.

Herbert untied the string from the largest box and opened it for me. I gasped and covered my mouth. "Goodness." From movies I'd seen, I recognized the riding dress—or riding *habit*, as they were called. Herbert opened more boxes to reveal a tall hat, a pair of boots, some gloves, and what looked like a scarf.

I pointed at them and asked, "This is all from Lord Shariton?"

He nodded. "I believe he is waiting for you in the stables. He wants you to begin your riding lessons this morning." He picked up the boxes, started for the stairs, then turned when he realized I wasn't following. I shook my head to clear the disbelief and followed him to my room. Annabeth was expecting my arrival, and helped me with the clothes and boots. After placing the hat on my head, I gazed in the mirror. An elegant, sophisticated lady stared back at me.

I made a mental note to find some way to repay him for this and all the other items he'd bought for me.

When I reached the stable, I paused outside the doorway, watching Lord Shariton speak to one of his horses. He rubbed its nose and looked into its big dark eyes, speaking low and soft. The memory of the night before caused my stomach to turn. *He must think I'm deranged.*

"My horse is ready, Charles," Ruth's voice called from somewhere within the stable. The tension in my shoulders relaxed, knowing she would be joining us.

I stepped into the stable. Lord Shariton glanced up, and our eyes met. My brain went momentarily numb. *He has such nice eyes.* "Er . . . Thank you for . . . this." I tugged at my dress, then touched my hat.

"You look stunning in that habit! Oh, Charles! How kind of you to get it for her," Ruth came running and hugged me. She giggled, then took my hand and pulled me to one of the horses that stood saddled and ready. "You will be riding Maggie—she is the gentlest mare, so you will not need to worry about a thing."

I pulled the glove off my left hand and reached for the horse. I impressed upon my memory the feel of her warmth and softness, never wanting to forget this moment.

"She likes you, I can tell," Ruth said, patting the mare on her silky neck. "She was the horse I rode a few years back, but my dear brother thought I needed to progress to something a little less tame." She walked to her horse, also saddled and ready to ride. "His name is Prince. Charles named him. He says now that I have my prince, I need nothing more," she laughed.

"I suppose he thought himself clever."

She laughed some more and nodded.

Lord Shariton chuckled. I turned to find him standing close behind me, his arm resting against a post above my head. My heart leaped into my throat at his strong, warm presence being so near. He slapped his glove against his leg and nodded toward the horse. "Are you ready for your first lesson?" He took hold of Maggie's bridle and led her to a near-by stool. I stepped onto it, and he helped me up into the sidesaddle with ease. I hoped he didn't see my blush when he lifted me. The sidesaddle felt awkward and uncomfortable. I had no idea what I was doing or how I should sit. Lord Shariton noticed my discomfort and instructed me on where to place my legs and how to adjust my weight. I looked around and found Ruth already astride Prince, but there wasn't another horse saddled.

"Which horse are you to ride today?" I asked Lord Shariton.

"I will not be riding. We will be staying inside the paddock today, so you can get used to riding first. Once you are comfortable and ready, we will go to the country and take you for a proper ride." He gave me a reassuring smile, then led the horse out of the stable. We went slowly most of the time, with Lord Shariton giving instructions on how to give the horse commands. Ruth galloped about and took jumps over low fences. She was a natural at riding. *Oh, how I envy her!*

By the time we were ready to go in for breakfast, I was feeling a little sore. I wanted to stretch my body when I dismounted, but knowing it would look odd to Ruth and Lord Shariton, I waited until I returned to my room. Annabeth wasn't around, so I undressed and laid on my bed to stretch. It felt glorious.

Once I donned a day dress, I headed for breakfast with a sketchbook in hand, hoping to sit in the library and draw afterward. Lord Shariton was missing from the party in the breakfast room. I assumed he was busy taking care of his estate. Pleased that the children were present for this meal, I laughed with them until it was time for their schooling.

"I see you have your sketchbook, Celeste. Are you planning to draw today?" Ruth asked.

"I am."

"I would love to watch you if you do not mind."

"Well, you could—but it would be better if I had someone to draw. You wouldn't mind sitting for me, would you?" I asked.

"I would be delighted."

We made our way into the library and sat by the window. I drew her with her soft strawberry curls framing her face. Her eyes reflected the light from the window. She held very still while I drew, and about an hour later, I announced that I was almost complete.

"All I need to do is finish the hair, which takes most of the time. I wouldn't want you getting a stiff neck while you wait," I said.

"Can I see it?" she asked, sitting at the edge of her seat. I nodded and turned the drawing toward her. "Oh! I look just the same as I do in the looking glass! It's perfect!"

"Here you two are," Lord Shariton interrupted at the open door.

"Oh, Charles, you must see this!" Ruth stood and waved him in. "Celeste drew a sketch of me. Is it not the most realistic drawing you ever saw?"

He stood over me and peeked at the drawing in my lap. "It is amazingly well done. You have captured her likeness perfectly." He placed his hand on my shoulder, then bent down and took the sketchbook from my hand to study it. "Amazingly well," he murmured, transfixed.

My heart was thumping, and my head spun at his gentle touch. I couldn't speak.

"We should have it framed and hang it on the wall," Ruth suggested.

"That we should, Ruth, but perhaps we should let her finish it first,"

113

he winked, handing the book back to me and sitting beside his sister in the window. I watched him relax—even slouch a little. Up until this moment, I'd never seen him look so *normal*. "Tell me, Miss Roberts, have you ever drawn a self-portrait?"

"Once. I no longer have it," I answered. I continued to sketch Ruth's hair, fixing my gaze on the page before me and thinking about the self-portrait that now lies with my father, six feet under.

"Where is it now?"

I shook my head. "I don't know."

"Well then, I want you to draw another, and we shall hang it beside Ruth's." He slapped his knee emphatically.

"And one of you also, brother!" Ruth exclaimed.

"I think Miss Roberts might not wish to draw me."

I opened my mouth to speak, but Ruth beat me to it, "Of course, she would, Charles—it is what she loves to do."

"I would be too grotesque a subject for her pencil," he said, raising an eyebrow at me.

I covered my mouth, stifling a giggle, and let out a small snort.

"You see, she agrees with me! Even now, she cannot hold down her breakfast at the thought of it," he waved an airy hand at me and spoke facetiously to his sister.

I laughed, "Do you really believe that?"

"Come now—admit it. You think me repulsive."

I shook my head and bit my lip, "No, I do not!" I thought quite the opposite. He was the most handsome man I had ever met. And smart, kind, and generous. My cheeks warmed with embarrassment.

"You are making her blush again, Charles! Now, if you will excuse us," Ruth stood primly and took my hand, "we need to prepare for the ball."

At the mention of the ball, my stomach dropped. I'd forgotten all about the Cromwell's ball! I grabbed Ruth's arm and stopped her. "Ruth.

I still don't know if I can dance. I haven't practiced enough—what do I do? I can't show up and not dance. What will people say? Or worse, if I do dance and end up stumbling over someone, what then?" I sputtered, panic welling up my throat.

She laughed. "You worry too much. I have seen your dancing. You will do splendidly."

"Perhaps, if I were to dance the first dance with you, it might help to calm your nerves," Lord Shariton suggested, stepping up next to me.

"There, you see. It will all work out," Ruth smiled.

"Can we practice all the dances once through before we change?" I pleaded.

"We will go straightaway," Lord Shariton held out his arm and escorted me to the ballroom. Stopping just outside the doorway, he looked at Ruth. "I suppose we will need music."

"No need. I will hum for you!" Ruth laughed. Lord Shariton led me to the middle of the room and stood before me.

Ruth began humming and tapping her foot, and we began to dance. The difficulty I now experienced wasn't in trying to remember the steps. Rather, it was in trying to keep my mind on them. With each touch and glance, I became overcome by self-consciousness, and heat continued to flush my cheeks. Dancing with an attractive man wasn't easily done.

Once we'd made it through the dances, Lord Shariton stopped and bowed while I curtsied. "You are a natural," he said.

I shook my head. "I disagree. I must look as though I'm walking through mud. I feel so stiff."

"You are graceful, Celeste. Do not be so hard on yourself," Ruth took my hand, and we started toward the door.

I looked back over my shoulder at Lord Shariton and smiled. "Thank you, my lord, for helping me. You've been so kind . . . in so many ways."

He lowered his head and cleared his throat. His expression confused me. Many emotions flickered across his face before disappearing in a small smile, "I am glad to be of service to you, Miss Roberts."

I wished, not for the first time, that he would call me Celeste as he had once done.

* * *

Celeste

Annabeth stood ready to make me beautiful when I arrived in my room. She helped me into my cream-colored gown and satin slippers. She redid my hair and added a few flowers to the curls. While she prepared my hair, another servant brought in a food tray. Since we needed time to travel to the ball, we needed to eat while we readied ourselves. My stomach turned all a flutter. Food didn't appeal to me. I took a deep breath and held a steadying hand over my abdomen, then checked myself in the mirror. I applied a thin layer of lip gloss to my lips before sliding it into my dress for later. When I reached the top of the stairs, I found I was the last to join the group. Ruth sat in a chair near the door, talking with Lady Garrison. Lord Shariton and Sir Garrison stood off to one side, speaking in low, solemn tones. I held onto the railing and made my way down the stairs.

I had taken only a few steps when Ruth glanced up and stood. "You look lovely, Celeste."

Lord Shariton's head rose, and he stopped speaking mid-sentence. His eyes widened for a moment, then he turned his back to me, continuing his conversation.

"You look lovely as well, Ruth—even more so," I replied, striving to keep my voice even.

Sir Garrison chuckled behind his hand as I passed. Lord Shariton cleared his throat and approached me, holding a short satin cloak with a hood. I knew there was a special name for this, but I couldn't remember it. My attention was drawn to Lord Shariton's eyes, but he would not meet my gaze.

"Here you are, Miss Roberts," he placed the cloak over my shoulders and helped me tie it in the front, gently arranging the hood over my head, "The rain may come at any moment, and we would not want your hair to go flat, now would we?"

I couldn't find my voice for a brief moment, but somehow I let out a feeble, "Thank you." I watched him avoid eye contact with me at every turn of his head. I felt deflated. I had hoped he would mention something about my appearance. After all, he'd bought me the dress, and I wished to please him.

"You look radiant, my dear," Lady Garrison kissed my cheek.

"As do you, Lady Garrison," I replied, glancing back at Lord Shariton. He managed to continue avoiding my eye while at the same time offering me his arm to lead me outside. Some of my girlish fantasies were coming true when I spotted the carriage. I'd always wanted to ride in a carriage, especially dressed as I was. I almost felt like a princess.

When we arrived at the Cromwell estate, Lord Shariton escorted me into the entry, where a maid took my cloak. The house wasn't quite as grand and richly decorated as Shariton Park, but it still looked beautiful. We made our way into the hall, where two ladies stood to welcome their guests. Lord Shariton escorted both Ruth and me toward them. I tried to remember to hold my shoulders back and my head high at our approach.

"Ah! So glad you could come, Lord Shariton, Miss Elsegood." An older, dark-haired woman with a pointed nose greeted us with a smile and held her hand out to Lord Shariton.

Lord Shariton took it and bowed, "It was good of you to invite us, Mrs. Cromwell. And where is Mr. Cromwell tonight?"

"Oh, he is here somewhere," she gestured airily down the hall.

Slowly, she turned her attention to me, examining me up and down with evident disdain.

"Allow me to introduce our guest and dear friend, Miss Celeste Roberts, of London," Lord Shariton nodded at me. "Miss Roberts, this is Mrs. Cromwell."

I curtsied, "Thank you for—"

Mrs. Cromwell's voice overrode my own. "I see you've brought some other old friends."

"Yes. You remember Sir and Lady Garrison."

"I do. You are *most* welcome," she said warmly, holding out her hand in greeting.

Lord Shariton took my arm and led me to the next woman. She was young, maybe a few years older than me. She was almost the spitting image of her mother.

"Miss Cromwell. You look well this evening," Lord Shariton began. "This is Miss Celeste Roberts. She is my guest for the time being."

I glanced at Lord Shariton. *For the time being? Well, of course, he wouldn't expect me to stay indefinitely.* My mind raced over my future possibilities, and I curtsied to Miss Cromwell.

"I'm so glad you could come," she said, looking me over in much the same way her mother had and then turning to Ruth with an exuberant welcome.

At last, Lord Shariton led me into the crowded ballroom. My stomach flip-flopped, and I moved past the many groups of women and men richly dressed and perfectly poised. Some were beginning to dance, and I watched intently to see if I could recognize the steps. With relief, I discovered that I could.

Men and women gazed my way with interest, murmuring to their neighbors. Lord Shariton introduced me to a married couple who lived close by, but the small talk ended rather abruptly when their daughters rushed to them and stole their attention. Lord Shariton stepped away to speak with an older fellow, and I was left alone to meander about the room.

I wished I had my father by my side. He would have put his arm around me, making me feel warm and calm.

It appeared as though Ruth had found friends to mingle with. How I wished I knew more people here! My heart flipped when someone took my hand, squeezed, and released it. Lord Shariton stood stiff and tall beside me. "Relax and smile. Their attention will soon pass."

How could I relax when he touched me like that? My heart fluttered, but I tried to take his advice and look pleased to be there. One woman, I noticed, didn't seem happy to see me. Her frown intensified her long chin. I turned my attention to the dancing and the music. Just as the next song was about to start, Lord Shariton turned to me, "I do believe I promised you a dance." He held out his hand, only meeting my eyes for half a second.

He led me onto the dance floor, and I stood across from him, anxiously waiting for the music to begin. He glanced to the side, and my gaze followed. A young man who appeared to be in his late twenties stood next to Lord Shariton, and his eyes fixed on me. Before I could react, the music began, and I started forward, counting the steps in my mind. *One, two, three, up on my toes, and one, two, three . . .*

Now came the part when I would have to join hands with the man dancing next to Lord Shariton. My feet obeyed the music and moved toward the stranger. He took my hand and stared at me. I chanced a quick glance at him, then returned to my place and moved toward Lord Shariton. As the dance continued, I felt the man's gaze still upon me. *Ok, ok, I get it. I'm the new girl, now can we move on? You are handsome—I'll give you that. But please stop staring at me.*

My face twisted into a scowl. When I looked back at Lord Shariton, he was smiling—almost laughing—at me. My eyes searched his questioningly.

I was relieved when the song ended, and Lord Shariton returned me safely to the side of the room, but I had only just caught my breath when the man who so liked to stare approached.

"Lord Shariton, I am compelled to introduce myself," he bowed. "I am Mr. Jenkins—Jonathan Jenkins." When his head rose, his eyes lingered on me.

"Good evening, Mr. Jenkins. Where do you hail from?" Lord Shariton replied shortly.

"Bristol. I am a distant cousin of the Cromwells," he replied, giving Lord Shariton a cursory glance before returning his gaze to me. "And who is this enchanting creature you brought with you?"

"This is Miss Celeste Roberts, my sister's guest at Shariton Park," Lord Shariton replied.

"Would you mind if I claimed her for the next dance, Lord Shariton?"

"If she is willing," Lord Shariton now appeared bored.

Is it some unspoken rule that all wealthy, high-ranking men must appear bored and prideful at such parties?

Mr. Jenkins took my hand. "Would you do me the honor of dancing with me, Miss Roberts?"

I could only nod. His stare was intense, and I found myself speechless. He held his head high and his shoulders back, pulling me gently away. I glanced back at Lord Shariton. He gave me a small nod and turned to walk in the opposite direction.

Mr. Jenkins and I joined in the dance after it had already begun, and I found myself immediately flustered. I hesitated momentarily, thought hard, then joined in the steps at the right place. When we met in the middle, Mr. Jenkins rested his hand on my waist, and my face flushed. All his attention was locked on me, and he didn't look anywhere else the entire dance. My mind was clouded with confusion. I'd never been near someone who behaved this way toward me. Each time we moved together, he seemed to get closer and closer.

At last, he leaned his head in and whispered in my ear, "Would you find me too bold, Miss Roberts, if I said you were the most beautiful woman I have ever laid eyes upon?" His warm breath tickled my ear.

I very nearly snorted aloud, trying to hold my laughter in. *How absurd! How could he say such a thing?* The dance demanded we move apart, and I felt a sudden wave of relief, but he leaned in close again when we moved back together.

"Please say something. I must hear your voice."

My mind raced through all the old movies I'd seen and the books I'd read. What would one of those young ladies say at a moment like this? I took a breath, "I am at a loss for words, sir."

He smiled. "Your voice is that of an angel. Please say you will dance with me again?"

"I . . ." I couldn't answer before we moved apart once more. When the steps brought us back together, I studied his face. "Are you sure you want to dance with me again? I'm afraid I'm a very poor dancer."

"How can you say such a thing?" he exclaimed earnestly. "You are like a soft, sweet flower petal carried by the wind."

The music ended, and he took my hand in his. "Please say you will dance with me again?"

I nodded slowly, wanting instead to find Lord Shariton or Ruth. Lady Garrison bustled up with a tall man by her side.

"Miss Roberts, forgive my interruption, but I wish to introduce you to a friend of my family, Mr. Edward Stewart. Mr. Stewart, this is Miss Celeste Roberts."

A slight tug on my arm nearly threw me off balance as I curtsied. It seemed Mr. Jenkins was anxious to start the next dance. I ignored him.

"Miss Roberts, may I have the next dance?" inquired Mr. Stewart. His thick auburn hair matched the heavy sideburns running down his cheeks.

"I'm sorry. I'm already engaged for the next, but perhaps the one after?" I replied, forcing a tight smile.

He bowed and Mr. Jenkins led me onto the dance floor once more.

Chapter Sixteen

Charles

"What have you learned, Henry?" I watched Miss Roberts from across the room. With each step she took, I ached to be the one dancing with her.

"Well, she is the talk of the evening, without a doubt," he spoke in a low voice, pretending to watch the dancers. "At first, it was only her beauty the men could talk about, then word spread of her vast wealth."

I jerked my head around to look at him. "Then they know?" *Drat that, Mr. Evens!*

He nodded, "No one knows the exact amount, but they all agree it is one of the largest dowries to be had."

My shoulders stiffened. "What of this Mr. Jenkins? What have you found out about him?"

"Not much, I am afraid. The only thing I could get out of Mr.

Cromwell is that he is a distant cousin who has come to stay to hunt on the estate for a time. Cromwell claims he is a good lad, brought up a gentleman. I do not know if he owns any property or has any prospects yet."

I listened to what Henry had to say while I watched Celeste dance her eighth dance in a row, three of them with Mr. Jenkins. She was beginning to look weary.

"See if you can find out anything more. I would like an excuse to be rid of him." I moved toward Miss Roberts.

When I stepped to Celeste's side when the song ended, her shining eyes found me. Her shoulders slumped, and she pressed a palm to her heart as if relieved to see me. A young man stepped up with lips parted to request the next dance, but I waved him away, "Miss Roberts needs some fresh air."

"You've saved me just in time," she breathed, raising a hand to her head. I led her to the stone courtyard to take in the cool breeze. She leaned against the stone railing and sighed.

"How are you getting on?" I asked, peering out at the dark grounds. Ever since she had walked down the stairs tonight in that gown, I'd had to work hard to keep from staring at her. If I did more than glance her way, I might not be able to suppress the urge to kiss her. I could not let her see the longing in my eyes. Throughout the evening, I continually reminded myself why we were here. She needed to find someone worthy of marriage, who could care for her. Once she found that someone, I could forget her. It would be easy to do once she was out of my home and life.

She peered up at me. "I'm tired. Can we leave?"

Surprised at her remark, I made the mistake of looking down at her. The light from the open doors glistened off whatever she might have applied to her lips. I leaned in only half an inch, then stepped back. "I . . ." I glanced away and cleared my throat, "I thought you were enjoying yourself."

She huffed. "I'm not one for large crowds, especially men crowding around me."

I looked at her. She was blushing as she stared toward the open doors.

"You do not enjoy their attention?" Hope soared within me, but before the dream of any future with her could take shape, I pushed the feeling aside and reminded myself of my duty.

She shook her head, "No. And I especially dislike Mr. Jenkins' attention."

Her comment caused the joy deep inside me to ripple out into laughter.

A smile pulled at one corner of her lips. "He's a little too bold for my taste."

I turned back to the doors and held out my arm. "Well, I am afraid you will have to endure it a bit longer. Ruth would be furious with me if we left so early."

* * *

Celeste

The moment we re-entered the ballroom, Mr. Jenkins hurried to my side. I stiffened.

Before he could speak, Lord Shariton moved to block his way. "I was just escorting Miss Roberts to a soft chair. Her feet need a rest."

"Allow me. I know the perfect place!" Mr. Jenkins moved to my other side. "Miss Roberts," he held out his arm.

I mentally pleaded with Lord Shariton for help, but any hope of deliverance from him was dashed when he leaned in and spoke low and soft, "See what you can find out about him." Then without another word, he strode away.

"It seems I am all yours for the moment," I said to Mr. Jenkins, then immediately wished I hadn't.

He grinned, leading me to the farthest corner of the room, and found a seat for two beside a tall window. A large potted plant nearly hid us from view.

I sat, but I didn't take much comfort in it. My back and feet ached terribly. I wished I could lay back with my feet in the air and let myself slouch. Oh, how I wished I could slouch.

Mr. Jenkins leaned in and rested his arm on the back of my chair. "Are you well, sweet lady?"

"Just tired, I guess."

He laughed.

I scowled at him. "What's funny about me being tired?"

"It is the way you talk. You are not like most girls. Where do you come from?" his eyes moved from my eyes to my mouth, then down my neck.

I scooted away from him a bit. "London."

"Tell me about yourself, Miss Roberts."

"There's not much to tell."

"I do not believe that," he smiled, moving closer.

"You don't?" I moved away again.

"I see it in your eyes. You have secrets." He touched my cheek with the back of his hand.

I moved to block his hand from touching me again. "I have no secrets."

"I think you do, Miss Roberts."

I was beginning to feel threatened by him. *Change the subject. Do what Lord Shariton asked me to do.*

"Tell me, Mr. Jenkins. What do you do for work?"

He laughed, looking down at my hand and touching it softly. "At the moment, I am working on some business that I hope will put me in a better position to purchase some land of my own. I hope to have a grand estate by next year."

"Oh." I didn't know what else to ask. I knew almost nothing of what men did for a living in this time period. "Hold on a minute. Scooch back a bit," I waved, shooing him away. "Criminy, I can hardly breathe," I muttered. *You'd think he's been lost at sea for years and starved for a woman's attention. There. Much better.* "What did your father do?"

He chuckled. "Do you want to talk about my father, Miss Roberts?" Despite my efforts, he leaned closer so his lips tickled my ear. "I can think of better things to talk about."

I breathed in fast and deep, then jumped to my feet. "I . . . I'm feeling as though I might need some refreshments. Right . . . refreshments."

He stood, "First, we should dance the supper dance together, then I can escort you in to dine."

I scowled. *Did all the men of this age believe women couldn't move about the room on their own?* "No. I'll be okay. I wanted to find my friend, Ruth, anyhow." I started to move away, but he took me by the arm.

"Can I call on you soon?" Hope lingered in his words. "I can see your answer in your eyes. I will be at your doorstep without delay, Miss Roberts." I wasn't sure what he thought he'd seen in my eyes, but it was not what I had tried to convey. His lips curled up, then he moved his fingers down the length of my arm and held my hand to his lips. The warmth of his kiss crept through my glove. If I had ever imagined a gentleman kissing my hand at a ball, I was sure it would've ended with me swooning in his arms. No such feeling came over me now. I must admit, he was handsome, but I knew his type. Or at least, I knew the type he would be in my own time. He was a player who used women to build his ego before moving on.

I hurried away from him, only to find myself in the hands of yet another young man all too eager to escort me. Searching the room for any sign of Lord Shariton or Sir Garrison, hoping for some relief, did me no good. This night wasn't what I had expected. I thought I would be sitting in a corner, watching the more beautiful girls in the room surrounded by men. Surely I couldn't be the most beautiful girl here.

The young man at my side had red hair and sideburns. Mr. Stewart, if I remembered correctly, was the only gentleman thus far who didn't seem too pushy. His only downfall-- his large teeth. I couldn't imagine kissing a person with teeth like his. I felt sorry for the poor guy. He led me gallantly into the room where everyone had gathered to dine and sat beside me. Ruth moved into the seat on my other side the instant I sat.

"Am I ever glad to see you," I leaned into her.

She leaned in and whispered, "I have so much to tell you." Her mouth opened to continue when Mr. Stewart asked a question beside me. Before I could answer him, the man across from me introduced himself. I could only smile helplessly, turning to Ruth for assistance. Her head turned away as she spoke with the gentleman next to her. Someone began playing the piano, making it difficult to hear.

"Do you play, Miss Roberts?" Mr. Stewart nodded in the direction of the pianoforte.

"I do," I answered.

"I would love to hear you play," he said.

"Oh! Yes please, Celeste. You must play," Ruth joined in.

Fear swept through me. "I . . ."

The woman at the piano finished her song, and Mr. Stewart stood and helped me to my feet, "Come. I must hear you play."

My legs felt like they were full of lead as Mr. Stewart escorted me to the piano and helped me to sit. The room quieted, and everyone's attention was on me. My ears and cheeks were as hot as a parking lot on a blistering day. I closed my eyes. *Think of them in their underwear.*

128

When I opened my eyes, I cringed at the thought of these people in their underwear. *Who would come up with such an idea?* I shook the image out of my mind and searched the room. Lord Shariton's eyes fixed on me. He gave me an encouraging nod. With a deep breath, I placed my shaking hands on the keys. Throughout the classical pieces I played, I thought about how I might escape the ball without making a scene. When I had made it halfway through the last piece—which was a long one—I stopped.

"I'm afraid I don't remember the rest," I shook from head to toe, and sweat dripped from my forehead.

The guests at table slowly clapped, stunned looks on their faces. *Why are they staring at me like that? Surely I wasn't that bad.*

"If you would please, Celeste, play one of *your* pieces," Ruth said from across the room.

My face grew even hotter, and I wanted to protest, but several other voices joined in, urging me to play more. There was no way out but to play. Again, I placed my fingers on the keys, closed my eyes, and I pictured myself in my home in London. I envisioned our old living room with the window behind me and the sofa off to the side of the grand piano. It didn't take much effort to picture my father sitting on the sofa with his head back, resting his eyes as he'd often done while listening to me play. Everyone in the room seemed to disappear the moment I began. I opened my eyes, focused on my fingers, and I played a modern song. It was one I had played during the night at Shariton Park, but had not yet played in front of anyone.

When I'd finished, I sat with my lashes wet. This piece always moved me. Thinking of my father, I smiled, then lifted my head to see if he had enjoyed it. To my embarrassment, I realized my father was not there, only a room full of regency ladies and gentlemen. For one long moment, the only sound was the tinkling of a glass. Clearing my throat, I lowered my head and let my lips droop into a frown. Seconds later, the clapping began, slow at first, then faster and louder, until everyone applauded enthusiastically. I stood quickly, hoping not to play again, and moved across the room, away from where I had sat with Ruth. Whispers surrounded me about the song's origin, astonishment, and questions.

When Ruth approached me, I held my hand to my head, "Ruth. I need to go home."

She looked at me concerned. "Is everything alright, Celeste?"

I shook my head. "I'm not feeling well." *Oh, please, let me go back to Shariton Park.*

"Miss Roberts, what could be wrong?" Mr. Stewart stepped up beside us.

I shook my head, "I am sorry I could not sit with you longer, and I hope I haven't been a bore."

"On the contrary, I enjoyed your music and your company. I must say, I have never heard anyone play so beautifully."

"Thank you, Mr. Stewart," I gave him a slight nod. *I want to leave!*

"I wish you well and hope to see you soon." He smiled widely, making me cringe. I moved my hand to my head again, hoping he would attribute my expression to my headache and not his smile. *Poor bloke.*

"Over there . . . see. There is Charles," Ruth pulled me in Lord Shariton's direction. She stopped in front of him and announced that I was taking ill.

Lord Shariton tucked my hand under his arm and hurried us out of the room. He motioned to Sir Garrison, telling him I felt unwell. As we walked to the door, a man with tall hair who appeared to be in his fifties immediately started heading our way with a look of determination directed right at me. His furrowed brow could have put any grumpy old man to shame. I noticed with amusement that his brows were long enough to braid them. We rushed outside before he could reach us through the crowd, sweeping into the waiting carriage. Mere seconds later the horses trotted briskly toward Shariton Park. Guilt about using such tactics to escape washed away when the carriage rounded the bend.

* * *

Celeste

I woke early—my inner alarm clock demanded it—and hurried outside, leaving my bonnet behind. I wanted to feel the wind gust through my hair, which I had pinned just enough to be presentable. The morning dew kissed the hem of my dress as I walked past the gardens, up the field along the forest, and stopped at the top to look back. Knowing I'd need to be back for breakfast, I didn't go far. I lay spread-eagled on the damp grass and let my breathing slow. The clouds overhead soothed me, and I thought about my time in this mysterious place. Despite all my worries about the future, I felt happy. I had friends I could talk to and had something in common with. I felt at home here if I didn't count the dances and the awkward social affairs. In my own time, I was often perceived as strange. I spoke and acted strangely—at least, compared with everyone else. I only behaved the way a lady should. The way my father and grandmothers had taught me. Of course, I had my wild moments. Yet I was seemingly too formal to live comfortably in the twenty-first century.

I smiled at the thought of my father, then stopped, realizing it was the first time I'd smiled while thinking of him instead of wanting to cry. With a deep breath, I said aloud, "You know what, Papa? This place is healing me. It's been hard, but I think it's healing me."

I blinked when a raindrop fell on my cheek. I laughed and sat up. The sky behind me grew dark from a looming storm cloud that gathered and stretched itself to the ground. The rain started to pour. Glad I'd had the sense to don my Spencer before I left—not that it helped much—I buttoned the frog clasps with cold, wet fingers. I would be soaked to the bone in this rain within five minutes. *No matter!* I giggled and spun around with my arms out and my head back. I reached up and pulled the two large pins from my hair, letting it fall down my back.

I sang as I danced around with my arms out, "I'm singin' in the rain . . ."

Chapter Seventeen

Charles

After washing the dirt from my hands in the small creek, I mounted my horse and returned to the stable just as the rain began. I had only gone a short distance when I noticed movement at the top of the hill. The sound of Miss Roberts' singing lured me closer.

"Something . . . something . . . something . . . I don't remember the words to the song, but I'll continue to sing and be happy again!" Miss Roberts sang, twirling around in the downpour. Her hair hung loose and wild, clinging to her face and shoulders. With each twirl, drops of water sprayed off of her. I had never witnessed anyone enjoying the weather in such a manner. I pressed my lips together, trying to hold back my laughter, but I could not contain myself. She spun around at the sound, pushing her wet hair from her face and staring.

"What on earth are you doing, Miss Roberts?" I asked breathlessly.

"Singing in the rain," she replied timidly. Mortification spread on her face and made me laugh harder. She broke into a smile and joined me in the laughter.

"Do you sing in the rain often?" I asked after our laughter had died down.

"No. Not for a long time," she admitted, wiping the rain from her face. "Have you ever sung in the rain?"

I tilted my head to the side. "I am afraid not."

"You should try it sometime." She held her head back, looked at the sky, and blinked rapidly in the falling rain. Glancing at me, she smiled mischievously. "Shall we race back?"

Startled by such a question, I stumbled over my reply, "I—I don't think it . . . wise.".

Her smile faltered. "Yes, of course, you're right." She turned to leave.

"Wait. Would you like a ride back?"

"I'm soaked—I'm very wet," she bit her lip and gestured at her dress.

"Come," I waved her over and helped her up behind me into the saddle. She had a difficult time, and I thought I heard the sound of fabric tearing when she settled in.

I nudged Apollo into motion. Despite the cold rain pelting down, my body flushed with warmth at the touch of her hands on my waist. She started to slide off but righted herself and clung tighter, with her arms around my middle. *Lud, my heart is nearly bursting through my ribs!*

Near the side door, I reined in and helped her carefully down, then slid off behind her to be sure she was steady on her feet. "Are you well?"

"Sure. Er, yes, thank you." She stepped closer, "Thank you so much for letting me stay here." Her soft lips pressed against my cheek as quick as a blink, then she turned and ran toward the house before I could catch

134

my breath.

I stood there with mixed emotions. She had kissed me, though not as I had dreamed she would. Her kiss felt friendly, like a kiss to a brother, but something else was in her eyes as she stepped away. *Does she feel something more for me? No. Of course not.* I shook my head and led Apollo to the stables. *Why does she seem so happy today? Is it the result of last night's ball? Has someone wooed her?* All these questions weighed heavily on my mind throughout the day.

* * *

Celeste

My cheeks flushed from that cheeky kiss. I knew he hadn't seen it because my head was turned, but something strong burned deep within from that simple gesture of thanking him. *Am I starting to have feelings for him? I do overheat a lot whenever he's near. But I did it with nearly every man I met last night. I suppose I'm a natural blusher. Still . . . the feeling is different with him. He's the only one who makes me want to sigh and fall into his arms.* When I reached my chambers, I shut the door behind me and leaned against it. *Am I falling for Lord Shariton?* I shook my head. *He's almost ten years older than me—plus he's trying to get me married off.*

I pushed the thoughts aside, dressed in warm, dry clothes, brushed through my hair and pinned it up, then headed to breakfast. At the bottom of the stairs, I was stopped by Herbert once again. This was becoming a bit of a pattern.

"Miss Roberts, you've received several deliveries this morning. They are waiting in the blue sitting room." He tried not to grin when he saw my mouth drop.

"Er . . . thank you, Herbert." I walked to the blue room and stopped short. Around the room were several vases full of flowers of every variety.

"They are not all yours. Those on the left are for Miss Elsegood," Herbert said.

The flowers for Ruth were set together on one of the tables. She had five beautiful arrangements. When I counted my own, I gasped. Twelve? I'd never received flowers from anyone other than Papa in my entire life. How—why would I receive this many?

The arrangements held cards with names and messages written upon them. My face grew hot with embarrassment. Some names I recognized more than others. All of them were men I'd danced with the night before. Concern grew when I discovered that three of the bouquets were from Mr. Jenkins. Surely one would have been enough. I blushed harder, reading what he had written. *How can he speak of love when he hardly knows me? Is he daft?*

I needed nourishment to help steady my legs, so I headed to the breakfast room. When I entered, I found Ruth staring listlessly at her empty plate.

"What is it Ruth?" I asked right away.

She looked up at me, and tears filled her eyes. "It is little Mary. She has taken ill."

My heart dropped. This was a time before vaccines and antibiotics. It was much more serious when children got sick. I peered into her eyes, fidgeting with my dress. "How sick is she?"

"She was not feeling well last night, and now she is *much* worse. They sent for a doctor before first light."

"What is it? What does she have?"

"The doctor left just a moment ago. They believe it to be Scarlet Fever." She wiped at her eyes.

I studied her in silence for a moment. With new determination, I hurried from the room, taking the stairs two at a time. When I approached the hall where the children stayed, I was stopped by Lord Shariton. He, too, was breathing hard, as if he had just run up those same stairs.

"Miss Roberts, you cannot come down here. This hall is quarantined. Little Mary is sick."

"I heard." I moved past him, but he sidestepped and blocked my path.

"She has Scarlet Fever. You cannot go to her." His voice was firm.

I tried to pass him on the other side, but he took my shoulders and held me. "You will fall ill if you go near her."

I shook my head stubbornly, "I'll be fine."

"I will not let you near her. I could not bear it if you were to . . ." His voice cracked, and I glanced into his eyes and wondered at his depth of feeling. He lowered his head and cleared his throat. "I am responsible for you, Miss Roberts, and I cannot let you fall ill." He loosened his grip on me and gently pushed me toward the stairs. "Go and eat your breakfast."

I walked reluctantly back the way I'd come, thinking about soaps, disinfectants, and medicines. I couldn't let Mary die when I had so much knowledge that could help. But modern medication that could save her had yet to be invented. An idea suddenly struck me when I reached the top of the stairs. I had no idea if it were possible, but I had to try. I hurried to my room, found my riding habit and boots, and crawled under my bed, gathering some coins and identification I'd stashed under the wood frame. I rushed out of my room and found Ruth at the bottom of the stairs, pacing the entry.

"Ruth. I need your help. Go get something warmer on and come back here immediately."

"But why? Where are you going?"

"I will explain on the way. Hurry, for Mary's sake."

She practically ran up the stairs while I took my turn pacing the

137

entry hall, hoping Lord Shariton wouldn't find me. When she returned, I pulled her outside.

"What are you planning, Celeste, and what does it have to do with Mary?"

"Just help me with this saddle. I need you to take me somewhere since I don't know how to ride well, and I'm not sure where to go."

She nodded and helped me saddle her horse. When the stable hand appeared, Ruth waved him off. "I can manage."

"Where are you heading, Miss Elsegood? It might rain again." He ignored Ruth's rejection and began tightening the cinch for her.

"Just taking Miss Roberts for a ride."

I turned my face away, hoping he would not see the worry in my expression.

Ruth pulled herself up onto the horse and reached down for me. I was able to get on with the help of the stable hand. I reached my arms around her as she guided Prince out of the stable.

"Where to?" she asked.

"Out onto the road."

We moved at a brisk pace toward the road. "Now, will you tell me what you are doing?"

I sighed. "I know how to heal Mary, but I need a special medicine. I know where to get it, but you might not believe me . . . I'll explain more when we get closer." Telling her before we reached the arched tree would only make her want to turn back. I needed her to get me as close to the place as possible. After that, I could walk back if I had to. I hoped the time portal would work and that it wouldn't send me to a different time than the one I came from.

* * *

138

"What?" I roared. "Where are they? How long have they been gone?"

"Just a few hours. I went to look for them, my lord, and when I came out of the stables, I followed their tracks leading to the road." The stable hand stood holding his hat, looking very nervous.

"To the road?" I peered out the window across the grass to where the road began. "Fetch Mr. Evens and get three horses ready."

He nodded and hurried away.

Where on earth could they have gone? Why would they ride at a time like this? Did their disappearance have anything to do with that Mr. Jenkins poking about my land?

Dear Celeste, I hope you are well and safe . . . and Ruth as well, of course.

Chapter Eighteen

Celeste

"Try over this way," I said, pointing to our left.

"We've been wandering through these woods for hours, Celeste," Ruth sighed, pulling on the reins to stop. "If you do not tell me every-thing, I will turn around this minute."

"Please, we're so close. Keep moving, and I'll talk."

She urged the horse to the left, and I scanned the woods around us, searching for the large tree. "The medication I'm trying to get is called an antibiotic. It kills bad bacteria in the body, bacteria that cause illnesses like Scarlet Fever. Do you understand?"

"No."

"The medication will cure Mary in no time if we can get it and give it to her."

"So, where do you get this medication?" she asked.

"In the year two thousand twelve . . . where I'm from," I said quietly.

She stopped the horse and turned her head to stare at me. "If you are teasing me, it is not funny. Mary is dying, and now is not the time for jesting."

"I'm not teasing. I'm completely serious."

Her eyes grew wider as she studied my face. "How is it possible?"

I shook my head. "I don't know. One minute I was in my own time . . . the next, I was here. I only know that I walked through an archway made of tree roots, and things changed."

"This is impossible," she shook her head and urged the horse forward. Any minute now, she'd turn for home.

"Ruth, please believe me! I'm here, somehow, and it must be possible because it happened! There are things beyond our comprehension. Don't you think that maybe the impossible could be possible?"

"I do not know," she said in a low, sad voice, shaking her head.

"There! Ha ha! We've found it!" I sat up in the saddle behind her, gesturing wildly at the tree, relief washing over me. Now she would see! And we would save Mary! Joy filled my every cell. I could fix this. I could save her. I slid off the horse before he stopped, stumbling forward and then pausing to look back at her. "Here's the tricky part," I said nervously and she looked doubtfully on. "I don't know if my time passes differently than yours, or if going back through will send me to a different time altogether. I don't know how this works at all. If I'm not back by nightfall, leave without me. I'll try to be gone for only a couple of hours, but if I don't make it back . . . tell everyone I'm sorry, and thank you." My eyes pooled with tears.

She stared at me blankly, as if she couldn't comprehend and didn't believe it.

"I'll bring you back a treat," I tried to smile. I turned and passed under the archway. When I glanced back, I could see the bottom half of Ruth atop the horse, but the rest of her was gone. Ruth's faint gasp brought me back to her. "What is it?" I asked, stepping toward her.

"You were gone," she said, holding her chest. "Your head. It was missing!"

"Yes, so was yours."

She looked at me, then laughed. "It is true, then?"

I nodded. "I need to go. Stay here. If all goes well, I'll be back soon."

Ruth slid from her horse and stood in front of me. "So what you are saying is, at the risk of losing Mary, we may lose you, too?"

I hesitated. She threw her arms around me and held me tight. After a minute, I pulled away. "I need to get going. Wait for me here."

"You had better come back." She frowned at me and wiped the tears from her cheeks. "Wait." She stepped closer to me. "Can I not go with you?"

"No!" I panicked. *Would she follow me through?* "As I said before, I may not make it back, and I may not be going where I think I'm going. Stay here, Ruth." I moved under the arch and started running to make up for the time we'd lost wandering the woods. Right away, the cold overtook me. My breath clouded before me when I stopped to rest. My heart hammered in my chest, and I worried about what I would find ahead. My mind raced when I thought of all the movies I'd seen of the future. Perhaps the world was now run by robots, or there might've been a great war and cities and countries were in ruin. Possibly there could've been a famine and there wasn't enough medicine to go around.

With each thought, I hurried faster. My lungs burned, and I stopped to catch my breath once again. A sound I'd not heard in days delighted and surprised me—a car's engine. As I continued, the noise of road construction thundered up ahead. I stepped out of the woods and onto the road. Crewmen worked hard a stone's throw away, paving the road on the right side. A few workers directed the cars driving by, one at a time.

The road wasn't busy, so the vehicles quickly moved around without waiting.

One car drove past me slowly, then pulled over. A woman in her thirties opened the door on the driver's side and stepped out. "Wow! What a dress you've found. I had to stop and ask you where you bought it."

I must have looked ridiculous in my period gown, grinning from ear to ear . . . "I'm not sure, someone found it for me."

"Well, it looks very authentic." She leaned closer to study the details.

"Um, could you give me a ride? My car broke down, and I really need to get into town," I said, hoping she wouldn't refuse me.

"Oh, of course." She straightened, fixing her intent gaze on my face. "Hop in." She turned and led the way back to her car.

I slid into the passenger seat and folded into the heater blowing on me. I sighed and put my cold hands up to the vent. On the dashboard display, I read the date and time—only a few days had passed from the time I left. Relief swept over me.

As we pulled into town, I had her drop me off at the bank. She was a kind lady who liked to talk about Jane Austen and the clothes of that era. She asked me why I was dressed this way, so I fabricated a story that I would use while here: a group of us were staying in a cottage in the woods. We were crazy about Jane Austen and wanted to experience the time period, so we dressed up and played pretend. She expressed interest in joining, but I told her we were packing up to head home.

She bought my story, and I hoped others would as well.

When I walked into the bank, I almost laughed out loud at the looks I received. I made my way to the teller and placed a few of my silver coins on the high counter in front of him.

"I need to trade these coins in," I stated.

The teller looked me over. "I'll need to check the value first, if you can wait." I agreed and waited far too long for the transaction. Once I had the cash in hand, I profusely thanked the teller and asked him where the nearest pharmacy was located.

When I found the pharmacist, I explained that one of the members of our Regency group was a child who had caught strep. Her father refused to take her to a doctor, but the fever and sore throat were unmistakable. The pharmacist hesitated to help, insisting she needed to be seen and properly diagnosed. He couldn't hand out medication without a prescription. "Please," I begged, "it's a very bad case, and her father doesn't believe in medicine. You'd be doing a kindness, and I can pay . . ." I slipped him three times the money required, then added one of the silver coins. "This is very valuable. Please help me."

He hesitated, then brought two bottles to the counter.

I quickly left that pharmacy and went straight to another, telling the same story, handing over the same bribery, and getting the same results. My success surprised me, but the old saying rang true: money talks. Being so dishonest left me feeling shaky and ashamed, but knowing it was for a good cause, I pushed on, feeling justified in my deceit. Before leaving the second pharmacy, I also bought some Tylenol, toothpaste, a toothbrush, bottled water, a few granola bars, and candy bars. The Mars bars were my favorite. I downed the water immediately and sighed. I hadn't realized how much I missed drinking water. No one drank water in the nineteenth century due to impurities. They boiled and drank it as tea. Tea had become monotonous.

On my way to the bus stop, I ate one of the candy bars, savoring every gooey, delicious morsel. It tasted even sweeter after not eating all day and a few days without milk chocolate. I found the route to take me back to the woods and boarded with time to spare.

As the driver neared the strip of road dotted with orange cones and construction workers, I asked him to stop, giving the excuse that I had forgotten something and would like to walk back and retrieve it. He thought it strange, I could tell, but as we were already pausing for road work, he stopped the bus and opened the doors for me.

Once out of sight, I jogged through the trees to keep myself warm and compensate for lost time. Worry weighed heavily on my shoulders. Would I make it back in time to save Mary? Would Ruth still be there waiting for me? What if I were stuck forever in the twenty-first century? I slowed my hesitant footsteps. I had been thinking as if I *belonged* in the 1800s. Was I really giving up my life to live in the past? None of this made sense. I shelved the thoughts that swam in my mind and threw myself into racing the clock instead.

I couldn't help a cry of relief when I found the tree again. Tears flowed down my cheeks when I spotted Ruth's skirts moving back and forth through the arch.

"I did it!" I exclaimed after I stepped through.

She threw her arms around me and cried on my shoulder. "You worried me so! I thought you might never return."

"How long was I gone?"

"Too long." She wiped her tears. "You look chilled to the bone."

"Look," I laughed, pulling a candy bar from the plastic bag and holding it out to her, "I told you I'd bring you a treat!"

She tilted her head to the side and pursed her lips. "What is it?"

I pulled the wrapper off one end and held it out again, bouncing on my toes, waiting for her reaction. "It's called a candy bar."

She took it and smelled it. "Chocolate? You eat all of it?"

I laughed again and nodded.

"What is this material it is wrapped in?" She rubbed the wrapper between her fingers.

My smile faded when I peered at the plastic. I hadn't thought about the strangeness of the wrapper or the plastic bag I carried. Even the plastic bottles that held the medicine, printed words, dates, and names would look like something alien to the people here.

145

"Can I use your reticule?" I asked.

She looked down at it, then held it out to me. I transferred the contents of the plastic bag. There wasn't quite enough room, so one of the candy bars stuck out the top.

"Let's get going." I moved to the horse's side and turned back to Ruth, who was still studying the chocolate.

She took a bite and moaned with delight, "This is the most amazing thing I have ever tasted! But far too rich to eat much of it, I imagine. But, mmmm. So divine."

I laughed and helped her mount the horse. She pulled me up behind her and we started toward the house. I sat astride so that I wouldn't fall. It might not have been ladylike, but it was secure. I occasionally asked Ruth to stop while I tied small strips of plastic bag to the tree branches as markers, just in case I needed to return.

"Next time, can I go with you?" Ruth mumbled, chewing a granola bar.

"What makes you think I'll be going back?"

"Why would you not? I would go back simply for the candy bar," she laughed.

I took her by the shoulder and turned her slightly to see her face, "You'll never go there. Never." I paused, then added in a whisper, "I'm not sure whether I want to go back."

"Why not?" she asked curiously.

"It's a very different world. You're far too innocent for it. The clothing alone would cause you to faint," I laughed, then my expression turned serious. "You would be lost and confused, my dear friend."

"You are jesting. It cannot be so terrible."

"I suppose it would depend on how open-minded you could be. There's more violence and heartache than you know," I said solemnly. "Promise me you won't try it."

"Well, it is no wonder you are considering never returning if it is truly as bad as that," she said sympathetically. She urged Prince on, and he broke into a trot, maneuvering through the trees. I tightened my grasp around her waist.

We made better time getting back through the forest, but it was growing dark long before we made it to the road. When we reached it, I spotted someone on horseback up ahead.

"Who do you suppose that is?" Ruth stiffened.

"Well, it couldn't be your brother. He's not riding fast enough," I replied dryly.

"What shall we do?" Panic rising in her voice.

"Remain calm. Perhaps he'll not bother us."

As the rider approached, I recognized his silhouette in the fading light of day. "Oh, no. It's Mr. Jenkins."

"That handsome man that gave you so much attention at the ball last night?" Ruth asked.

"Yes. Keep your voice down." I didn't want her saying anything out loud that might encourage him.

I hid my face behind Ruth's head, hoping he'd move on by. I wasn't so lucky.

"Good evening, Miss Elsegood . . . and is that Miss Roberts there with you?" he asked, sounding too pleased.

I turned my head and peered at him.

"Good evening, Mr. Jenkins," Ruth and I said simultaneously.

"Now, what brings you out here without an escort at this hour?" he inquired, moving his mount closer so that my leg was nearly smashed between the two horses. I felt suddenly self-conscious of my unladylike position astride Prince.

"Nothing important. We were only heading home," I said, nodding briskly. "We should be going. Have a good evening."

He leaned over, took my hand, and held onto it. "Allow me to relieve you, Miss Elsegood, and let me escort Miss Roberts back to

Shariton Park for you." He kissed my hand, his eyes never leaving my face.

I pulled away. "That won't be necessary, Mr. Jenkins. I'm quite comfortable."

"Good night, Mr. Jenkins," Ruth said quickly, spurring Prince into an abrupt trot. I jerked forward and nearly dropped the reticule. Once I regained my hold around Ruth, I glanced back and saw Mr. Jenkins looking down at the road as if discouraged. *Poor sap.*

"The nerve of him," Ruth said over her shoulder. "If he believes I would give you up and place you at his mercy, then he is more of a simpleton than I thought."

"A real charmer, he is," I laughed.

"A real rake, more like."

I urged her to slow down when we reached the edges of the estate. The moon glided behind a cloud and a blanket of darkness fell around us. The once bright and familiar grounds were now black and foreboding. "Just drop me off here, and I'll sneak in. You go on to the stable—and Ruth, please don't tell a soul where we were or what we did."

"I would not dare speak of it," she whispered loudly, then said more softly, "Be careful. If Charles catches you, he will be furious and will not allow you near Mary." She helped me down first, then dismounted and wished me luck before heading to the stables.

If my supposition was correct, Lord Shariton and Sir Garrison would be searching for us. I was banking on that hope. I made my way across the lawn and thanked the heavens above that I wore dark clothes that blended in with the darkness around me. I watched the windows anxiously, hoping nobody would be peering out. When I reached the door, I opened it carefully, grateful it made no sound.

I moved inside and slowly shut the door behind me. Someone pacing in the drawing room made my muscles stiffen. The door hung slightly ajar, so I hurried past on tiptoe and climbed the stairs softly, hardly daring to breathe. Just as I reached the hall where the children's rooms were located, I heard footsteps around the corner. Swiftly, I ducked into the nearest doorway when a preoccupied servant hurried by carrying a large pitcher. I reached Mary's room and opened the door to find Lady Garrison sitting beside her.

I shut the door behind me and watched her slowly look up.

"Goodness! Miss Roberts, where have you been?" She stood and rushed to me, "You should not be in here." She started to push me out, but I held my ground.

"I went for medicine. One that will cure her." I moved around her and opened Ruth's reticule. My heart dropped when I noticed the last candy bar was missing. *Where could it have gone?* No time to cry over lost chocolate. I pulled a bottle out and turned to Lady Garrison.

"Do you have a spoon handy?"

"I cannot allow you to do this. What kind of medicine is that?" She stared at me as if I were some stranger she didn't know.

"It's new medicine that will cure her," I repeated, hoping she wouldn't press me further. She opened her mouth to respond but was interrupted by the thunderous sound of a gunshot outside, causing us both to jump. I swallowed nervously and asked, "What was that?"

"The signal that you've returned." She moved to block me from reaching Mary. "First, answer me. Where have you and Ruth been?"

Pushing the concern of the gunshot out of my thoughts, I turned my attention back to Lady Garrison. "I can't tell you. You'll just have to trust me."

"How can I? You deliberately took advantage of Lord Shariton's hospitality by running out into—who knows where—with his sister." Her voice rose in anger.

"I only did it to save your daughter." I tried to keep my voice calm and sincere.

Her voice and face softened. "Miss Roberts, we have already had the doctor come, and he says it does not look promising." Her chin quivered, and she continued, "It would not do her any good now."

"Then it won't do any harm! I can heal her. Please let me," I pleaded. "I don't want to see your heart break over losing a child. I couldn't live with myself if I knew I could save her and didn't do everything I could." I stepped toward her and looked into her eyes. "I know this is hard to understand, but I didn't risk my life—and Ruth's, and the chance to stay here for nothing."

She studied me for a moment, then stepped aside. "She has been burning up for hours now."

I went to the bed and threw the covers back from the sleeping child. "Well, it's no wonder with her so covered up and the heat in this room." I went to the window, "She needs to cool down to get better."

Lady Garrison gasped when I threw the window open. "Oh, but she will die if you do that!"

I shook my head. "No, she won't. Do you know how many times I've seen children survive this illness, Lady Garrison? Myself included. Of course, it was never allowed to get this bad." I moved to little Mary's side, opened the bottle, and poured thick liquid into the lid. I opened her mouth slightly and carefully poured it in. Mary swallowed and licked her lips while she slept. I did the same with the fever reducer, giving her a little bit more, hoping it might work faster.

I closed the lids and placed them back into Ruth's reticule. "Her fever should lower soon . . . maybe half an hour. Keep her uncovered until it does, and then only cover her lightly so it doesn't rise again."

"How do you know all this?" She didn't take her eyes off her daughter.

"I know you don't understand, and you may not trust me now, but wait. She'll get better if I keep giving her the medicine. She'll need to take it for ten days."

"Will it take only ten days for her to be well?" she asked, surprised.

I shook my head. "She'll be back to normal in a few days." I walked to the door, then had a horrible thought. I stopped and turned back to look at her. "Lady Garrison, please don't tell anyone of this. If people knew what . . . what kind of medication this was, then . . . well, I don't want to think what would happen."

Her eyes squeezed shut before they rested on me. "Is there something wrong with the medication? Should I be worried?"

"If you can keep silent, there'll be nothing to worry about," I said, then I opened the door, only to run into Lord Shariton. "Oh!"

He took hold of my shoulders, his eyes searching mine. "You're not hurt?"

I shook my head—a lump formed in my throat.

He sighed, and his hands slid to my elbows, his head dropping. A whispered "thank God" passed his lips before he let go and stepped back, but he kept a firm hold on one of my arms. His eyes narrowed, and his voice deepened, "Where have you been and why?"

Chapter Nineteen

Charles

Her shoulders drew back, and her chin rose. "Medicine."

"Medicine? What do you . . . What?"

"Ruth helped me to find some medicine for Mary."

"You left without a word, causing us to traverse the countryside in search of you—and for medicine? Miss Roberts, that is why we called for the doctor. He administers medicine, not—" I pulled her through the open doorway and down the hall, stopping just outside her own room. A torrent of new emotions washed through me. *How dare she! I could have lost her!* "Where have you been?" my words came out with more force than I intended. I felt ashamed, but determined to know what she was hiding.

Her eyes searched mine. Hurt is what I saw in them. "I only went to get some medicine for Mary." Her voice was soft and steady.

"I had already sent for a doctor—and the last I checked, you are not one."

"She could have died had I not gone." She still looked at me like a wounded pup.

She whimpered then, and I realized my grasp was too strong upon her arm. I loosened my grip and again felt shame over my anger. "She is dying now. Nothing you can do will change that," I said harshly.

"She will live . . . now that I've given her what she needed."

"Where did you go?" I barked.

"I . . ." she shook her head.

I thought of my brief encounter with Ruth before I rushed to find Celeste. Ruth had shut her mouth and given me that look I knew all too well. Nothing would get her to talk. "Did you make Ruth promise not to tell me? Now you both feel inclined to keep secrets from me?" I was so angry that bits of spittle flew from my lips and into her hair. My voice weakened, and I prayed she did not hear the hurt I felt by her deceit.

"It wasn't my intention to hide things from you, but there are some things you can't understand." She shook like a leaf, standing before me. "If you feel the need to throw me out, then do so. I only wanted to save a life." Her voice cracked, and her face twisted into a sob. She reached up and covered her mouth, turning away from me. "I couldn't let her die," she pleaded softly.

I felt my anger subside. I took a step back and let go of her arm. Her shoulders shook as she cried.

"Are you going to tell me where you went?" I sighed in defeat, already knowing the answer.

She shook her head.

I groaned in frustration and pulled my fingers through my hair. "Why did you drag my sister into this? Do you not realize that if things go wrong, you could be charged—it is not your place to dispense medications."

She glanced at me, then turned away again. The sadness in her eyes nearly pulled me to her. "I took her into the woods, she waited for me in a safe place, and then we returned. She was safe. Nothing happened."

There was more that she was not saying. "I do not believe you."

She lifted her chin, and her eyes met mine. "That's all that happened to Ruth. I can't tell you what I did; you wouldn't believe me. I assure you I did nothing that would disgrace this house." Her voice was firm, and her eyes held my hard gaze.

I had to do something to make her understand the damage she could have caused. "You are forbidden to speak to Ruth, and you will not go near Mary or any of the other children again until I can sort through this mess. Do you understand?"

She lowered her head, and her chin quivered, but she did not answer.

"Do you understand?" I repeated through clenched teeth.

She shook her head. "Mary will die if I don't give her more medicine."

My attention dropped to the reticule tied around her wrist. I reached to take it, but she hid it behind her back and glared at me.

"Miss Roberts, please."

"No."

"Give it to me," I demanded. All refinement had ceased the moment she resisted me.

"No," she whispered.

I reached out and grasped her forearm tightly. She twisted her arm, pushed against my thumb and freed herself, looking up at me defiantly. I stood for a moment in shocked silence. *What am I doing? How dare I treat her this way! I needed to calm myself.*

"Please stop. I can't let you have this. You'll have to kill me to keep me from saving Mary's life, for I will not give up!" The forcefulness of her words struck like a dagger to my heart. How could she imply that I would kill her? I opened the door behind her, and she backed slowly into her room, staring at me mournfully.

I closed it firmly, considering locking it once I had the key. At least I could keep her from sneaking out. The look in her eyes in that last moment between us before the door closed melted my heart. Despite her impulsive flight, evasive lies, and her aggravating stubbornness, I still loved her. The thought angered me.

As I walked away, I could hear her crying grow louder, then muffled, as if she had covered her head. My heart broke once again. I wrung my hands through my hair and stormed down the hall.

How could I love someone so entirely uncontrollable?

I paced the halls for quite some time before suddenly remembering Mary. A cool breeze greeted me as I opened the door to her room. The window was partially open, moving the curtains in a soothing manner. Little Mary's blankets had been pulled back, all except for one thin sheet.

"Lord Shariton!" Lady Garrison cried. "You will not believe it. Her fever has broken!" She smiled through tears of joy. "Whatever that dear, sweet girl has given her is working already."

Henry and Susan stood smiling at me from the other side of the bed. My heart dropped to my toes, then leaped into my throat. Many emotions shot through me at once. Joy at the news of Mary, concern for her, but most of all, shame. I had caused the woman I loved pain and heartache when she truly did tell me the truth—albeit not all of it—and it appeared she had saved young Mary's life.

Throughout this ordeal, I knew one thing for certain: despite all Celeste's strange behavior and shortcomings, I loved her and could never live without her. And I behaved like the cad I am.

* * *

155

I sat up, feeling my head spin. *What had woken me?* The darkness in my room didn't disappear when I blinked. Had only minutes gone by since I rested my head? My head continued spinning as I moved slowly to the wardrobe. I retrieved my robe, slipped my arms through the sleeves, and I walked across the sitting room. With a shaking hand, I reached for the doorknob which jerked open, nearly hitting me in the head.

"Miss Roberts," Lord Shariton hesitated in the doorway, holding a candle before him. "I was told to fetch you. Lady Garrison is in need of your assistance again."

I nodded, moved to my bed, and retrieved the reticule. Afraid someone would take it while I slept, I had kept it close. Lord Shariton moved aside, and I silently followed him down the hall. When I entered Mary's room, Lady Garrison came to me and hugged me.

"The medicine worked for a time, but I am afraid her fever is returning."

I pulled away from her and moved to Mary. "What time is it?"

"Nearly three," she whispered.

Sitting on the bed, I pulled a bottle of fever reducer out of the bag and poured some into Mary's mouth. Mary opened her eyes and smiled at me, then swallowed.

"Does it taste good, Mary?" I asked.

She nodded, licked her lips, and whispered, "More, please."

I laughed and shook my head. "No, sweet Mary, if you have too much it could make your tummy hurt." Her head felt hot to the touch. I stood and put the bottle back in the reticule. Taking hold of the edge of the blanket, I lifted it up and down quickly, then up and down again.

"What are you doing?" Sir Garrison asked.

"I'm fanning her to cool her down more quickly," I replied.

"Better," Mary said with a sigh.

"When you are all better, would you play with me in the garden again?" I asked her, hoping I wouldn't be leaving in the morning. I had worried myself sick, believing I'd be thrown out. I didn't want to return to my lonely life in the twenty-first century, but I might have had no choice.

She nodded with drooping eyelids.

"Go to sleep, sweet child. You'll feel better soon." I continued to fan her with the sheet until my arms grew tired, which didn't take long. I was weak from lack of food and the emotions that plagued me. I folded the blanket and placed it next to her, then sat at her side and felt her head. "She's getting better already."

Lady Garrison hurried to touch her forehead. Her shoulders relaxed and fresh tears gathered in her lashes. She stood and hugged me. "Thank you, Celeste. You are an angel sent from above."

"She will need more medicine in the morning."

"I will send for you," Lady Garrison said.

I stood and turned to leave, pausing when I saw Lord Shariton in the doorway. *Had he been there the entire time?* I dropped my gaze to the floor and moved past him into the hallway. I had cried myself to sleep over him only a few hours ago, and being so close to him nearly undid me. When I felt him take my hand to stop me, my breath caught, and my heart constricted.

"Miss Roberts . . ." He paused.

Hearing what he had to say would only cause me pain. I pulled my hand free without looking at him and hurried away. Back in my bed with the covers over my head, I quietly cried myself to sleep for the second time that night.

* * *

When I finally woke the next morning, I felt too weak to sit up, so I stayed still until my maid arrived.

"Are you unwell, Miss Roberts?" she asked, her brow furrowed.

I blinked at her and stretched in bed. "I didn't eat much yesterday."

"Miss Elsegood is not feeling herself either. I will bring you something to 'elp you recover." She shut the door behind her. When she returned, I could only nibble on the bread. It tasted fine, but I had no desire to eat or to do anything. I would be leaving today.

Annabeth helped me into my day dress, and without putting boots on, I left my room to see about Mary.

She was sitting in bed, playing with a doll, and smiling happily, despite still appearing weak. Lady Garrison smiled at me and welcomed me in. "Does she not look beautiful, Miss Roberts?"

A smile pulled at my lips. "She does indeed. How are you feeling, little Mary?"

She frowned. "My throat still hurts."

"Does it hurt as much as it did?" I asked.

She shook her head. "It is getting better."

"Good. Can I give you more medicine?" I asked.

She nodded and opened her mouth complacently. I carefully poured the fever reducer and the antibiotic into her mouth, then replaced the bottles in the reticule. Earlier, I had pulled the labels off, but I still hid the plastic with my hands as much as possible whenever I took them out.

After talking and playing with Mary, I returned to my room and shut the door. I paced back and forth before the fire, packing and then unpacking my things, debating when to leave. The weight pressing down on me and all the crying I'd done caused a headache and tension in my shoulders. When I thought about Mary, I realized I must stay at least until she had taken all ten days of the medication. After that, I would leave. I would take only the things I had brought—minus the money. Lord Shariton could have it for all I cared.

My shoulder pressed against the window as I enjoyed the forest view when Annabeth came in. "Time to get dressed for dinner."

"I'm not going to dinner." I gazed steadily out the window.

"Lord Shariton is expecting you."

I huffed. "Sure he is."

She stood momentarily looking at me, then went to my wardrobe. "Come, now. Let's get you dressed."

"I will not go, and I won't be bullied into it," I said with my shoulders back and my head held high.

She hung the dress in the wardrobe. "I will 'ave someone bring you some dinner, then." Quietly she left the room and shut the door.

My heart dropped when the door shut. I hadn't been kind to Annabeth. That wasn't fair to her. The sunset pulled my attention to the window once more. The sky reminded me of a song. The song played through my head, but only part of it. I sighed, wishing I could listen to music once again—wait! My MP3 player! I rifled through the wardrobe and discovered my player nestled in the back under my old sweater. I slipped the earpieces into my ears and turned it on. As the music began, I laughed with tears in my eyes. Of all the things I missed, it was music I missed the most . . . and maybe running water. Sure, I had opportunities to listen to someone play the piano or sing, but it was nothing like modern melodies, with multiple instruments playing simultaneously, the harmonies blending beautifully. The familiar sound reminded me of my childhood and warmed my heart.

I realized then that I missed my own time. I missed it, but I knew I didn't belong there. When I arrived at Shariton Park, I thought maybe I had found where I belonged, but now I wasn't so sure. I didn't belong anywhere.

* * *

Celeste

The following day began much the same as the last when I went to give Mary her medicine. Now feeling much better, she was anxious to play in the garden. Her mother promised her she might go tomorrow. Mary tried to keep me, but fearing I'd run into Lord Shariton, I hurried back to my room to have my breakfast brought to me there. After breakfast, Ruth came to see me.

"You shouldn't be here. I've been forbidden to speak to you," I said.

She sat with me at the window and took my hands in hers. "My brother is not keeping to that punishment any longer. It is safe for us to talk."

I narrowed my eyes. "Are you sure?"

She nodded. "He's been moping around since yesterday. He regrets how he treated you."

I shook my head. "He has every right to be angry with me."

"No, he does not. Did you not see Mary this morning? Or even yesterday? She looks as good as new!" she laughed. "The doctor was baffled and could not explain her miraculous recovery."

I jerked my head around to glance at her. "Nobody told him, did they?" Fear swept through me with a sudden pulse of pain in my temples.

She shook her head quickly. "Charles has forbidden anyone to speak of it until he can speak to you again."

Until he could speak to me? I would have to make doubly sure not to be in his presence then. *Avoid him at all costs.*

160

"When Mary began to recover, he realized you really were just trying to help," she explained.

Only *after* Mary started to heal did he believe me. He still didn't fully trust me, and who could blame him? I hadn't been completely honest with him since I arrived. Although I felt he had a right to be angry, I was still hurt.

"I have come to convince you to join me for a walk. You will enjoy it," she said with a warm smile.

"I don't feel much like walking," I lied. In truth, I yearned to be in the sun with the breeze in my hair.

"You cannot sit around in this room any longer. You need to get out." She stood and held her hand out to me, "Let us get your hair pinned up and go for a nice walk."

I shook my head, but she pulled me up anyway. She led me to the chair in front of the mirror and played with my hair until it hung up in a loose bun with curls hanging out.

She sighed. "Well, I did not do a very good job, did I? Next time, we will leave it to Annabeth. How do the girls in your time wear their hair?"

"All sorts of ways. Mostly down and loose."

"They do not wear it up?"

I shook my head. "Not often."

"It would be a relief not to always wear it up." She dragged me to my feet and walked with me down the stairs and out the doors by the ballroom.

"What a glorious day," she breathed, heading toward the gardens. She led the way, and I answered her many questions. I couldn't enjoy the majestic trees or the birds twittering in their branches. I would soon be leaving all of this. I hung my head, watching the grass, pebbles, and dirt pass in front of my feet.

"Cheer up, Celeste. I hate seeing you like this," she said when we passed beneath the shade of a tree. She bumped me with her side, "You've had several visitors call on you this morning. Of course they were turned away due to the illness in the house, but they did leave more flowers and cards."

I didn't respond, or try to smile for her sake. I couldn't do it. Footsteps marched nearby, and I peered up just in time to see Lord Shariton storming toward us. His head stayed down, watching his step. The veins in his neck bulged like the night he had been angry with me.

I quickly took a breath through my nose and stiffened. My heart thumped as though it might fall to my knees at the next beat.

Was he still upset with me?

He mumbled and turned past the hedge toward the stables. Seeing him and knowing he disliked me caused such heartache. I wanted to hide forever so I wouldn't be forced to face him again.

Chapter Twenty

Celeste

Ruth and I found the children out playing on the north side of the gardens. The two boys ran about with sticks while Mary sat to the side, wrapped in a light quilt. Ruth excused herself from our walk and informed me she had a morning visit planned. I waved her off and joined the children.

"Miss Roberts, I am happy to see you are feeling better and are out of your room," Susan said, while George attached himself to my leg. She frowned at him. "George, Miss Roberts is not a tree."

"Actually, I'm feeling a wee bit willowy today," I smiled and winked at him. He giggled, but not because he understood my joke. I played freeze tag with Thomas and George, and at one point, I coaxed Susan into joining us. I ran and tumbled to the ground when George pulled at my leg.

George jumped on me and cried, "Got you, princess."

"Princess?" I laughed and tickled him. "Am I a princess?"

He nodded.

"Are you my prince, then?"

He grinned and nodded with his chest puffed out and a sparkle in his eye.

"Well, now that I'm frozen, you should get Thomas. He's looking proud as a peacock over there." I laughed and watched George scowl, then run to catch his brother. I laid back and looked up at the sky, wishing I had the paints to capture the hue of the white clouds against the blue. I let that desire tumble out of my thoughts and lifted my head to find Mary sulking in her chair.

"Little Mary, why are you crying?" I asked and knelt beside her.

"George was poking fun at me." She rubbed her eyes.

"Come here," I said gently. "Perhaps you need some girl time." I took her by the hand and helped her climb onto my back. Pretending I was a horse, I headed into the library and sat her on my lap in the soft chair. Her sweet laughter brightened my heart.

"Would you like to hear a story about a princess?" I whispered in her ear. She nodded eagerly, and I began to read her multiple versions of princess stories. After the sixth one, her eyelids grew heavy, so I began to hum. Her breathing drew in deeper, and she soon fell asleep. I wished I had propped a pillow under my arm. It ached while I held her, but I didn't dare lower her head in case I should wake her.

Footsteps echoed in the hall just outside the door. Lord Shariton walked into the library and then froze, his brows raised. I wished I could have blended in with my surroundings, the same as a lizard in the rainforest.

Lord Shariton looked at the sleeping child on my lap, then gave me a slight smile. It was a strange smile. Only his lips moved, but his eyes remained elusive.

I wanted desperately to stand and hurry from the room, but I didn't have the heart to wake little Mary. My attention moved to the window, where a slight breeze rustled in the nearby trees. I focused on those trees, finding them riveting. *Don't look at him.* With each footstep, I stiffened more. He lifted something heavy and then moved toward me. From my peripheral view, I saw him placing a chair directly across from me. *Grr.* I couldn't help but glance at him. My eyes widened when he sat, leaned back in the chair, and looked at me.

He had me cornered . . . *blast him!* The trees became fascinating once again. My heartbeat quickened and my hands began to sweat, knowing he watched me.

He reached across and took the book from my hand. "Were you reading her a story?" he whispered. His voice was so gentle I had to look at him and study his face.

Slowly, I nodded.

"May I tell you a story?"

I didn't know what to say. It was the last thing I had expected from him. He waited for a moment, then continued when I didn't answer, "When I was very young, this forest out front here," he pointed to the forest outside the front grounds, "belonged to my family—it still does, of course. My mother repeatedly scolded me for playing in that forest. She warned me that the townspeople had set traps for hunting—illegally."

He gazed out the window, as if he could still see times past. "I was a stubborn little boy. I went out in that forest daily and played with my favorite dogs. When my mother learned I had disobeyed her, I received a scolding the likes of which I had never received before. She sent me to my room and confined me to the house for nearly a fortnight." He lowered his head and shook it. "I was angry with my mother and did not understand why she was so adamant about my staying out of the forest. I was sure I could look out for myself and stay out of the way of any traps.

The moment her back was turned, I snuck into the forest again. But that was the day I stepped on a trap and was badly injured. I might have lost my foot if the injury had been higher up my boot." He turned and looked at me, "The pain and suffering I endured was enough punishment to understand why my mother had repeatedly warned me not to venture out in those woods. She cared about me and did not want to see me get hurt." He glanced back to the window.

"I know I reacted harshly when you returned from your trip to the woods. I was harsh and overbearing." He leaned toward me, placing his elbows on his knees and looking directly into my eyes. "I should not have reacted as I did, and I apologize." He huffed, smiled, and then looked at his feet, "Now I know how my mother felt."

I wiped away a tear and swallowed. *He cares! Oh, I love this man!*

He reached out and took my hand in his. "Please say you will forgive me, and we can be friends again."

I breathed in slowly, then held my breath while he held my hand. *Can he hear the hammering of my heart?* He watched me, waiting for my answer. I slowly blinked and nodded, not trusting my voice. He smiled, and my heart fluttered faster. His eyes drew me in, and I struggled for air. For a moment, I wondered if I read something more in theme than concern for me. For a moment, I could imagine he loved me. *Don't be stupid. It would never work out.*

The pain in my arm from holding Mary brought me out of my fog. I cleared my throat, "Could you please . . . I need a pillow for my arm."

"Oh, yes. Of course." He stood, found a pillow on the sofa, and slid it under my arm. I carefully laid Mary's head down and eased my arm out from under her. I sighed, moved my arm in a circle, and stretched it across my chest.

"Are you in pain, Miss Roberts? We could take her upstairs if you wish." He reached out as if to take her in his arms.

"No. Please, my lord," I whispered, "I enjoy holding her."

He sat back down on the chair and watched me. "You would suffer simply so she may nap?"

I smiled and brushed a stray hair from her face. "She's the dearest little child . . . and it's a blessing to have this special moment." I looked at him, "It's like a piece of Heaven in my lap."

"And you would risk your life for this child, as well?" he asked.

"Wouldn't you, my lord?" I answered him with a question.

"Of course, but it is different for you to risk your life."

"How so?"

"I am a man and can protect myself. You . . . are so young and . . . fragile. It was careless of you to venture off into the woods." His voice still sounded calm and soft, but I saw worry and accusation in his eyes.

"I had Ruth to help me. We were fine."

"And together, you could overcome a group of ten men with weapons—if there per chance might be some? Not that there are any." He softened and looked almost playful.

I tried to hold back my smile and lowered my head, "I see your point. It won't happen again . . . unless someone else falls deathly ill." I couldn't help my crooked grin. My heart flew when a laugh broke from his lips.

"If that happens, I will escort you wherever you need to go, and you leave Ruth out of it."

My heart fell. I couldn't take him along on a trip like that. He'd insist on going through the portal with me, and then who knew what might happen.

He watched my reaction, then stood to leave. "There are so many mysteries about you, Miss Roberts. When will you trust me enough to share them with me?"

I gazed out the window again, letting my silence answer for me. I couldn't entrust my secrets to him. Not now. Maybe never.

Chapter Twenty-One

Celeste

Later, after Mary awoke and returned to the nursery, one of the servants came to inform me that I had a visitor. When I arrived in the sitting room, I found Lord Shariton with a gentleman I'd never seen.

"Mr. Davis, may I present Miss Celeste Roberts. Miss Roberts, this is Mr. Davis," Lord Shariton said. "He is from the Bank of England."

"Good afternoon, Miss Roberts," the stranger nodded curtly. He was short and balding, with bushy sideburns. He looked exactly how I would picture a banker to appear.

"Good afternoon," I replied.

"Please sit down," he said rather forcefully.

I sat on the sofa and watched him slowly sit as though he had problems with his hip. His breath came out in one big gush and the chair squeaked. His breath reached my nose from across the short distance between our seats. I coughed once, held my breath, and waited for the foul stench to pass. How I wished I could give him my toothpaste and brush. It would make life bearable for those he came in contact with. I hoped my discomfort wasn't evident. From the corner of my eye, I could see Lord Shariton beside the sofa, watching us.

"Miss Roberts, I have come to inquire about some coins we recently acquired at the bank."

My hands started to sweat. I didn't like where this was heading. Lord Shariton's eyes on me added to my discomfort.

Mr. Davis continued, "We have traced the ownership of these gold coins to you, Miss Roberts." He paused and looked at me as if expecting an answer. I was silent. He continued, "We are very curious, Miss Roberts, how you came to own such unusual coins."

"Unusual coins?" my voice squeaked.

"*Very* unusual. They do not look like British coins nor resemble any foreign coins we have ever encountered, not to mention the incorrect dates. It is all . . . very puzzling. I must say, there is no doubt as to their purity, however. They are solid gold. We made sure of that before the exchange—which I presume you received . . ." He studied me appraisingly.

I nodded in the affirmative, but not a word escaped me. What could I say? I couldn't tell him the truth. I glanced at Lord Shariton. He still watched me.

"Where did you get such a strange collection of coins, Miss Roberts?" Mr. Davis asked again.

"From my father." I felt like I could have a heart attack at any moment.

"And your father's name?" he pressed.

"Her father has passed on, Mr. Davis," Lord Shariton intervened.

Mr. Davis let out an annoyed breath. "I see. And his name?"

"Sir Roberts . . . Damian Roberts," I said quietly.

"Do you know where your father acquired the coins, Miss Roberts?" Mr. Davis looked at me as if daring me to lie to him.

"I don't know, sir."

He sighed. "Are you quite sure?"

I nodded.

"Well . . . If you remember anything that might be helpful, send me a letter." He stood, gave me his card, and quickly left the room, nodding briefly to Lord Shariton.

Lord Shariton glanced down at me before following the man out. I had seen that look many times before. He knew I wasn't telling the truth.

* * *

Celeste

That evening, everything returned to normal. I dined with my friends and enjoyed playing songs for the children to dance to—most of which were children songs. We all laughed and talked and grew tired late into the evening. When the evening ended, I stopped Lord Shariton in the hall. "Lord Shariton, would it be alright if I went back and played the piano a bit longer?"

He looked conflicted for a moment, his brows pulled together and his head slightly cocked. "Do you not need your sleep?"

I shook my head. "When my father was alive and I couldn't sleep, I would play the piano late at night. It helped me relax."

"And did your father not mind?" he asked.

I shook my head again. "He would join me and listen to me play. Sometimes he would even fall asleep." I smiled at the memories.

"If it helps you to relax, you may play. Although I will not have the privilege of listening to you, as your father did," he said, then added, "Sweet dreams, Miss Roberts."

"Thank you. Good night, Lord Shariton," I said and hurried to my room, where I waited for everyone to go to bed.

* * *

Celeste

In the morning, I received a note from Lord Shariton. He wrote that he would be waiting in the stables and wished me to join him in a riding lesson. With anticipation bouncing in my limbs, I asked Annabeth to help me with my hair and into my riding habit. When I arrived, Ruth was already galloping around the fenced-in field, jumping over the obstacles in her path. I found Lord Shariton waiting for me with the mare, ready to ride.

"Good morning, Lord Shariton," I smiled at him and stepped to his side.

"Good morning, Miss Roberts. How did your piano practice go last night?" he asked casually.

"Well, you should know," I said, then chuckled when he snapped his head around to look at me with a slack jaw. "Yes, I knew you were there."

The tips of his ears reddened, and he ran his hand through his hair. Was he nervous about being caught?

"I don't mind if you listen."

"Maggie is ready for you to mount if you are." He changed the subject and moved Maggie to the mounting step.

After I climbed on, he mounted his horse and rode alongside me, giving instructions. After about thirty minutes, I pulled Maggie to a stop

171

and gazed beyond the fenced area. "Can we go for a real ride now?" I asked Lord Shariton.

His handsome face lit up. "Are you confident enough to handle her?"

"Yes."

"Then let us go." He waved the stable hand over to open the gate, letting us out.

Ruth and Lord Shariton stayed alongside me as we rode slowly toward the fields and a grove of trees where a small river ran through the property. I was able to see more of Shariton Park than I had by walking to the top of the hill. It stretched on farther than I had thought previously. When I looked over the valley, I recognized the way the country moved. Two hundred years from now, beyond the field, there would be a main carriageway. To the north, there would be a larger city with lights that would glow in the night sky. It was strange and magnificent to see the glory of this land from this time and compare it with what I knew. I preferred it like this. It was peaceful and beautiful.

"We should head back. We need to eat a large breakfast if we are going to the Foster's ball this evening," Ruth announced, pulling her horse around.

The grandeur of the moment melted away at her words. I sighed, "I forgot about the ball."

Lord Shariton smiled, gladdened to see my lack of enthusiasm. "You are not excited to go?"

I shook my head. "Not if it's going to be a repeat of last time."

"Well, prepare yourself. It will be," Lord Shariton chuckled.

* * *

Celeste

Just before I retired to my room that afternoon to prepare for the ball, a package arrived for me. It was another gown of light blue satin. I blushed and wondered why Lord Shariton would buy me yet another dress after all he'd already done for me. I hurried to my room, where Annabeth helped me into the new gown and pinned flowers into my curls. When she had finished to her satisfaction, I made my way into Ruth's room.

"Ruth. You have to help me tonight."

"Goodness. You look stunning. Where did you get that dress?"

"It came for me a little while ago," I replied, feeling my cheeks redden.

"Charles surely intends to see you married right away, I believe," she laughed.

I nearly choked. *Is he trying to make me look good so I can be married off and out of his hair?* The thought disturbed me. I cleared the emotion from my throat, "Please, Ruth. Last time I was overwhelmed by all the men asking me to dance. I need you to stay by my side, especially when Mr. Jenkins is around."

"Mr. Jenkins? Now why would that be?" she inquired with a crooked smile and put on her earrings.

"He's an accomplished flirt."

"Never fear, Celeste. I will be at your side as often as I can. She reached into her desk, pulled out a necklace and a few other pieces of jewelry, then stood, "Here, your neck is too bare. This will match perfectly with that gown." She clipped the necklace around my neck and put the earrings in. They were heavy and hung halfway to my neck.

"Thank you, Ruth. I will take good care of them." I didn't want to be rude and refuse her sharing with me, but I wasn't one to wear large jewelry. It felt heavy and foreign.

We made our way to the stairs and found everyone waiting for us.

Lord Shariton only glanced at me before holding a cloak for me to put on. When I turned around, he stared at my gown, saying gruffly, "You look lovely this evening, Miss Roberts."

"Thank you." I hoped he knew I was thanking him for the dress, as well.

Chapter Twenty-Two

Charles

I watched Miss Roberts' face turn pale when we entered the ballroom. For a moment, I thought she would be sick, but I realized she was simply nervous. The color returned to her cheeks as soon as the first gentleman approached, asking her to dance. She looked up at me for help, but I only nodded for her to go. She needed this chance to find someone. Matchmaking happened at balls, and that was why I despised them.

I danced more than I would have liked, only so that I could be near to her. She seemed more relaxed with me nearby, and Ruth saved her a few times so she could rest. I felt sorry for the poor girl.

"Dear brother, why do you wear a scowl like that? Are you not enjoying yourself?" Ruth slipped next to me and sipped her drink.

"You know how I feel about dances," I mumbled.

"Yes, I do," she chuckled. "I have been talking with my friend, Miss Georgia Marshall."

I stiffened at the mention of the name.

"I am sorry, Charles. I know how you feel about her, but the family she has been staying with has turned ill. I felt I could not help but invite her to stay with us. She will be coming to us in the morning."

I resisted the urge to groan out loud. "Very well."

I watched Miss Roberts move about the dance floor and then turned to Ruth, "I do not remember you having a gown like that. It was kind of you to let her borrow it before you could wear it yourself."

Her lips curved down. "I thought you gave her the dress."

I stiffened, and my eyes narrowed. "What do you mean?"

"She said the dress arrived this afternoon. We assumed it was from you." She studied my expression and covered her mouth in horror. "You do not suppose it is from some admirer?" She looked around the room in a panic.

It was one thing for a gentleman who acted as a lady's guardian to provide a gown for her, but when there was no connection, it was another matter entirely. She had accepted it without hesitation and worn it to a ball. The young man could use this circumstance to force her into marriage.

I swiftly excused myself and hurried to find Henry.

* * *

Celeste

"Miss Roberts, may I sit with you a while?" Mr. Jenkins asked. Without waiting for an answer, he joined me on the sofa. How I wished the young lady sitting there moments before hadn't moved.

"You look exquisite in that color, Miss Roberts." He leaned closer, "I have been unable to take my eyes off you all evening."

I cleared my throat. "Thank you, Mr. Jenkins."

"I was afraid I would not see you here, what with the sickness at Shariton Park." He caressed my hand with his fingers.

"Yes. Mary has fully recovered, and the others are safe." I shifted nervously, wishing he would stop touching me and move away.

"Strange. Does she have no side effects?" His gaze followed his fingers moving up my arm to my elbow. With a glance around the room, I noticed a few looks and whispers of disapproval. I moved my arms away, not knowing what to do with them to keep them from his wandering fingers. He took hold of my hand and brushed his thumb back and forth over my knuckles.

"Side effects?" My head felt cloudy, but not in a good way. Nobody had ever touched me like that. I wasn't so sure I liked it.

"Does she not have hearing loss or weakness?"

I shook my head.

"Strange. I have been thinking about you since seeing you in the forest." He leaned in and touched my cheek. I moved away. "What were you doing in the night with no escort?"

I cleared my throat. I couldn't come up with an excuse quickly enough.

"You will not tell me?" he frowned.

"I . . ."

"Where did you come from? One minute I saw only one dark silhouette waiting amongst the trees, and then there were two."

"You think I appeared out of nowhere?" I tried to laugh to make light of his questions.

"You are a mysterious woman, Miss Roberts. As mysterious as the universe, and I intend to discover all your secrets." He raised my hand to his lips and kissed it while peering into my eyes. Chills ran down my

177

spine, not because of the kiss, but because of what that comment sounded like. *He couldn't possibly guess my secret . . . it would be impossible.* That would mean he meant his comment in a more . . . flirtatious way.

"Oh dear, please stop." The words slipped out in French without my realizing it.

His eyes grew, as did his smile. "I knew there was more to you, my blushing flower," he replied in French.

My face grew hot, "Please, Mr. Jenkins. Don't speak like that. You're making me uncomfortable."

He leaned back, a wicked smile taunting me. My fist balled, ready to plant it into his nose.

"Celeste! I have found you."

Ruth waved a fan at her face, her brows drawn together, glancing between the two of us.

"Mr. Jenkins, I hope you will excuse Miss Roberts. I would like to introduce her to someone." She held out a hand to me and helped me up.

Mr. Jenkins still had a hold of my other hand. When he didn't release it, I looked down at him.

"Kisses are the unspoken words of love," he said in French, then pressed his lips to my hand. I pulled away and turned my head. *Confound it. Why can't I control this excessive blushing?*

"I'm afraid I've neglected my study of the French language, but now I wish I had not. What did he say?" Ruth whispered while we walked away.

"Nothing. Only nonsense."

"It does not look like nonsense." She studied the blush on my cheeks, "I hope you are not becoming ensnared by him, Celeste. I am not sure he is the kind of man my brother would approve of. We know nothing of him."

"*Believe* me, Ruth, I'd rather not be in the same room with him. He frightens me more than anything," I said to her, pulling her out into

178

the hall where fewer people were. "I get the sense that he might know something . . . something about our secret," I whispered the words so softly into her ear that it made the secret feel eerie.

"But that cannot be. Surely you have misunderstood. We saw him when we came out of the woods, so he could not have followed us out or in."

I nodded. "Perhaps you're right."

"Celeste, I need to ask . . . was there a card that came with the dress, or had a name been given?"

I shook my head. "It came with no name or card. Just like the other ones."

She sighed. "It was not Charles who gave you the dress."

I looked at her in confusion "Then who?"

"It could be anybody, but I am putting my cards on Mr. Jenkins."

"Oh." I didn't like someone else buying me clothing, especially Mr. Jenkins.

"Do you not see the seriousness of this? If he talks and makes everyone believe he has bought that dress for you, then everyone will assume he has asked for your hand."

"But he hasn't, and if he did, I would refuse him," I stated simply.

"But the damage will be done. People will believe you led him on, and your name could be tarnished."

My stomach turned. "I want to go home now."

"Miss Roberts. Allow me to introduce myself."

I jumped at the sound of a deep, unfamiliar voice. I turned and looked into the face of a man I only vaguely recognized. I remembered that he attended the last ball. I also remembered catching a glimpse of him as we left in a hurry that night.

"My name is Mr. Chapman. I tried to speak with you at the Cromwell ball last week," he said.

"It's a pleasure to meet you, Mr. Chapman." *Oh I hope he doesn't*

179

have any intentions to woo me. He's as old as Papa!

"I had the pleasure of listening to you play last week, and I was moved to tears when I heard the last piece. From that moment, I knew I must speak to you. I told my wife I could not rest until I learned where you received such inspiring music."

Phew. He's married. "I received the music from my father. I'm afraid I don't know the composer," I lied.

His face fell. "Are you sure?"

I shook my head. "I'm sorry."

He grinned at me. "There is no need to be modest with me, Miss Roberts. I have been taught to recognize those with talent at composing masterpieces, much like what you have created thus far. With your talent, combined with some of the current composers, you could change music as we know it. Come. I must have you play more." He held out his arm for me.

I glanced at Ruth, but by the bewilderment in her expression, I knew she would not be any help. *Great. What have I gotten myself into? If I stuck to playing something familiar, none of this would be happening.*

He led me into the room set for the guests to dine. In the corner stood the piano. Only a few people gathered in the room, and they watched us when we entered.

"Sit and play that song once more, Miss Roberts," Mr. Chapman said, leading me to the bench.

I reluctantly sat, touching the keys of the piano. I took a breath and played the song he requested. When I finished, I casually looked around the room, discovering that a large group had gathered to listen. I noticed Lord Shariton among them and quickly lowered my head.

"You must play another, Miss Roberts," Mr. Chapman urged with a slight touch on my shoulder.

"Just one more." I took another breath and played a song by Bach that I knew he would recognize. When I'd finished, he frowned his dis-

180

satisfaction.

"You played that well, Miss Roberts, but I want you to play something like the last one you played. Something *new*."

My eyes sought Lord Shariton's, and I read concern in them. "I will play one more," I said, playing a simple tune from my time. By the time I finished, practically everyone in the room had grown silent.

Mr. Chapman clapped his fingertips to his palm, hardly making a sound. "That proved tremendous, Miss Roberts, but I believe you are holding back on us. I can see it in the way you move your fingers. You know much more than a simple song such as that."

I peered at Lord Shariton and Ruth with pleading eyes. Lord Shariton stepped forward. "I believe you look as though you need some refreshment, Miss Roberts." He held out his hand to help me stand.

"Thank you for sharing your talents with us, Miss Roberts. I hope someday you will put on a concert and invite me. If you do not, I may search you out," said Mr. Chapman.

I didn't know how to respond. I couldn't possibly say, "Sure. I would love to." It wasn't my place to throw parties or concerts at Shariton Park. I could only nod slightly and let myself be led away to a seat beside Ruth.

"That was grand, Celeste," Ruth said.

I gave her a weak smile.

"I have a friend I would like to introduce to you. Miss Marshall," Ruth waved a girl about our age over. I stood and watched her glide across the room. She had blond curls, naturally rosy cheeks, and blue eyes. She looked like the type that could attract a man merely by batting her eyelashes. She flashed a closed-mouth smile.

"Miss Marshall, this is Miss Celeste Roberts. Celeste, this is Miss Georgia Marshall, a friend of mine," Ruth said and motioned to me.

"It's a pleasure to meet a friend of Ruth's," I curtsied.

She curtsied in return. "I am delighted to meet you. I have heard so much about you that I feel we are already close friends," she giggled.

My mind raced at what she could have heard about me.

"Georgia will be coming tomorrow to stay with us for a few days," Ruth told me. "We will get to spend more time together—is that not grand?"

Chapter Twenty-Three

Celeste

While we were eating breakfast the next morning, Miss Marshall arrived. From what Ruth had told me, Georgia came from a respectable, upper-class family. She had been staying with her aunt and uncle nearby when a sickness fell on their small children. When I heard about the illness, my heart sank. How I hoped the children would survive, but I couldn't share the antibiotics with everyone.

"Ruth, I cannot tell you how relieved I am to be here. We should have thought of this idea sooner. I have always loved being in your company." She exchanged hugs with Ruth, followed by introductions to Sir and Lady Garrison. She greeted me in almost the same way she had Ruth. I was surprised by her willingness to be friends with me. She reminded me of the overly friendly girls who were all sugar and spice to one's face, but behind their backs was an entirely different matter.

When we had finished our breakfast, Ruth suggested a walk around the garden to show Georgia its beauty. I hurried to retrieve my bonnet and met them in the entryway. While we walked, Georgia asked Ruth questions about her stay in London. It seemed Georgia had been there at the same time as Ruth. She expressed her delight over the dances she had shared with Lord Shariton.

"I was lucky enough to dance with him last night. Your brother is a slippery one," she giggled.

"He dislikes balls. Always has," Ruth said.

"I have to say I agree with him on that one," I smirked.

"You dislike dancing, Celeste?" Georgia turned to me for the first time during our walk. "You danced enough last night!"

"I become a bundle of nerves when men are near. I'm not graceful like the two of you."

"Well, perhaps not, but I am sure you have other admirable qualities." She paused with her head held high. "Tell me about your family, Celeste. Who is your father?"

Ruth interrupted, "Celeste does not remember much, Georgia. She had an accident and cannot remember her past, but I am afraid her father has passed on."

"Surely you can remember *something*." Her lips pressed together as if the idea were hilarious. How could she laugh after being told my father had passed on? Shouldn't she be telling me how sorry she was?

"I remember some things better than others," I replied stiffly.

"Then tell me, do you have an admirer waiting for you in London?" Georgia asked with a mischievous grin.

"No."

"Celeste believes herself too young to marry," Ruth teased.

Georgia laughed, "Too young? How old are you?"

"Twenty-one—but you must know, I'm accustomed to women marrying when they are older," I answered.

184

"Really?" Ruth raised her eyebrows. "You never told me so. What do the young women do all that time? Sit around waiting to find a wrinkle?" she laughed. Her face fell when she saw the warning look on my own.

I breathed out nervously. "No. They continue their schooling."

"I have never heard of such a thing!" Georgia exclaimed in astonishment.

"Oh look! There is Charles," Ruth cried out, pointing to her brother astride his horse.

"Oh! He looks so handsome on his steed," Georgia exclaimed. With her attention drawn to something else, I glanced at Ruth. We let Georgia walk ahead, and Ruth stepped to my side.

"I am sorry," she whispered. "It was foolish of me to talk so."

"Shh," I hushed her.

When Lord Shariton noticed us, he waved and dismounted.

Georgia whipped around. "How do I look?" she asked Ruth nervously, pinching her cheeks. She didn't wait for an answer, but whirled around at Lord Shariton's approach.

"Good morning. I see you have arrived promptly, Miss Marshall." He gave her what I suspected was a forced smile. My footsteps felt suddenly lighter.

"It is kind of you to open your home to me, Lord Shariton," she batted her eyelashes. *Humph. Just as I thought.*

"Good morning, Ruth. Miss Roberts." He nodded at each of us in turn.

"Good morning," we said together.

"How is your mother, Miss Marshall? The last time I saw her, she was not faring well," Lord Shariton continued.

"She is well enough," Georgia waved a hand dismissively, moving closer to him. "Would you like to join us, Lord Shariton? Your sister was just showing me around the gardens. I am sure you could tell us about the wonderful grounds here." She took his arm, and they began walking. Ruth and I followed behind.

"How are the Williams children faring?" Lord Shariton asked Miss Marshall.

"Oh, those Williams boys are beastly. Running simply wild, without a care for others' feelings."

"I thought they were ill?" I asked, now worried I'd been misinformed.

"What?—Oh, yes. They are ill. I was referring to before." The look she threw me from beneath her perfect curls and rose-colored bonnet caused my step to falter.

Is she angry with me?

The true reason Georgia had come to Shariton Park was apparent. She flirted shamelessly with Lord Shariton, laughing at everything he said, hanging on his every word, tossing her delicate head, and pouting her rosebud lips. I lost count of how many times I rolled my eyes and sighed in exasperation. I disliked her more and more as time went on. Ruth and I didn't speak while we walked. We listened silently as Georgia went on and on about her own family's gardens, peppering Lord Shariton with questions and complaining about one thing or another.

The sound of children playing nearby tempted me to join them, but I didn't want to leave Ruth as the third wheel. I felt relieved when we arrived back inside, and Lord Shariton excused himself. He smiled at me when he left.

"Now what? Should we explore inside now?" Georgia asked, as though she were already bored to death.

"We should save that for tomorrow. We only have a few hours until dinner. Why do we not go to the library, and Celeste can draw a portrait of you, Georgia," Ruth suggested.

Ugh. Fiddlesticks. I had hoped to go off alone for some peace and quiet.

"Are you talented at drawing, Celeste?" Georgia asked.

"Is she ever!" Ruth exclaimed with a clap of her hands.

"I find drawing rewarding as well. I have been told by many that my art is the best around—though perhaps they are exaggerating," Georgia said in a rather haughty tone.

Ruth appeared surprised at her comment.

"Really?" I asked with sudden interest. "I love finding friends who enjoy art as much as I do. Have you ever visited art museums in Rome or Paris?" I inquired.

She glanced away. "No. I am afraid not. Have you?"

I nodded and almost began telling her about my trips when I caught myself, realizing how easy it would be to slip up and talk of things that might not be of this era.

"So you have traveled, then. I must say I envy you. I have always wanted to travel." Her smile faltered, and she appeared rather put out.

"I would love to see your artwork. In fact, you should draw a picture for us," I suggested.

"I do not have any supplies with me," she frowned.

"You can borrow mine," I said. "I'll go retrieve them and meet you in the library."

I went to my room, found my art supplies, and hurried back downstairs, but when I entered the library, I found only Ruth there. "Where is Georgia?"

"She decided she needed to rest after her long walk." She gave me a knowing look. "Honestly, I never knew her to be interested in art at all. At least, she never mentioned it before."

I sat beside her on the sofa. "Perhaps she's not as good as she claims."

"I apologize for her behavior. I must say, I do not remember her being quite so forward." She leaned into me. "Of course she has always flirted with Charles, but we both thought her harmless."

187

"Perhaps she's just overly enthusiastic," I said.

"Perhaps."

We rested our heads together, watching the clouds float across the blue sky. I wondered what Ruth thought of me. She was the closest thing to a sister I'd ever had. I couldn't help wondering what the future held for the both of us.

* * *

Charles

Oh, how I wish she were not here. This was a new level of agony. Her mother's absence made it a little more tolerable. I only wished Miss Roberts did not have to witness the excessive flirting of Miss Marshall. Nor Henry. If his grin were any indication, he was rather enjoying my misery.

Miss Marshall now sat at my right hand at the dining table, with Miss Roberts on my left. Ruth gave up her place to Miss Roberts to sit closer to the Garrisons. We were forced to listen to Miss Marshall's near-constant chatter, but finally she paused to take a bite of her food, giving Miss Roberts a chance to speak.

"Did you enjoy your rest earlier, Miss Marshall?" Miss Roberts asked.

Miss Marshall swallowed, then spoke as if forced to. "Yes. I apologize I was not able to join you in the library. I felt too tired to do any portraits."

"We can do it some other time. Perhaps tomorrow," Ruth said.

The prim smile slowly faded from Miss Marshall's face. "I would like that."

I suspected a bit of nervousness from her, so I decided to dig deeper.

"Was Miss Roberts going to draw a portrait of you, Miss Marshall?"

"Actually, Georgia was to draw Celeste," Ruth supplied.

"You have never mentioned an interest in drawing, Miss Marshall. It seems you have something in common with Miss Roberts." I winked at Miss Roberts. She returned a look of surprise. I laughed inwardly, thinking art might be the only thing they had in common. The difference between the two women astounded me. Miss Marshall was loud, conceited, and overbearing. Sometimes I wondered how Ruth could have befriended such a person. Miss Roberts was quiet, kind, shy, self-sacrificing, and full of love for life. I could see it in everything she did. Both women were beautiful, but Miss Roberts was breathtakingly so.

"Should we retire to the drawing room, ladies?" Ruth spoke up, interrupting my thoughts. The women stood with a rustle of cotton and taffeta and left the room.

Both Henry and I breathed an audible sigh of relief, then laughed when we realized what we had done.

"Remind me how she came to be here?" Henry asked me.

"That was all Ruth's doing," I grumbled.

He chuckled. "I do not envy you, my friend."

We took our time before joining the women in the drawing room. Upon entering, we found Ruth playing the piano. Miss Roberts had her eyes closed, as I knew she would. I smiled, knowing she was enjoying every note played. On the other hand, Miss Marshall looked bored—until she noticed me entering the room. She moved over in anticipation of my sitting beside her. Instead, I went to stand before the fireplace, pretending I needed to tend the fire.

Ruth stood when she had finished her song and sat beside Miss Marshall. At that moment, the children entered the room. George and Thomas went to sit with their parents while Mary skipped to Miss Roberts' side. Miss Roberts' face lit up, and she promptly pulled the child onto her lap and kissed her cheek.

"Tell me a story, Miss Roberts," Mary begged.

"Maybe now isn't a good time," she replied.

"Then play us a song!" Thomas begged.

"Yes, please," Mary and George said together.

I smiled when Miss Roberts glanced at me and stood. Mary moved across the room and wiggled herself between Miss Marshall and Ruth. Miss Marshall wrinkled her nose and moved away to make more room for the small girl. My eyes narrowed. When Miss Roberts began to play, I noticed displeasure on Miss Marshall's face. The more I observed of this woman, the more I was ashamed of her.

Chapter Twenty-Four

Celeste

I was asked to play two songs by Lord Shariton. The moment I finished, Georgia stood and came to my side.

"That was very lovely," she said stiffly. "May I play?"

I stood and let her have my place. She played a Mozart piece I knew well, although she played it too quickly and without any emotion. It was as though she tried to prove she could move her fingers faster than me, and in doing so, she fumbled her way through several notes. When she had finished, she seemed very proud of herself.

"Singing is where I perform best," she said to me, then she began a piece on the piano that moved slower. After a moment, her voice joined in. She wasn't exaggerating. She did indeed have the voice of an angel. In fact, if she had been born in the twenty-first century, she could be quite famous with a voice like that.

When she finished, I clapped with enthusiasm. "I love it. Your voice is angelic, Georgia."

She gave me a dismissive nod, then batted her eyelashes at Lord Shariton.

He nodded at her and said, "That was indeed lovely, Miss Marshall. You have great talent."

She beamed at his compliment, and my heart sank. But why shouldn't Lord Shariton compliment her? After all, she could hold her own at singing. It was natural for him to say something to her about it. I wasn't the only one in the room—and I wasn't the only one with talent. Why, then, did I feel this way?

I stood by the window, and Miss Marshall began another song. Mary came to me and held my hand while she watched Miss Marshall play and sing. I could only give the child a small smile. When I glanced at Lord Shariton, I noticed a puzzled look on his face. My cheeks warmed, and I turned my attention back to Mary. I moved to a seat close to the window and pulled Mary onto my lap. Mary's eyes drooped. When Miss Marshall finished her song, I stood and held Mary's hand.

"This little one is ready for bed. I'll go with her and tell her a bedtime story," I announced.

Miss Marshall giggled with her hand over her mouth as though she thought I was silly for wanting to spend time with children. Susan and the other children followed me up to bed.

After telling the children the story of Aladdin, I went to my own room, readied myself for bed, and read a little. Instead of getting under the sheets, I pulled my robe on and made my way back downstairs to the dark and empty drawing room. When I sat at the piano, I sighed, wondering what song would best fit my somber mood.

Maybe it would be best to return to the modern world and take my chances at life there.

I played a song and sat quietly, looking at the piano keys. Self-

192

doubt crept through me when I pondered my future. Tears rolled down my cheeks. I wiped them away and began another slow song, which I could only play halfway through before losing enthusiasm. I stopped, placed my head in my hands, and cried. *I miss you, Papa. Tell me what to do.*

Confusion clouded my thoughts. I didn't know if it was best for me to stay, or return to my own time. I turned to the window and stood with my forehead resting on the cool glass. I cried for a few more minutes before giving up and heading to the stairs.

* * *

Charles

I paced my room, pondering Miss Marshall's cruel laughter. Surely Celeste couldn't have been hurt. She was stronger than that. I ached to hold her close and tell her I loved her—but doubt held me back. Would she welcome my words and loving embrace?

I could faintly hear the piano drifting up the hall outside my door. The melody of it knocked on my heart and tempted me to follow it down the stairs. The piano stopped, and footsteps sounded from below. When I reached the top of the stairs, I saw something white move from the corner of my eye. I did not have a chance to see what or who it was before I hid in the hall's darkness and waited, thinking Miss Roberts would head this way at any moment. I didn't expect to see Miss Marshall appear around the corner. I slipped behind a drapery just in time. The two women's footsteps met.

"Miss Marshall?" Celeste's voice reached my hiding place. "You nearly scared me to death!"

"If only," with Miss Marshall's mumbled response, I knew her to be closer to me, though I couldn't see her from around the corner. "What are you doing up so late, Celeste?"

"Er . . . Lord Shariton allows me to play at night. It helps me to sleep."

"I see." Miss Marshall paused. "How long do you plan to stay here, Miss Roberts?"

"I'm not sure."

"Do you have any hopeful designs toward Lord Shariton?"

My breath caught, waiting for Celeste's response.

"No—no. Of course not. And you? How long do you plan to stay?" Celeste asked.

My heart sank.

"Only a few more days, but I hope to return quite soon in a more permanent position," Miss Marshall's intentions were clear.

"Yes, that is obvious." Celeste's voice held strong, "Tell me, Miss Marshall, do you love Charles Elsegood the man, or Lord Shariton, the title?"

"What an impertinent question!"

"From what I can see, you're sweet on his land, money, and title— the name Lady Shariton might look good in your handwriting, yes?"

"Well! I never . . . I—"

"Miss Marshall, let me clue you in on a little secret that most women know where I come from. Women have so much more to offer a man they deeply love than they do a man they simply make a business agreement with. There's more to life than a roof over your head and pounds in the pocket."

Never had I smiled so broadly nor felt so proud as I did at that moment, listening to Celeste.

"Well, I never! You're just jealous! I know what men prefer, and you do not have it, Miss Roberts!" Miss Marshall's voice rose an octave, though she still tried to whisper, "You are nothing but a conniving ninny!"

Miss Marshall had gone too far. Impulsively, I stepped out of my hiding place but remained out of sight around the corner.

"I'm sorry you feel that way, Miss Marshall," Celeste replied. I thought I could hear the smile in her voice.

"Stop! I am not finished. If you so much as utter one word about this to anyone, I will personally see you ruined."

When I stepped around the corner, I found Miss Marshall blocking Celeste's way, giving me a full view of Celeste's surprised expression upon seeing me standing in the corridor. Her eyes shifted toward me for only a moment.

"I give my word I won't say a thing, but I have a sneaking suspicion I won't have to," she said. She fought back a smile, and her eyes again shifted to me. Miss Marshall turned her head to follow her gaze and stumbled back in surprise, a look of horror on her face. Her jaw dropped, and she began to stutter.

"Good evening, ladies," I said in my most formal voice. "I do believe it is too late for small talk in the corridor. Perhaps we should all retire to our bedchambers?"

Miss Roberts curtsied. "Good night, Lord Shariton."

"Sleep well, Miss Roberts," I said with what I hoped was a warm smile. Miss Marshall stood there in shock as Miss Roberts slipped away, so I nodded once at her, "Miss Marshall." Then I turned, took a step, and stopped. "Oh, Miss Marshall, there has been a slight change of plans in the duration of your stay. You will find the carriage waiting for you at first light. Good evening, Miss Marshall."

Chapter Twenty-Five

Celeste

I woke early, as always, dressed, then hurried outside to take a walk. A carriage following two beautiful horses had just pulled away from the entrance. Inside I caught a glimpse of the golden curls of Miss Marshall. *Good riddance. I hope never to meet anyone else like you.*

Riding my horse was what I wanted to do most, but I knew everyone would be sleeping in and wouldn't want to go for a ride so early. I needed to become a pro at riding so that I could ride as fast as Ruth and Lord Shariton. But it would have to wait until they were up.

I walked to the stables to say good morning to Maggie and offer her an apple. The sight of Lord Shariton already tending his horse caused me to stop short.

"Oh! Good morning, Lord Shariton. I didn't think you'd be up yet."

"Greetings, Miss Roberts," he nodded to me. "I am an early riser, like yourself, it seems."

"Yes. On rare occasions, I can sleep in, but when I do, I always feel lousy," I said, standing beside him and petting his horse.

"Have you recovered fully from last night?" he asked.

"I'm recovered," I said with a slight smile.

"Would you like to go for a ride, Miss Roberts?"

"Yes, I would, but should we not get Ruth? I mean, we need a chaperone, don't we?"

"The stable hand will come along."

"Yes. Of course." My cheeks warmed.

"Retrieve your riding habit, but hurry. I cannot linger long."

"I'll be so fast, your head will spin," I said and hurried out of the stables. I could hear him chuckling behind me.

I made it back faster than he thought possible. We rode along with the stable hand at a safe distance behind us. I was fidgety being somewhat alone with Lord Shariton. In my experience, this could be classified as a date, or as two friends going for a ride in the country. The problem was, I wanted it to be a date. I had begun to sense some chemistry between us, but I wasn't sure if he felt it, too.

"Was the Foster's ball the other night any better than the Cromwell's?" he interrupted my thoughts.

"Worse. I feel like a fox among hunters. All of them after my tail," I said with a frown.

"In a way, that is true." He stopped his horse, then looked at me and sighed. "The secret is out, Miss Roberts. I do not know how it came to be known, but every gentleman in England seems aware that you are worth a great amount." He paused, adding quietly, "Although no one knows your true worth."

I buried my face in my hands and moaned, focusing on only the first part of what he said. "So, I *am* being hunted for my tail?"

He raised his eyebrow, then nodded thoughtfully. "I am afraid so."

I looked up at him. "What do I do? I don't want to marry someone who only wants my money." I dropped my hands, tipped my head back, and groaned at the sky above me. I knew it wasn't ladylike, but I didn't care.

Lord Shariton moved his horse closer. "It is your choice who you marry. Let no one push you into it."

His eyes were so intense and penetrating that I couldn't breathe. My mind slipped into a daydream of kissing him, and slipped back out again. I'd never kissed anyone, and I didn't know how . . . but oh, I wanted to. For a long moment, we gazed wordlessly into one another's eyes. There was something there in those gorgeous eyes of his. The thought occurred to me that his eyes reflected the same deep urgency I felt at that very moment. Then Maggie threw up her head and jerked forward, enough to break the spell. *Hold on. What am I thinking? No. He couldn't care for me. He plays the part of a matchmaker, nothing more. My heart lies!* I cursed my heart, wishing it couldn't feel.

I shook my head and urged my horse forward. "I've lost my mind," I said in French.

"Would you like me to search it out?" he replied in the same language.

I blushed. I'd forgotten he knew French. I'd have to speak Italian more when I was around him.

"So, Ruth told me the gown wasn't from you."

He sighed and shook his head. "No. And despite my best efforts, I could not ascertain who might have given it to you. Other than the steadfast Mr. Jenkins, of course." His mouth twisted in amusement.

I huffed.

"Do not worry, Celeste. Henry and I will stand by you through all of this. He has been inquiring as well," he assured me seriously. He seemed to hesitate, then looked sideways at me. "Has Mr. Jenkins given you any trouble? Ruth mentioned something . . ."

198

I scowled. "He's a flirtatious nitwit."

He laughed. "A what?"

"Imbecile?" I tried again. He continued to laugh. "Blockhead?" He laughed harder. "Ignoramus." We were both laughing.

"You never cease to astonish me, Miss Roberts. Sometimes you say the strangest things."

Warmth crept up my neck, and I tried to hide my smile by chewing on my lip. It was at times like this when Lord Shariton seemed so much less formal, more warm and pleasant. It made me wonder who he really was. "Which university did you attend?" I asked.

A faraway look passed over his face. "Oxford."

"Do you have a place in parliament?"

"I do, yes, but I rarely attend."

"Why not?"

"What good would it do?"

"You don't believe that just one man—or woman—can change the course of the future?"

He lowered his head and pressed his lips together.

I knew I should stop—I was overstepping—but suddenly, I wanted him to understand. "Do you know what good you could do for so many less fortunate than you? In your position, with your power, you could do so much to make their lives better."

"Well," he straightened, "you have given me something to think about, Miss Roberts."

We rode silently for a short time before he interrupted my thoughts, "Do you think we should return? I had hoped I might sit for a portrait this afternoon."

I felt my heart thump hard. "You want me to draw you?"

"Of course. I would be a fool to pass up the chance to have a talented artist such as yourself take my likeness," he said with a warm smile.

We returned to the stables and found Mr. Evens there waiting for us.

"What is it, Mr. Evens?"

"'Tis the cows again, my lord, but this time I believe it was intentional. Some rapscallion youth playin' a joke," he said bitterly.

"I will ride straight over," Lord Shariton assured him. "I will see you later, Miss Roberts," he added, nodding to me.

"Thank you for your company, Lord Shariton. I'll let them know you won't be joining us for breakfast."

"Thank you, Miss Roberts."

I dismounted in the stables and headed for the house. I was halfway there when a movement in the trees caught my eye. A figure stepped out of the bushes. "Mr. Jenkins!" I gasped.

"Miss Roberts." His bow stopped short, and his eyes never left me.

"You startled me. Why are you hiding in the bushes?" I stepped back from him, and he moved closer.

"I am madly in love with you, Miss Roberts, and that fool Lord Shariton will not let me near you."

"And for good reason, I believe." I shifted, but not quickly enough.

He reached out and took my arm. "You looked mesmerizing in the gown I gave you. Did you like it?" I didn't answer. "Do you not feel it too, my love? I have seen your maidenly blush and know it to be true. You love me," he whispered in French, then pulled me in and kissed me on the lips.

No, no, no! My first kiss isn't supposed to be like this! Not with him! I kept my mouth closed tight and tried to push him away. When he loosened his grip, I stepped back and did what any twenty-first-century woman would do.

I lifted my knee swiftly, and with a groan, he doubled over, loosening his hold on me. I had only turned toward the house when I heard the click of a gun. I froze long enough for him to retake my arm.

"If that is the way you are going to be," he grunted and pulled himself up to his full height, moving his hands to my waist. I gasped when he jabbed the gun into my side.

"You're off your trolley," I said. His confusion gave me only a moment to think through my situation. *If only he didn't have a gun . . . I could easily escape then.* I looked up at the house to see if anyone could see us. My hopes were dashed. There were no windows facing this part of the yard that weren't blocked by trees.

"Let's get going." He held onto me tightly and we moved swiftly along the tree line beside the short stone wall toward the outer fence.

"Where are you taking me?" my voice didn't sound like my own.

"I will explain later, my love. As for now, stay silent, so I will not be forced to hurt you." He led me to a gate in the stone fence where his horse awaited. He pulled a rope from the saddle and tied it around my waist, then tied the other end in a loop around his own. "It is so you will not jump off," he winked.

He mounted, and the short rope pulled me against the horse's side, digging into my ribs. Then he reached down and pulled me roughly up behind him. I was hardly seated astride when the horse lurched forward, and I was forced to hold fast to Mr. Jenkins.

My breath came in short, panicked gasps as we trotted briskly down the trail through the forest. I peered back at Shariton Park and watched it disappear behind the trees, wondering if I would ever see it again.

"They will notice that I'm missing," I said quietly.

"I think not," he replied over his shoulder. "I took the liberty of writing a sweet parting note from you and left it in your room. They will believe you missed your home and left on your own."

"You were in my room?" my voice shook.

"Not long after you began your ride this morning, I was lucky enough to run into a friend. She helped me find my way into the house and into your room. You should not have crossed Miss Marshall, though I am happy you did. She was all too eager to help me get rid of you. I left the note and let out the cows, and here we are."

My anger grew at the mention of Miss Marshall's complicity. "They won't believe I would leave."

"Then their confusion will buy us some time."

"Where are you taking me?" I asked again.

"Do not fret, my love, all in good time." He reached back and placed his hand on my leg, and squeezed. I slapped at his hand as hard as I could. He only laughed and urged his horse faster.

Chapter Twenty-Six

Charles

"Where is Celeste?" Ruth asked when I entered the breakfast room.

"Is she not here?"

Ruth shook her head. "I have not seen her all morning."

"We took a ride this morning; perhaps she is in her room," I suggested.

"I will go look."

Before she could leave, Celeste's maid entered and handed me a note. My name was penned across the front. I pulled it open and read through it quickly. My heart dropped, and worry set in.

"What is it, Charles?"

"She has left us," I mumbled.

"That is preposterous," Lady Garrison said from across the room. "She would not leave. Not after what happened before."

"This does not make sense. Let me see the note." Ruth held out her hand. I handed it to her and watched her read. Her eyes narrowed. "This is not from her."

My eyebrows shot up. "What do you mean?"

Clair and Henry hurried to our side.

She showed it to me. "See, her name is misspelled. I know because I watched her sign her name on her drawings. Here it is spelled with an *i* instead of an *e*. Also, it doesn't match her signature."

Clair gasped. "Has she been taken?"

Anger shot through me. *This cannot happen. Not to her.* I hurried from the room with Henry, Clair, and Ruth at my heels.

"Do you believe it was Jenkins?" Henry asked me.

"I do. That jackanapes won't take no for an answer!" *I should have escorted the blackguard out of the country myself!*

"Charles," Ruth said, trying to keep up with me. I ignored her.

"Where do you suppose he has taken her?" Henry hurried beside me.

"Charles!" Ruth called again.

"I do not know," I answered. "We will get as many men out as we can in every direction."

"Charles!" Ruth screamed behind me. I stopped and she ran into me and almost stumbled backward. "I know where she has gone," she panted.

"What? How? Where?" The words tumbled out of me so fast I almost did not understand them.

"She thought perhaps Mr. Jenkins had guessed our secret. If that is the case, he has taken her into the woods with him," she pointed out the window.

"Come along then," I growled. "You'll take us there."

A few minutes later, Henry, Ruth, and I mounted our horses with a gun and sword at my side. I locked eyes with Henry. "When we come upon them, I want you to bring Ruth back here. Bring her *all the way back here, then join us.*"

He nodded, and we rode into the forest.

* * *

Celeste

"Here we are. This is the place where I found the first one," Mr. Jenkins said.

"The first what?" I moaned. *Ugh, he is so irritating.* Why couldn't he come right out and say what was going through that twisted, small mind of his?

"Why this, of course." He held out a piece of plastic bag for me to see. "I have been trying to figure out this puzzle since I saw Mr. Evens trading some unusual coins with even more unusual dates. When I discovered who they belonged to, I had to meet you. Little did I know what a jewel you would be," he squeezed my leg again.

"Keep your filthy hands to yourself!" I slapped his hand again.

He ignored my slapping. "I fell for you the moment I laid eyes on you, and I knew I had to have you. It was not until you dropped the Mars bar—is that what it is called? I watched it fall as you rode away from me that night on the road."

My heart stopped. *So, that's what he was looking at that night—he saw the candy bar!*

"When I saw the date on the coverings of the chocolate, I knew for certain you must be from the future."

"But that's preposterous!" I exclaimed, trying to keep the lie from my voice.

"Oh, sweet Celeste, let me tell you a story. When I was young, about ten years old, my friend and I came to this forest so we might check on his father's traps. He went in one direction, and I in the other. Before long, I found myself lost. It was suddenly dark out, night. I ended up on a hard black road of sorts. I was nearly run over by a giant metal beast with shining lights as I examined it. Loud music hailed from the beast for a moment before it stopped. A woman emerged and in a frantic state, began talking into a small black—I do not know what—that she held to her ear."

I closed my eyes and took a deep breath, knowing exactly what he had seen. The woman must have called someone. My stomach tightened in anxiety.

"Cold and frightened, I ran away and retraced my steps. It took me the better part of the night wandering about in the forest. I saw strange beams of light approaching me and people calling out, so I hid, but the oddest thing happened as I ducked into the arch of a tree. I found myself back in the light of day, in the quiet, familiar woods of home. I eventually reunited with my friend—but I never forgot the experience.

"You see, Celeste, I believed I had traveled through time somehow. Over the years, I've pondered it often, looking for a chance to go back. Luck would have it," he reached back and rubbed my knee, "I found you. You came with all the clues.

"After searching for days, I knew I needed you to help me uncover this mystery. I knew it had something to do with this white stuff." He held up the plastic again. "Am I on the right track?"

I didn't answer. Hot, angry tears dripped from my chin. I sniffed.

"No need to cry, my dear, sweet, Celeste. All will be well. You will show me the way into your time and I will find a way to get the money we need—or we could use your money—you do have more, do you not? Please tell me you do," he turned slightly so he could see me. I hid my face.

"Once we have the money, we can come back, buy Shariton Park or any other grand castle you wish to have, and live like kings and queens," he said happily.

"I don't want to live like that, and I certainly don't want to live with you," I growled through my teeth.

"I do not know why you would say that, my love. You have given me nothing but encouragement since I met you." He touched my leg again and said in French, "You are my blushing flower."

I slapped him, over and over, yelling in French, Italian, and English, calling him every degrading name I could imagine. He held his hands over his head while I pounded on him. After overcoming his shock at my behavior, he reached back, grabbed my arms, and held them around his body so I was forced to lean against him.

I pulled and yelled into his ear, "Let me go, you repulsive—horrible—hateful—deceitful—ahh!" He stopped my ranting by bending my finger back so that it nearly broke.

"Are you going to stop now?"

"Yes! Ow!"

He released my finger but held on tightly to my arm. He began wrapping my wrists together with what felt like a piece of leather. I pulled against him, but now I was stuck for sure. I huffed.

He rubbed my fingers gently with his. "I do not like hurting you, sweet Celeste. It pains me that I must force you to go with me. I had hoped you would be willing to be with me." He paused. "I suppose I have rushed things for us. Perhaps, in time, you will come to love me as I love you."

"Never." My voice was shaky from the anger surging through me.

He sighed and urged the horse forward. A few minutes passed, then faint, rhythmic thumping of a horse's hooves came behind us. A man on horseback rode fast toward us, in the distance through the trees. Mr. Jenkins kicked his horse's sides, and we launched into a gallop.

"Help!" I screamed.

We rode fast and hard. I turned and kept my eyes fixed on the rider behind us. *I know it's him. He has come for me!* My tears fell, a smile grew on my face, and I watched him draw nearer.

"Charles!" I cried out, not caring that I had used his given name.

My blood froze when I turned my head to see Mr. Jenkins' gun pointed directly at Charles.

"No!" I screamed, lifted my right leg, and leaned to the left, pulling myself and Mr. Jenkins off the horse and tumbling to the ground. Pain shot through my side, and I lay there gasping for breath. The horse galloped off into the woods. Mr. Jenkins cursed and fumbled to untie the leather at my wrists. Once free of my arms encircling his waist, he stood and the rope around my middle tightened sharply. He pulled out a knife and cut us loose. Before I had time to react, he pulled me up by the hair. I screamed. He held me close to him, my back against his chest. The click of his gun sounded in my ear just before I felt the cold barrel against the side of my head. He gripped me around my waist with his free hand, holding me tight.

"Stop, or I will shoot!" Mr. Jenkins shouted.

Charles was off his horse and had his own gun in one hand, a sword in the other. "Get your hands off her!"

"Drop your gun!" Mr. Jenkins ordered.

I shook my head. "No, don't!" Lessons from self-defense classes flashed through my mind. All I could think was the word *pinky*. I pulled back on his pinky, knowing his grip would then loosen. As I tugged, I leaned my body forward and started to slip out of his grasp and step away. At that moment, several things happened at once. I saw Charles raise his gun and aim. Two gunshots sounded, and I stumbled forward from the bullet's force entering the back of my shoulder.

* * *

208

"Celeste!" Charles cried out.

I fell to my knees. The jolt of impact caused pain to tear through my shoulder. I gasped. He dropped his gun and took me into his arms.

"You came for me," my voice sounded foreign and weak. I looked back and saw Mr. Jenkins lying on the ground.

"He's dead." Charles picked me up and went to his horse. His breathing was labored, as if he was trying not to cry. "We need to get you back home."

"No," I shook my head. "I won't survive if you take me back there." My teeth clenched in pain when he moved me.

"You have a better chance there than out here in the forest. Can you stand just for a moment?"

I mumbled and nodded my head.

He pulled a piece of cloth from his horse and pressed it against my wound.

I screamed from the pain.

"I am sorry, Celeste. It cannot be helped. I must put pressure on it."

"Please, Charles, you need . . ." I panted. "You need to do what I say. Take me in that direction," I pointed through the woods.

"There is nothing there for miles. Shariton is closer," he argued.

I reached up and placed my hand against his cheek. His sideburn tickled my fingers. "I know this doesn't make sense," I paused for breath, "but if you care about me at all, please trust me and go where I tell you."

"Celeste, if you . . . die . . . I will never be able to forgive myself."

"I have a better chance of living if you do what I say," I smiled weakly. He moved as if to lift me onto the horse. "No, on foot," I said. It's just up ahead. Leave your weapons."

"What? Miss Roberts—surely you cannot—"

"Just do what I say. Where we're going, people don't carry weapons." I gritted my teeth, pushing the words out with great effort.

He carried me in the direction I indicated. "Go that way," I pointed, "through the root arch there. Let me down."

"Why are we doing this?" He steadied me and followed me through the archway.

"The reason may shock you," I said, and I let him pick me up again to continue on. "The night you found me, I had passed through . . . that archway . . . and I found myself . . . in a different time." I spoke slowly, weak, and in pain. "I'm not from your time. I'm from the twenty-first century."

He glanced down at me with a scowl.

I ignored his scowl and pushed on. "You need to listen closely to me, because it will be a bit of a shock . . . to see the future. Things are very different in my time." I gasped when he adjusted his grip on me. "We will come to a road . . . it will appear different than any you've seen before. There'll be things that will be moving on the road—moving without horses; they're called cars. It will make no sense to you, but you must wave until one stops. A person . . . a person will be driving the car. You must tell them I've been shot and need help." I gasped again in pain and breathed shallowly. Each step he took jolted my shoulder, shooting pain through my ribs. He mumbled apologies and continued.
"Everything they do will . . . will seem strange to you, but you must act as though it's familiar to you. When a large car comes and they . . . they take me away, you need to go back to Shariton Park by way of that tree root."

"Take you away? I will not leave you, Celeste. You are in my care. Wherever they take you, there I will be."

My heart skipped. Tears formed. *Did he really say that?* "Are you sure? You can't stay with me the whole time, and I'm afraid of leaving you . . . on your own."

"I am not leaving you."

I could hear the noise of the road up ahead. "Then listen to me. They will ask you loads of questions . . . about what happened. Say, a hunter shot me in the forest. We don't know where he went, only that he ran away. Say . . ." I groaned, "Say we were filming for a school project . . . about the Regency era."

"Filming?"

My teeth were chattering by this time. "Yes, moving pictures. Long story. Oh, and people dress differently now. I should warn you . . . it will be a bit of a shock," I repeated. I could see the road and the lights of a town beyond. "Tell them your name is Charles Roberts, and I'm your sister, Celeste Roberts."

He stared down at me in confusion.

"They won't let you stay with me if we aren't related," I explained. "If they ask for an address, tell them one you know from London."

We stepped out of the woods, and he stopped at the side of the road. His eyes grew large, and he hurriedly moved back at the sight of a car speeding past. "What's this?" he murmured fearfully. Another car passed by, then slowed and stopped along the side of the road. A man jumped out of the driver's side and hurried to us.

"What's happened?" he asked Charles.

"She has been shot." His voice sounded weak and out of breath.

The man pulled out his cell phone and called for an ambulance. Charles' face contorted in confusion. The sharp pain prevented me from lifting my hand to his face, so I whispered to him, "Charles, it will be . . . alright now. It's normal . . . remember . . . it's normal."

We waited while the man stayed on the phone, studying us with confusion. The loud sirens cut through the air, and the paramedics appeared in hurried chaos. They took me from Charles and laid me on a stretcher, loading me carefully into the ambulance while taking vital signs and calling over the radio. People in uniforms questioned us. I asked the men surrounding me if Charles could ride with us. "I'm afraid . . . he's in shock. He can't make it . . . to the hospital on his own."

"Oi! Mr. Darcy!" One of the paramedics called out to Charles. "You with the ruffled neck! Hop in the front!"

I couldn't hold back a laugh. *Mr. Darcy!* But I regretted it immediately as pain shot through me. The doors slammed shut, and we began to move forward. Through the window that separated us, I heard Charles call my name. He sounded frightened, something I never thought I'd hear.

"Tell him everything is alright for me."

"Oi! Mr. Darcy!"

"His name . . . is Charles," I breathed.

"Oi! Chuck, she'll be fine now. Don't fret," the man called, putting steady pressure on my wound. They asked me several questions about how I felt and what happened. I started slipping in and out and could only remember some of what they said. Dizziness overtook me, and then everything went dark.

Chapter Twenty-Seven

Charles

I held tight to the seat as we sped down the road. The noise coming from all around was greater than anything I had ever encountered. My heart thumped fast inside my chest, and I felt as if I might lose my mind. Strange buildings and objects blurred by with numbing speed. We abruptly stopped in front of a very large building filled with odd, clear glass. When the men jumped out, I tried to follow but had difficulty getting out of the contraption that held me to the seat. Once out, I went to Celeste's side and found her unconscious.

"Celeste," I called and took hold of her hand. They began pushing her toward the glass windows, and I followed along. I jumped back, startled when the windows flew open of their own accord. The men beside me called out instructions that seemed in a different language, but may have been English. A woman grabbed my arm to prevent me from following Celeste.

"Sir. She'll be alright now. You need to stay here and answer some questions." I stopped resisting and followed her to a chair while I watched Celeste disappear through double doors.

I sat and worked my hands through my hair. Everything in the room looked as though it was from a different world. It was so bright inside, and there were glowing objects in every direction. I shook, and my breathing grew hard. I could not take in my new surroundings.

"Calm down, sir," the woman in unusual clothes said beside me. "Tell me your name."

"Charles El—Charles Roberts." My voice did not sound like my usual self-assured voice.

"Who is the young girl you came in with?"

"My sister, Celeste Roberts."

She moved a strange stick across a paper, and ink came out. She continued to ask questions about what happened and where. She inquired about our address, so I gave her my own house in London. The lady proceeded to ask questions regarding Celeste's health issues in her family history. So many of the illnesses she mentioned I had not heard of, and I could not answer yes or no. Once she had finished, two men in matching dark clothes with badges asked me about the accident. I gave them the answers Celeste had prepared me with. When they asked for my identification, I could only say I had none. They did not like it but left me alone.

The woman returned and directed me to a room where I was told to wait for news of Celeste. I waited and paced. People in perplexing clothes with abnormal hair moved from place to place. Some people had metal attached to their heads, like a pin cushion. The noises sounded all around and overwhelmed me. Some were like birds or bells, others were loud voices asking for this person or that person. It was so confusing. After what seemed like an eternity, a doctor greeted me.

"Mr. Roberts?"

I stood and shook his hand.

"Your sister will be fine. She's lost a lot of blood, but not enough that we needed to give her any."

Give her any?

"Thankfully, the bullet didn't hit anything major, and we were able to remove it and stitch her up without any problems." He held some black sheets of paper up to the light above our heads and pointed at what looked like a drawing of a skeleton. "See here? That's the bullet. It passed through here," he pointed, "and lodged itself here in the bone. It did little damage to the bone, but it will be difficult for her to take deep breaths for a few weeks while it heals." He lowered the black paper and grinned. "Considering what it could've been, I would say it's the perfect wound. You can breathe a sigh of relief now, Mr. Roberts. She'll be coming out of the anesthesia soon. The nurse will show you to her room." He shook my hand again and left with a smile.

Anesthesia? What was that image? Did they draw a picture of her insides? I sat and held my head in my hands until I was directed into another room. When I entered, a middle-aged woman sat upright in a bed reading. Around her sat boxes with blinking lights and strange clear ropes attached to her skin. A large curtain in the middle of the room stretched across the width of it.

Her eyes widened. "I'm dreaming. I've died and gone to Heaven."

I walked past and found a second bed with Celeste lying in it. Her right arm was held against her body with a kind of sling, and her left hand lay at her side covered in bandages and tubes.

"Celeste." I hurried to her side and took her hand. She did not respond.

"She's still asleep from the anesthesia. She'll be coming out soon," said the woman who had guided me there.

What do they mean?

The woman turned and started out of the room. I heard the woman's voice in the other bed call to her. "Hey. Who is that man?"

I saw the woman shrug. "Maybe he's Mr. Darcy." They laughed, and the woman left.

What are they talking about? Who is this blasted Mr. Darcy?

I waited for some time before Celeste made any sign of waking. She moved her leg first, then licked her lips. I watched every movement with anticipation, waiting for her eyes to open. When she finally did open them, she acted as if it were most difficult. She laughed, then sighed, then laughed again.

A sound of stringed instruments sounded in the room, along with horns, deep and low. It played a tune, then abruptly stopped. The lady in the next bed spoke a one-sided conversation to no one.

Several times Celeste called for her Papa. I started to wonder if her father was still alive. She would want to stay here and find him if he lived. If he truly had passed on, then maybe she had lost her mind because nothing she said or did made sense for a long time. She waved at me and laughed when I talked to her, but fell asleep for over an hour before she woke up.

* * *

Celeste

Lifting my eyelids felt challenging, but once I could keep them open, I found someone sitting close by. I turned my head, and the room spun. "Charles. You're here?" I smiled at him, then stopped when I saw the slump of his shoulders and the unease in his eyes.

"I have been here the whole time," he said from the windowsill. His eyes stared at the end of the bed.

216

"What did the doctor say?"

"You will recover." He looked at me as if I were a stranger, then returned his gaze to the end of the bed.

I moved and felt a tug on my hand where the IV had been taped. I studied it for a moment, then lowered my hand.

"What is that?" he asked, nodding at it.

"It's called an IV. It's a tube that puts liquid into the body to help it heal." I tried to give him the best answer without complicating it.

He didn't move or make a sound. I worried about him. He wasn't the confident, proud man I knew him to be. His hair was a mess, and blood still stained his jacket. He looked broken.

"How are you taking all of this?" I asked.

He didn't answer for a minute, then quietly, he said, "I am losing my mind."

I reached out to him, but he didn't move. Sadness washed over me, and I lowered my hand. "I'm sorry. I should have insisted you go back."

"I still would have come. I had to know if you would live."

I searched for the button to raise the bed. When I pushed it, Charles jumped. I stopped and said, "It's okay. It's only the bed moving." I pressed the button again until I sat up straighter.

"Even the beds make noise," he said, still looking away from me.

"I imagine the world here sounds very different to you," I whispered.

He nodded. "There is a constant hum."

I scratched my head and realized my hair was down and free of the pins I had grown accustomed to. Me sitting here with a light hospital gown on and my hair down must look strange to him. This wasn't exactly something he was used to. It wasn't proper, for sure.

"I need to get back. Sir Garrison will be wondering where we are."

I lowered my head. "You can go, then."

"Do you wish to stay here?"

217

I took a moment to ponder his question. I didn't belong here. I knew that much. The words Ruth had said to me weeks ago came back to me in full force. *Marriage is the only future we women have been allotted.* Even knowing I had little choice in my future if I returned with him, still, I could not live in a world without him. I shook my head. "I have no one left. My family—my father—they're all dead. I don't even have any friends here—well, no close friends." *How pitiful I must sound.*

"Then you wish to return to Shariton Park?" he met my gaze briefly, then looked back at the end of the bed.

"I . . . you . . ." I sighed. "You would ask for me to come back?"

"If you wish to."

"I've caused you so much trouble, though. How could you want me back?" I felt myself losing control of my emotions.

"Miss Roberts, someone needs to look after you."

I felt a tear roll down my cheek. I wiped it quickly away. In another moment, I would lose myself entirely. "I could not live without—" I gazed at him beseechingly, but I couldn't bring myself to say the words—"without Shariton Park. I'd miss Ruth and—everyone—too much. I'm at home there."

"Then we will go back together." He glanced at me, then returned his eyes to my feet. "The doctor came in not long ago. He said you are responding well to the antibitium—"

"Antibiotic?"

"Yes. Quite," he nodded. "He relayed such nonsense which I did not understand. Seems I am . . ."

A nurse bustled in, interrupting him. "Okay, Celeste. Time to take the catheter out." Without warning, she began pulling the blankets back.

I looked at Charles with wide eyes. "You should go."

He hurried from the room with flaming red cheeks.

"Your brother seems very worried about you," the nurse said, glancing toward the door.

"Oh, well . . . he has trouble understanding things. He relies on me pretty heavily." Poor Charles. Now I was giving him a mental disorder.

"Ah," she nodded, as if that explained it.

I relaxed and elaborated, "He sometimes believes he's from a different time."

"Sounds like you have your hands full."

I nodded, "I do. I take care of him now that our parents have passed on. He makes life interesting."

Chapter Twenty-Eight

Celeste

The next day while I ate half of my lunch—I shared my meals with Charles—two police walked into my hospital room. After discovering why they were there, I was relieved Charles had left the room. He was using the water closet down the hall, and I hoped he would take his time until the officers could leave.

"We have not been able to find any record of your brother," one of the officers stated.

Uh oh.

The first officer mumbled something under his breath, then looked at me, "Where is this so-called brother now?"

I fought the urge to look out the doorway. "I'm not sure. I think he went to get lunch."

Officer number two narrowed his eyes at me. "You know what I think? I think you fibbed and said he was your brother so he could stay with you here . . . didn't you?"

I narrowed my eyes right back and didn't respond.

The first man shrugged in exasperation and walked out. The other followed. I heard them talking on the other side of the closed door, then silence.

When I was sure they were gone, I pushed the food tray away and closed my eyes tight in frustration. The tears had almost come when I was interrupted by a nurse.

"How are you doing today, Celeste?" she asked in a kind voice.

"Loads better," I forced a smile. "Can I go now?"

"I'm sorry. Not for another day or so," she replied. "I've come to bring you your painkillers."

"Do you know what happened to my clothes?"

"I'm not sure. They were covered in blood. They might have been thrown away."

My heart dropped. How could I return to Shariton Park wearing modern clothing? She must've noticed the disappointment in my eyes.

"I can go check for you if you like."

"Yes, please."

She gave me my pills with a glass of water and entered the infor- mation into the computer at my side. Charles joined the room as she finished. He bowed a greeting, then sat down beside me. I gave him a weak smile and pushed the tray of food over to him. The nurse smiled at me and slipped out of the room.

"You did not eat," Charles said, watching me closely.

"I didn't feel like it," I replied.

He sighed. "What is wrong?"

I glanced at him quickly, then turned my face away.

"What has you worried? Has the doctor said something?" he sound- ed on the verge of panic.

"No." I lowered my voice. "The police came by." I looked at him with a heavy heart. "If we don't get out of here soon, they may arrest you, me, or both of us. Or, at the very least, take us in for questioning."

He stiffened. "But why?"

"I was shot. You don't have any way to prove who you are, they don't believe you're my brother, and you gave them an address that doesn't belong to you anymore. They're investigating, and our story has too many holes," I explained helplessly.

He took my hand. "Let us hurry, then."

"I can't go wearing a hospital gown!" I protested. "Wait until the nurse comes back. She's looking for my clothes."

He paced the room for thirty minutes until I verbally forced him to sit and eat the rest of my meal. Once finished, he pushed the tray aside and stared out the window.

"I'm sorry you had to sleep in that chair. I know it must not have been comfortable," I said.

He barely acknowledged my apology. His face was lined with worry. The urge to touch his furrowed brow and lighten his mood pushed through me. I wanted to tell him all would be well, but I wasn't sure it would be.

"Here you are, Celeste," the nurse whispered, peeking around the curtain. She held my riding habit, my boots and stockings, and even my undergarments in her arms.

I smiled with relief. "You found them!"

"Shh. The woman next to you is sleeping," she laughed quietly. "I was informed that the nurses couldn't see such a fine costume going to waste. So they washed it as best they could." She set the neatly folded stack on the foot of my bed. I glanced over at Charles who had his eyes fixed on the window. I peered down at my undergarments and blushed. He was a gentleman through and through.

I thanked the nurse and told her to give my thanks also to those who had washed my clothes. When she had gone, I stuffed the undergarments at the bottom of the pile and turned to Charles. "I will change as quickly as I can, then we'll sneak out."

"How will you go about changing in your condition?" he whispered back.

"I don't know, but it must be done. Maybe you should stay on the other side of the curtain in case I fall." I gave him a wan smile. He hesitated, seeming to struggle, then nodded and stepped around the curtain.

I carefully loosened the tape on my left hand, then held my breath and swiftly pulled out the needle. It began to bleed. From a nearby medic trolley I grabbed tape and a handful of gauze to hold against it. Charles paced quietly on the other side of the curtain. "I'm ok," I murmured. I took several deep breaths and sat quietly for a minute. I thought about the medicine I still had hidden at Shariton Park. *Thank heaven for small mercies.* I checked my hand, then used it to carefully sort through the pile of clothing on my lap. What did I really need here?

I eased my right arm out of the sling, stabilizing my shoulder. I would need both hands for this. I pulled the stockings on, wrapped the ribbons around my thighs, and tied them tightly. I avoided moving my right arm as much as possible. Then I hiked my skirt up, thankful it was a two-piece riding habit. I couldn't imagine donning a tight gown. I kicked the train out of my way and studied the top pieces with determination. Putting on my short stay brought me to tears. It was very loose, and I had to tie it to the side. Getting my arms through the sleeves of my shirt was most painful. I pressed my lips together and quietly cried, so Charles wouldn't hear my suffering. I fumbled with the buttons, not bothering with the bottom half. Next, I put the jacket on, easing the sleeve over my right arm first, then tugging it across my back with my left hand. It was tight, and I couldn't button it. I wiped the tears from my cheeks and moved around the curtain. My hands shook when I reached out for Charles.

"Celeste," he whispered, taking my hand and steadying me around the waist. "You are as white as a ghost."

"Can you help me with the buttons? And my boots?" I pleaded. He nodded curtly and helped me sit back on the bed, then buttoned my jacket and donned my boots with businesslike efficiency.

When he had finished, he carefully helped me to stand and we made our way slowly past the sleeping patient in the next bed. Charles peeked out into the hall to make sure it was clear before leading me out. We found our way to the stairs and out the back door. I sighed once we reached the sidewalk and crossed the street. Charles must have noticed that the sudden cold air had slowed me down because he slipped his coat off and placed it over my shoulders. I thanked him and leaned into him for support, and because I needed comfort.

Moments later, Charles helped me onto a bus, and I sat down, weak and in pain. I watched for the next stop, then stood.

"Are we getting off here?" Charles asked.

I nodded.

"But why?" He stood and followed me off the bus, then quickly held me close to his side.

"I need to take care of my money while I'm here. I don't know if I'll get another chance," I explained. Doing this without the aid of painkillers would have been impossible. As it was, I found it difficult to stay alert.

"But is this really necessary? You have more than enough to take care of yourself." He sounded more worried than usual. I didn't respond.

It was well over an hour of interviews and a few phone calls to Papa's acquaintances before I was able to gain access to my account. I instructed the teller to withdraw most of my money, over five million pounds, and donate it to the rebuilding of Shariton Park. I didn't tell Charles about my reason for visiting the bank. I didn't want him talking me out of it, so I asked him to wait for me on the couch by the window.

With the money taken care of, we boarded on a bus and headed out of town. When we neared our destination, Charles asked the driver to stop because I felt ill. He let us off, and I waved for him to continue without us. Reluctantly, the bus driver drove away. We hurried into the trees and out of sight.

"I do not wish to offend, but you do look very unwell." Charles picked me up and cradled me in his arms.

"I don't feel so good," I admitted. "The painkillers are wearing off—not that they've helped much with all the moving I've been doing."

"What did they give you in the hospital? It was not only painkillers, was it?" He carried me through the trees.

"One helps dull the pain. The other gets rid of the infection."

He stared at me with surprise. "Is it the same kind of medicine you gave to Mary?"

I nodded.

"Now I see why you left." He paused. "I am sorry I caused you heartache over it. You knew what you were doing then, as you do now."

I nodded. "Hospitals are a lot different in my time. They can take a heart from someone who has passed away and place it in someone who needs a healthier one."

He nearly choked. "You are teasing me now, Miss Roberts."

"I'm not. You'd be shocked at what they can do. People survive all kinds of illnesses and injuries."

"Well, perhaps we can talk about it later. I am a little overwhelmed."

"Sorry," I said, then groaned in pain. He loosened his hold on me. "We're nearly there."

We were surprised to find Sir Garrison and Ruth waiting for us when we passed through the root. Upon seeing them I relaxed. I would be home soon. *Home.*

"Oh! Charles. Celeste. You are okay!" Ruth leaped up from the stump she had been sitting on.

225

"What on earth happened to you?" Sir Garrison called, running to us and taking me from Charles.

"You are hurt?" Ruth asked, looking me over anxiously.

"I was shot, but now I'm on the mend." I tried to laugh to make light of it, then winced in pain.

"Shot!" Her hand flew to her mouth. "But where is the blood?"

I opened my mouth to explain but was cut off by Charles.

"How did you know to wait for us here?" Charles asked his friend.

"After searching for nearly two days, Ruth explained everything to me. We even went through the root but decided to wait here, for we did not know where you went after passing through it," he explained. He looked down at me. "I always knew there was something different about you, Miss Roberts, but I had no idea it could be anything like this."

I could only grin, for I was afraid to laugh and feel the pain it would cause.

Charles mounted his horse, which stood nearby, then insisted I ride with him so he could make the ride as smooth as possible for me. We rode slowly back while Sir Garrison and Ruth peppered us with questions. I didn't want to give too much away about the future, so I made my answers very general and brief. Charles didn't say much about what he thought of my time. He only said it was noisy and frightening.

"I would love to take a look for myself one day," Sir Garrison said when we came within sight of Shariton.

Charles stopped his horse and turned to him. "Do not do it, I beg you. It is a dangerous place and could cause you to go mad with the things you would see!"

"He's right," I said, then moaned. The constant movement was getting to me. I felt exhausted. "I saw how it affected Charles. There's no good reason for you to go."

Ruth's eyes were on me. She appeared concerned, but there was a spark of something else I didn't understand.

Oh, I hope she's not planning to go back.

Chapter Twenty-Nine

Celeste

I didn't remember passing out, but I must have. I awoke in my bed, Annabeth sitting beside me. The overcast daylight shone through the window and rested on her light hair and cheek.

"You are awake. I was so worried." She dabbed at her eyes with a handkerchief.

"Annabeth. It's good to see you." I tried to move, but it hurt. I moaned.

"Are you in pain, Miss Roberts?" She bent over me and placed a cool towel on my forehead. "What can I do for you?"

"In the trunk," I pointed toward the end of my bed, "is a reticule with bottles in it."

She opened the trunk and pulled out the cloth purse. "Is this what you need?"

I nodded. She set it beside me, and I pulled out a few bottles. I nearly sighed with joy that I had had the foresight to pick up so much medicine when I returned the first time. Had I not, I wouldn't be able to take anything to dull the pain, nor could I take antibiotics to ease my worry of infection.

"Thank you."

"What 'appened to you, Miss Roberts?" she asked. "Lord Shariton said Mr. Jenkins shot you, and he 'ad to take you to a 'ospital in London. I cannot imagine 'ow he got you there and back so quick without you dying along the way."

"How should I know? I was unconscious." At least I could use that excuse.

"Well, at any rate, I am glad you are back, miss," she squeezed my hand.

Over the next week, I stayed in bed and let my body heal. I found I didn't bounce back as quickly as I hoped. Ruth visited me every morning and afternoon. Lady Garrison brought the children to see me often, as well. Charles only came a few times with Ruth. His visits only made me sad. He didn't look at me the way he used to. He almost didn't look at me at all. It seemed as if I were a different person to him now. *I'm not different. I'm still me.*

I received flowers several times from Mr. Stewart, the redhead with bad teeth. I let Mary have the flowers.

After the eighth day, I decided to go down to breakfast.

"It is so good to see you out of your room," Clair said happily, kissing my cheek. Some of the anticipation I felt in escaping my room lessened when I realized Charles was not coming to breakfast.

"Thank you, Clair," I replied. Upon my return, she insisted I call her Clair, and she said that I should consider her a sister now. In addition, I was instructed to call Sir Garrison by his given name, Henry. In return, they called me Celeste, as I had always wanted them to do. I had expected Charles to start calling me Celeste as well, but he continued to call me Miss Roberts, and not wishing to offend him, I continued to call him by his title. Although, in my mind, I still thought of him as Charles.

After breakfast, I walked with Ruth to the library to sit for a while. I found a book and relaxed into the large, soft chair, pulling my feet under me.

"When do you suppose you will be ready to attend a ball again, Celeste?" Ruth asked.

"Oh, I don't know," I said vaguely. I didn't want to attend another ball, ever, but knowing Ruth would want to, I answered her. "Perhaps another week, at least."

"Good. I will get started on the invitations."

"Oh, do you mean to throw a ball?"

She nodded. "We had to cancel the last one, of course, because of what happened."

"Yes . . . I'm sorry about that."

"You should not be. It was not your fault," she replied.

"Does Lord Shariton wish to throw a ball?"

"He never does." She smirked, then let her smile fall and stared at me hard. "You know, when you and Charles first came back from your time, you called him by his given name. When I heard you use it, I thought perhaps he had offered you his hand."

My face grew hot. "I should explain so you understand the situation we were in. When we went to my time, he had to pretend he was my brother to be allowed to stay in the hospital with me. And as you know, brother and sister call each other by their given names."

"Oh, I see. So it was only for that reason?"

I nodded.

She sighed. "I had hoped there was an understanding between the two of you. I had hoped I could call you my sister."

I blushed. "I don't believe . . ." I didn't know what to say, "That's

230

not going to happen." I hid my face behind my book. I believed what I said. It couldn't happen, not with the way Charles behaved toward me.

That night I dressed and went down to dinner. Charles escorted me into the dining room and sat me at his right as he always did. During the dinner conversation, I soon realized that Clair did not know what had truly happened and where I was truly from. I wondered how Henry could keep a secret like that from his wife.

Charles said little to me directly but included me when he spoke, which was better than avoiding eye contact altogether. When the topic of the Napoleonic Wars surfaced, I listened hard, trying to remember my history lessons, so I wouldn't make a fool of myself.

When there was a pause in the conversation, Henry mused, "I wonder what war will be like in the future?"

Everyone—excluding Clair—turned to me. I swallowed hard. This was a topic I didn't want to get too deep into. "Very different . . . I imagine."

"How so?" Henry persisted.

"Inventions will—could—change everything," I answered evasively, taking a bite of my meal.

"What kind of inventions could change warfare so much?" he asked, hastily adding, "I wonder."

I shook my head. "How could I know? I'm no inventor."

"It is good we don't know too much of the future. Knowledge of what may come could be damaging," Charles declared heartily, looking directly at Henry as if warning him. He must have gotten the hint and kept silent on the subject.

When we had finished dining, Charles and Henry stayed behind for a drink while the women retired to the drawing room and were joined by Susan and the children. The piano drew me in the moment I entered the room. The keys felt soothing to my soul. Oh, how I had missed this. I moved my fingers across the keys and played my father's favorite song.

Tears poured down my cheeks, feeling lucky to be alive and thankful Charles hadn't been hurt. I jumped at the sound of applause; I had forgotten I wasn't alone. Henry and Charles had joined us. Henry smiled and clapped with the rest, but Charles turned toward the fireplace. His eyes looked red.

* * *

Charles

I turned my head to hide my tears. It had been so long since I had heard her sweet music. Seeing her there with a smile and tears on her cheeks caused all the feelings I had pushed deep inside to resurface.

I stood before the fire, enjoying the heat on my legs. The children behind me begged her to play again. She agreed and began another song, one I had heard her play late into the night. I thought of those nights she played secretly, and I could see it in a new light. They were songs from her own time. I understood now that she had been a scared young woman when she came. Afraid of being alone. Fearful of a new place and time. She had to change so much. I turned and watched her play. Yes, she had been scared when she first arrived . . . but now . . . she was by far the bravest woman I knew. She dared to go back through the roots, not knowing what might happen, to retrieve medicine for Mary. She weathered through the dances that must have been completely foreign to her. She had fought Mr. Jenkins most valiantly and stayed strong through the whole ordeal. She was even resilient during recovery. She did not complain about pain, though I could see it in her eyes at times.

She was brave and beautiful, and now I loved her even more.

I sighed and turned my head. I could not have her. She had shown no sign of feelings for me, and I could not force my own on her. If I did, she might believe she must marry me out of obligation, and I did not want that.

The children danced to the music and I continued to struggle with my feelings. The sooner she met someone else, the better, then I could go about my life without seeing her and being reminded of her every hour of every day.

* * *

Celeste

The sun shone perfectly after almost two weeks of rain. I sat in the library wishing I could go out and enjoy the weather. I had already walked the gardens with Clair, Ruth, and the children, so I had no energy to do it again. I looked around the room and held my sketchbook to my chest, wishing I had something new to draw.

Footsteps grew near and Charles stepped inside. He stopped when he noticed me.

"Lord Shariton. Just the person I wanted to see." I patted the chair across from me, "Come sit and be my muse." I hoped the friendly sound of my voice would let him know I was still his friend—even though I was strange to him. I had felt, since our stay in the hospital, that he thought me to be some kind of alien. He rarely talked with me anymore. It seemed he spent most of his days out in his fields. He only showed up for breakfast long enough to grab something before heading back outside. He didn't even sit in the hall and listen to me play the piano late at night.

"Your muse? Would Ruth not be a better muse than I?" he asked.

I shook my head. "I've already drawn her twice. But I've not had the privilege of drawing you."

He appeared conflicted.

"If you don't want me to, I—" I moved to gather my things.

He walked into the room. "We did talk about you drawing me, did we not?"

I nodded, and my smile grew.

In the chair I had indicated, he sat and peered at me. "How do I sit?"

"Well, not stiff and formal like that. Relax. I like my portraits to be more natural."

His shoulders moved down slightly.

I laughed, leaned forward, took his arms, and pulled him inward so his forearms sat on his knees. "Now relax . . . and don't scowl at me."

He chuckled and shook his head. "How do you want me to look?"

"Well . . . as nice as your smile is, drawing someone smiling directly at me feels too much like someone saying 'cheese' to the camera."

"Camera?"

"Er . . . never mind. So . . . smiling is out unless it's a small one."

He tried a small smile, but it looked like he was trying too hard.

"How about this? Think of something that makes you happy."

"Like?"

"I don't know," I sighed. "Think of something you would like most in all the world and run it over and over in your mind while I draw you," I said while I watched his face. "There. That look. Hold onto that thought."

I leaned back in my chair and studied his face. I drew the basic shape and measured with my pencil to get the eyes, nose and mouth set in the right areas. When I drew his eyes, I wondered what he was thinking about. Curiosity grew, but I was too shy to ask. It was very personal if he thought of something he wanted most in the world. Expressing something personal wasn't his style. My face grew hot when I drew his lips, and my heart started to thump faster when I thought of kissing those lips. *Focus.*

I was impressed by how still he could sit. He seemed content at the moment to sit and look at me. He hadn't looked at me this much in weeks. I finished his face and started on his hair. One unruly lock was out of place, so I leaned in and reached to smooth it down. He stiffened and stopped breathing. *Is he so uncomfortable around me?* I quickly sketched an outline of his hair.

"Well, I'm far enough along that I can finish on my own. You can move now." I gave him a small smile. "Thank you for being the perfect muse."

* * *

Charles

I sat back and stretched my neck and shoulders, to get my heart to settle down. This last hour had been very difficult for me. My heart writhed in agony when she leaned in and casually placed my arms on my lap. To be near her and not touch her or kiss her caused me pain. When she asked me to think of something I wanted most, I thought of kissing her—holding her. Her fingers moved the pencil across the paper with ease. Her brow furrowed in concentration when she gazed at me. I watched her bite her bottom lip and tuck a curl behind her ear. Then, near the end, I nearly lost it when she leaned in to smooth back my hair. I had been dangerously close to pulling her into my arms and kissing her. I was in agony.

I took a deep breath and stood. "Can I see it now?"

She shook her head, "I'll finish the hair, then you can see."

"Inform me when it is completed." I smiled briefly and turned to leave the room, forgetting why I had ventured there in the first place.

Chapter Thirty

Celeste

That evening after dinner, I went to my room for my sketchbook before the men joined the women in the drawing room. When I returned, I found that Charles and Henry had already joined us. The children were not coming, as they were deemed too tired.

Charles very nearly jumped out of his seat when he saw the sketchbook in my hands. He sat quickly beside me. "Have you finished? I have been anxious to see it."

Ruth, too, sat beside me. "Finished what?"

I opened the sketchbook to the portrait I'd drawn of Ruth. Everyone oohed and aahed over it. I turned the page to Charles' portrait. Henry chuckled when he saw it.

"What is so humorous? I think it is quite good!" exclaimed Ruth.

"It is funny because I know why he has that look on his face. It could only mean one thing." Henry chuckled again and smiled at Charles.

I stared at Charles, but he only glared at Henry.

"Ah! I know what you mean," Ruth giggled. Charles shot her a similar look and remained silent.

"Look at the detail in the eyes," Clair changed the subject, holding up Ruth's portrait. "We need to frame these right away."

Charles stood. "I will be back in a moment." He quickly left the room without explanation.

I sat watching the door he had disappeared through. The conversation went on around me while I pondered what had happened. It was obvious that Charles' closest friends and family knew him better than I did. They knew what that look in his eyes meant, but I was at a loss. What had he been thinking about?

A few minutes passed before he returned with frames in hand. "Miss Roberts, I have a selection of frames that may be large enough for those portraits." He held them out to me. "What do you think?"

"Perfect," I said, moving to stand beside him. He held one of the portraits in a frame to see how it would fit. His shoulder rubbed my own, and I smelled his masculine scent. How I wished I could be in his arms right this moment.

Charles laid the frames and pictures on the table, and the two men debated the best way to frame them. I picked up one frame and studied the wood. "If you had slivers of metal, you could tap it into the edge here, then bend them back to place the glass in, then the picture, then the backing," I stated, smiling. My suggestion was met with perplexed looks, and my smile fell. "Do they not put glass over the pictures in this time?"

There was a pause. Charles and Henry raised their eyebrows in alarm and exchanged furtive glances. Ruth stood frozen as if she wasn't sure what to do. I studied them in confusion.

"What do you mean, *this* time?" Clair asked, glancing around at us

all suspiciously.

"Oh fiddlesticks!"—more surprised looks—"Sorry, I forgot! I mean, I didn't mean *time*, I just meant, where I'm *from*—"

Charles closed his eyes and took a deep breath, shaking his head slightly. "You may as well tell her everything—after all, she is your wife. She should know."

Henry nodded.

"Tell me what?" Clair sounded hurt and angry.

Henry paused and took a deep breath. He approached Clair and took her hands in his. "Celeste . . . is not from here, my dear. In fact, I know this is difficult to believe, for I could not at first believe it, but we have seen proof that she is from another time altogether," Henry said hesitantly.

Clair laughed. "Oh, what a good jest!" she exclaimed.

"She is from the future," Charles interjected seriously. He described his journey with me through the archway. Clair grew sober with each word, then fearful.

With wide eyes, she looked at me. "Celeste, practicing witchcraft?"

I swallowed hard, shaking my head vigorously. "No, of course not, Clair! I didn't even mean to come here. It was an accident!" I pleaded.

"I think it's time for me to turn in." She stood, avoiding eye contact with anyone. "I bid you all goodnight."

Everyone was silent for a few moments. I cleared my throat. "I apologize . . . sometimes I forget where I am and say things I shouldn't. I have tried hard not to give myself away, but it's difficult—" I studied the pattern in the rug. *I'm ridiculous.*

"Of course it is. We could not expect you to keep such a secret. And we are grateful to you for trusting us with it," Charles spoke softly, gazing into the fire. After a moment, he lifted his head to Henry. "Will she keep silent?" he asked soberly.

Henry nodded. "I will explain it all to her. I am sure she will see the

truth." He bowed and followed Clair upstairs.

That night, I paced my room, worrying about what Clair might think of me. When I could no longer stand it, I threw on my dressing gown and slipped downstairs to the piano. I sat down and softly played a few notes. The tune reminded me of a song by one of my favorite singers. I slowly picked out the melody, searching for the right keys. Then I started to sing, soft and low. "Everybody loves somebody sometimes . . ."

I sighed and stopped playing. Maybe everybody loves somebody sometimes, but not everybody can sing Dean Martin. I played a little Bach instead. I was just beginning another piece when I heard a throat clear in the doorway. Clair stood there in her nightgown and robe with a candle in her hand.

"My apologies for interrupting. I heard you playing and wanted to speak with you."

I stood, not knowing what to say.

"Can we sit?" she waved toward the sofa. I nodded and went to sit beside her.

"First, I need to say something." She took my hand, "I am sorry for doubting you. I should never have thought you could be practicing witchcraft," she said and shook her head. "My imagination can get away with me sometimes."

"I'm the same way," I said kindly.

"Henry helped me see the proof of what you claim—how you came here so unexpectedly with your sometimes strange words and views and the odd coins you traded at the bank. Then there is the way you rode off to find a mysterious medicine that healed Mary and the greatest feat of all, your survival of a gunshot wound to the shoulder—I believe you are telling the truth." She covered my hand with hers, "I would also like to say thank you for loving my daughter enough to want to save her. I owe you my life and my silence. I will never speak of this to anyone—for I understand the dangers that could befall you if I do."

"Thank you, Clair. You're a true friend, and I'm so glad I don't have to hide this anymore!" I hugged her, then pulled away and dabbed at the tears in my eyes. "I hated keeping this secret—mostly because I despise lying. It's better now that I can talk more freely about my true self, but next time, I'll be more careful about what I say around people who don't know."

"Learning you came here by accident was a bit of a surprise," she laughed. "I must admit I thought you were a young lady wishing to marry Lord Shariton and that by playing lost and helpless, you planned to win him."

I coughed and laughed. "I'm only twenty-one! In the twenty-first century, it's unusual for a girl as young as I to marry—not unheard of, mind you, but not common. Most women don't marry until their mid to late twenties."

"So you are not after Charles' title?" She peered at me with one brow raised.

I shook my head and laughed.

"Well, though you may be young, you can still fall in love." She paused. "Is there someone, Celeste?"

I lowered my head to hide my warm cheeks.

"A Mr. Stewart has called many times over the last fortnight. You must miss the opportunity to converse with him."

I furrowed my brows. *Does she think I'm blushing for Mr. Stewart?* When I raised my head to say something to the contrary, she was grinning impishly at me. I smiled. *Ah, the joke's on me.*

She stood and held out her hand, "Well, I'm very glad we could talk tonight. And now we must both get some rest."

* * *

Charles

I stood in the entry hall at the bottom of the stairs and talked with Clair about the final touches for the ball she and Ruth had planned. The guests would begin to arrive at any moment, and Ruth and Celeste were still dressing. I felt uneasy. Over the last few days, I learned of Mr. Stewart's intentions toward Celeste. He was an upstanding gentleman who stood to inherit an estate with great prospects. He had enough money that he need not pursue Celeste in order to secure his wealth. He was the kind of man who could make Celeste comfortable and happy. And take her from me.

Clair interrupted my thoughts, touching my hand and nodding at the stairs. I turned and found Ruth and Celeste standing at the top. With the flowers in her hair and the flowing silk of her gown accentuating her fine figure, Celeste looked like an angel. I could not breathe, move, nor take my eyes off her. Her cheeks darkened to a nice pink shade as she descended the stairs toward me. I closed my eyes and cleared my throat, then reopened them. I tried to keep my eyes trained on Ruth, not to reveal my feelings toward Celeste.

"You two look stunning," I said to Ruth, glancing briefly at Celeste. "Come, it is time to greet our guests."

The guests flowed through in groups. It had started to rain, and many of the ladies came in fretting about their hair or gowns. When I spotted Mr. Stewart, I greeted him warmly. He moved on quickly, a little too eager to greet Celeste.

Celeste blushed as she always did when someone complimented her appearance. Mr. Stewart spoke kindly to her, and she to him in return. He asked for a chance to dance with her, and she accepted before he moved on.

Watching the exchange pained me. I did not want him to speak to her again, yet I encouraged it.

* * *

Celeste

I was glad when the receiving queue ended. How many times did I have to hear how sorry everyone was over my injury? However small, my relief was short lived, for it seemed I had promised to dance with every eligible bachelor. I danced the first several with men I'd never met. They all flattered me, though thankfully not in the same manner as Mr. Jenkins. I pushed the thought of him away, trying not to remember his awful end. I accepted the gentlemen's compliments with grace, although it was difficult. They were all full of the same blasé lines, the same insipid praise, empty and forced. How I wished I could roll my eyes and walk away.

As I danced with Mr. Stewart, I began to grow weak. I had made it halfway through the dance when he noticed my discomfort.

"Miss Roberts, are you unwell?" he asked earnestly.

"My shoulder aches. I haven't healed as well as I thought," I replied through tight lips. "I wish to rest."

He took me by the arm and led me to a sofa. "Please sit, Miss Roberts, for I could never forgive myself if I were to see you faint during a dance with me." He sat down beside me, looking concerned.

"Thank you, Mr. Stewart," I sighed gratefully, leaning my head back into the softness of the sofa.

"Are you in pain, Miss Roberts?" He took my hand and patted it nervously.

"Only when I move my shoulder. I'm fine now," I assured him. I considered pulling my hand out of his sweaty clasp, but I was afraid to hurt his feelings. He was a nice young man, after all. It wasn't his fault he had such teeth.

"I have been very anxious about your recovery, Miss Roberts. I hope you have not been in too much pain."

How thoughtful. "No, I have not."

"Did you receive the flowers I sent you?" He appeared hopeful and nervous. As I studied his demeanor, I came to understand him better. He was a bit awkward, much like me, when conversing with the opposite sex. He really wasn't so bad . . .

"Oh, how forgetful of me! I should have thanked you sooner. I did receive them, and they're lovely. Thank you."

He smiled, leaned in, and spoke softly, "I had hoped to give you your favorite flowers, but I am afraid I do not know what they are. And if it is not too forward of me to say, perhaps I will have the opportunity to get to know you better, Miss Roberts."

I swallowed. "Yes. Perhaps."

"Good evening, Mr. Stewart. How are you enjoying yourself?" Clair interrupted us brightly.

"It has been an exceptional evening. Thank you, Lady Garrison," he replied.

"I am glad to hear it. I hope you will not mind my stealing Miss Roberts from you, for I am in need of her assistance."

I gave Clair a smile of gratitude, then stood before he could answer. "Thank you for the conversation, Mr. Stewart. I hope you will have the chance to dance some more before the night is over."

"I will if you are well enough?" he replied.

"Oh no, I think I must not push this shoulder too far. I thank you, Mr. Stewart!"

I nodded at him and fled swiftly away with Clair. She leaned into me and spoke softly, "I have been instructed to watch out for you, Celeste. How are you?"

"A bit tired and stiff in my shoulder, but I'm well enough, I sup-

245

pose." That statement was more lies than truth.

"You looked a little uncomfortable sitting there, so I thought I would ask." She led me to the side next to a window.

I sighed, "Clair . . . to tell you the truth, I'm terrified."

Her eyes opened wide. "Why, Celeste?"

"I glance around at all these men and believe that every one of them could end up being exactly like Mr. Jenkins." I lowered my head, trying to hold back my emotions. "Not so much Mr. Stewart. I suppose he's harmless enough."

"The likelihood of that happening again is so small, I would not worry about it, dear," she said, taking me gently by the arm.

"But all these men are only here for my money. I don't want to be sought after for my money. I want to be *loved*. How can I possibly know what their true intentions are?" I fought to keep the tears at bay.

"You will know, my dear. You are young and have time to find the love you seek. Listen to what your heart tells you, and follow it." She patted my arm, "I do believe that you are perfectly safe with Mr. Stewart. When he inherits, he will have twelve thousand a year, so he is not likely to be looking for a fortune."

I smiled weakly back.

Just then, a young man I had met previously approached us, took my hand, and kissed it in greeting. I could not recall his name. "Miss Roberts, may I persuade you to dance with me?" he asked expectantly.

I shot Clair a look of uneasiness and then nodded at him. I danced several more dances, one of which was with Mr. Stewart. Well after two in the morning, I felt run down. After ending one dance that became especially long, I went in search of Charles. I found him talking with Henry at the side of the room.

"Lord Shariton, I wanted to ask if it would be alright if I retired for the evening." I didn't look up at him, because I didn't want him to see how weak and tired I truly was. I didn't want him to worry and fret over me.

"Are you unwell, Miss Roberts?"

Fiddlesticks, he sees right through me. "I am well. Only tired." I stared at the door, longing to be away from here.

"Well, if you need your rest, you may go."

I nodded, thanked him, and walked out of the room. Only a few steps up the stairs, I felt dizzy and had to sit. I rested my head against the cool marble banister and struggled to regain my strength. The room dimmed with each dizzy spell.

"Celeste, you should have told me you were this undone!" Charles' sudden appearance next to me caused me to jump. He had used my given name. I wanted to smile, but I felt too weak. I knew my eyes were moist already, so I didn't hold back the tears.

"Forgive me, my lord."

"Enough of this lord business. You may call me Charles. We have been through enough together to warrant it, don't you think?"

A smile pulled at my lips.

He reached for a handkerchief and dabbed at my cheeks. "I should have known better than to let you dance all night," he said with a scowl. He tucked his handkerchief away, put his arm around my waist, and lifted me to my feet. "Come, Celeste. Let's get you to your room."

My legs shook as he guided me up the steps and down the hall. I may not have needed to lean into him so heavily or to bury my head into his lapel—oh, but I loved the way he smelled of fresh-cut wood and spices.

He spoke softly to one of the servants, instructing her to fetch Annabeth, then he bid another to follow us into the room. When we reached my bed, he helped me lie down. I sighed and smiled with my eyes closed. His fingers touched my forehead softly as he brushed my hair from my face. I opened my eyes and saw the pain in his expression. *What could have caused that look?*

"Sleep well, Celeste," he said and quickly left the room.

Chapter Thirty-One

Celeste

Although I was exhausted, sleep eluded me. I had repeated nightmares of men like Mr. Jenkins appearing everywhere, all around me. There seemed no way I could get away from them. It was midday before I felt rested enough to get out of bed. Annabeth appeared to help me dress and fix my hair, so I made it down for tea. Charles, Henry, and Clair were there already; everyone was quiet in their own thoughts. I supposed it was due to the late night. Ruth came in a little while later and yawned through her refreshment. Charles announced that he would be helping the servants mend a fence in the south fields. I wanted to go with him and watch him work, but felt it wouldn't be prudent.

"The children are outside playing if you would like to join them, Celeste," Clair told me before leaving the room.

I nodded. "I will." I made my way slowly outside.

I played a brief game with the kids before they were called in to do their reading lessons. The sun was out, but I felt a storm coming, so I took advantage of the weather and went for a short walk. I stayed in the gardens where I felt safe, in view of the house. The balls were all over, and knowing no other dances would take place anytime soon relieved me. I sang.

Singing lifted my spirits, and soon I was whistling, too. Amid a popular tune from the twentieth century, I turned to find Clair bustling toward me alongside Mr. Stewart.

Trying not to appear flustered, I curtsied a greeting.

"Good morning, Miss Roberts," said Mr. Stewart.

"And to you, Mr. Stewart." We stood there in silence.

"It is kind of Mr. Stewart to wish to join us for a walk, is it not?" Clair asked, nodding pointedly toward Mr. Stewart, who took no notice of her. Her eyes gave the message that she wished me to begin something, whether walking or talking, I did not know. I nodded politely.

Mr. Stewart held out his elbow. I took his arm and glanced back at Clair, who fell into step some distance behind us.

I tried to relax, but my guard was up. I feared he might try something like Mr. Jenkins, and relief came over me with Clair coming along. With each backward glance, I saw Clair silently urging me to speak. But what could I say?

"Oh, I do believe I see Lord Shariton. There is something particular I wish to ask him . . ." she trailed off and hurried away. I searched in the direction she had gone but didn't see any sign of Charles.

Clair! Get back here! Don't leave me with him!

We walked in silence for some time. Mr. Stewart cleared his throat and fidgeted. I almost commented on his nervousness when he finally opened his mouth to speak.

He paused and turned to face me. "Miss Roberts, I have come . . . to tell you how much . . . Miss Roberts, it would please me greatly if you would accept my hand and be my wife." His words at first were broken, then rushed out so quickly I thought he'd faint.

My jaw hung slack. *How can he ask this question when he hardly knows me?* He studied me anxiously, waiting for an answer. He hadn't even mentioned loving me. Shouldn't that be the first thing a man says when proposing?

I wanted to laugh at the absurdity of the situation. This was exactly what I'd always wished for—when I was ready, of course. My entire life was filled with daydreams of a young man proposing to me in a beautiful garden, no less, beside a picturesque country manor. What were the odds?

I glanced up at him and gave him a quick smile. He didn't fit into my dream. "I'm sorry, Mr. Stewart. I can't say yes." I shook my head, "I don't love you . . . and you deserve to be loved. You're a great man and . . . I'm so sorry."

His gaze fell for a moment, then something new brightened his eyes. "Miss Roberts, perhaps if you thought it through, you might come to understand the great courtesy I have taken to bestow this offer on you. Perhaps—"

"Mr. Stewart, I can't—"

"You will have a title—a connection with a distinguished family." He stepped closer, and I moved back.

"You don't understand—"

"No! You don't understand!" He moved closer, and I backed up. I held up my hand to keep him at a distance. My heart raced as he began to list all the reasons I could live comfortably with him.

"No, hold on!" I raised my fists in defense, ready if he came any closer.

"Mr. Stewart!" Charles' booming voice at my side gave me a start.

Mr. Stewart's eyes bugged, and he turned with a jerk.

"You may leave, Mr. Stewart, before you find it quite difficult to ride your precious horses again." Charles' shoulders rose and fell with labored breathing as if he'd run far. His fists were balled, ready for any reluctance on the part of Mr. Stewart.

Mr. Stewart huffed, his face blanched, and he exited the garden. In the next instant, I rushed into Charles' arms. My body shook with emotion. *He's saved me again!*

"All is well now, Celeste," he said, and I cried into his lapel. His left arm encircled my waist, and his right hand brushed the loose hair from my face.

My tears subsided, and I settled into the safety of his embrace. *I am home.* Impulsively, I turned my face into his neck and kissed him under his chin. "I love you."

He froze, and his breath stopped.

My eyes flashed open. *What did I just say?* My heart clenched. I moved to step back, but his arm remained tight around me.

He lifted my chin, forcing me to meet his eyes. I bit my lip, waiting for his response. A smile spread across his face just before he leaned in and touched his lips to mine. He pulled away long enough to whisper, "And I love you."

His soft kisses warmed me through and were even more heart-melting than I could have imagined. My knees weakened when his fingers brushed my cheeks and pressed against my back. When we pulled away to catch our breath, we gazed into each other's eyes and laughed.

"I thought I disgusted you," I said.

"How could you believe that?" He touched my chin softly with his fingers.

I sighed at his touch and closed my eyes. "You would hardly look at me, and when I got close to you, you stiffened up like I was something loathsome."

He chuckled, kissed my lips again, then pulled away and looked at me. "Every moment you were near, I had to keep myself from rushing to you and kissing you. Whenever you were close, I had to freeze to keep from pulling you into my arms. I love you, Celeste. I have fallen more deeply in love with you since I first saw you and every day after."

New tears streamed from my closed eyes, and I laughed again. Joy burst from within. I sighed and waited for him to kiss me. When he didn't, I opened them to see him smiling. "What?"

"You are more beautiful than words can say . . . but you are more than that. I have watched you for so long and thought about how brave, intelligent, accomplished, and kind you are. I dreamed of the day I could hold you in my arms and kiss your sweet lips." His fingers touched my lips.

I knew I must be blushing madly. "Then why were you trying so hard to marry me off and get rid of me?"

"I did not think you loved me, and I wanted you gone so you would stop tormenting me."

"Tormenting you?" I frowned, "You were the one doing the tormenting."

He laughed. "When I heard from Clair that Mr. Stewart had come, I had to do something . . . I feared I had lost you."

"But my heart belongs to you."

He laughed and kissed me once again. When he pulled away, I breathed softly, "Wow."

* * *

Celeste

All that afternoon, I avoided Ruth and Clair. I didn't want them to guess why I was smiling so much. Charles was the only one missing when I entered the drawing room that evening. Clair hurried to my side and pulled me to a corner.

"Celeste, I apologize. I heard that Mr. Stewart behaved very wrongly. I did not know he would behave in such a manner." She patted my arm reassuringly.

I grinned stupidly. "You needn't worry about that anymore."

"Well, I do worry. I am concerned you might wish to leave us, especially after all that's happened," she said.

"I won't be going anywhere, Clair," I said, my eyes following Charles as he entered the room.

My heart skipped a beat when our eyes locked. Henry intercepted him and began to speak, but Charles kept his eyes on me. After a moment, he said something quietly to Henry, stepped past him, and came to me.

"Celeste, I cannot hide this from them any longer. Shall we tell them?" He took my hand in his. I smiled and nodded. He turned to Henry, Ruth, and Clair and cleared his throat. "I have an announcement . . . I have asked Miss Celeste Roberts for her hand in marriage, and she has *somehow* found it in her good heart to accept."

I softly hit his arm. "Somehow?" I laughed.

Ruth was the first to react. She squealed with delight and ran to us, throwing her arms around us and kissing our cheeks. Once Clair and Henry had recovered from the shock, they, too, kissed our cheeks and congratulated us. I looked at those around me, overwhelmed with joy. This was my family now.

* * *

Celeste

"Do you think about the future much?" Ruth asked me the next day

254

as we sat in the library together. She watched the rain fall outside the window while I finished a drawing.

"What do you mean? What will happen in this time or the future time I came from?" I asked.

"The time you came from."

"Only when I think of my father."

"What else do you miss?" she asked.

I laughed. "Running water, music, chocolate-covered caramels, personal hygiene products, and health security."

"Security of health?"

I nodded. "It scares me a little being here and knowing that I could catch an illness and die from it at any moment. In the twenty-first century, our knowledge of how bodies work and our overall health is much more advanced."

"Oh." She paused, confusion written across her face. "What is 'running water'? And we already have music—what do you miss about that?"

"Hold onto that thought," I said, hurrying from the room. When I returned, I had my MP3 in hand. I sat down next to her and carefully placed one earbud in her ear and the other in my own. "This is what I mean by missing music. I can press a button and . . ." She jumped when the music began, clutching my hand.

Her eyes went wide, and she listened in silence for a moment; then she smiled with delight and laughed aloud.

"What are you two doing?" Charles asked, coming into the room. When he spotted the device in my hands, his brow furrowed in confusion.

"Come listen to this, Charles. It is amazing." Ruth held her hand out to him. He sat next to me and put his arm around my lower back. I motioned for him to lean in and then placed the earpiece in his ear. His eyes lit up with wonder, and he smiled widely. I couldn't help myself.

255

He sat so close I couldn't resist kissing his cheek. He blushed and looked at Ruth.

She laughed and stood. "I will let you two have a moment alone, but I am leaving the door open, and I'll be right outside." She smiled mischievously and skipped out of the room.

I leaned into Charles and hit the buttons on the player until I found the song I was searching for. It was one of those sappy songs people play at weddings. Now, when I listened to the words, I smiled at him and felt the truth of each one. The lyrics spoke of deep and undying love and the desire to hold each other close. He watched the title of the song move across the screen. I turned his chin toward me to see the love in his eyes. He took hold of my hand and kissed it. When the song ended, another louder song began, and I quickly turned it off.

"Sorry. Some music can be annoying at times."

"That song was amazing." He hesitated, then asked. "You feel that way?"

I nodded. His smile faded, and a troubled look crossed his face.

"What is it, Charles?"

"I remembered the first time I met you, and something has been bothering me." He stroked my hand.

I touched his lips. "What is it?"

He kissed my finger. "You said something about Shariton Park."

I stiffened.

He watched my reaction. "You do know something, do you not? What happens to Shariton in the future?"

I sighed. "It's damaged during a war more than one hundred years from now. It's been in bad shape ever since. Your descendants have struggled to maintain it."

His shoulders were hunched and he thought for a moment. "Then I must do my part to help them keep it." He looked at me. "Thank you for telling me."

I smiled at the thought of what I had already done.

"What? You have that look again as if you are hiding something."

I giggled, "I can't hide anything from you. You've always known when I spoke untruly. When we went to the bank after the hospital . . . you remember?"

He nodded.

"I donated all of my money—well, not all, but most of it—to your descendants toward rebuilding Shariton Park."

"You what?" He laughed, "You did not even know what kind of future you had, and you gave your money away?"

I nodded, and he kissed me.

When he pulled away to catch his breath, he asked, "Why?"

"Because I love Shariton Park. This is my home, and it's where I belong. All my life, I've never felt like I fit in anywhere . . . until I came here."

"And you will always belong here, my darling." He kissed me, then pulled out the sketchbook tucked next to me on the couch. "What have you been working on?" He flipped through the pages and found the picture I had just finished. His mouth dropped open, and his eyes nearly bugged out of his head.

"Do you like it?" I asked.

He closed his mouth and nodded. "It looks just like you." He gazed at me, then back at the drawing.

"It's your wedding gift," I said.

"After what you've done for Shariton . . . I am speechless," he said.

"As I said, I love you and Shariton Park, and I was only too happy to help your descendants restore it to its former beauty."

"*Our* descendants," he corrected me and smiled. "After all, you are marrying me." I laughed, my heart so full at that realization. My great-great-great-great grandchildren would someday receive the money I had donated. It warmed my heart incredibly, knowing I had a direct hand in my family's life—joyful tears formed in my eyes. I threw my arms around Charles' neck and kissed him until I nearly fainted from happiness.

Thanks for reading!
If you enjoyed Celeste's story, please leave a review and check out Ruth's story in the next book, *A Season for Shariton Park*
(Don't worry, you don't have to wait long for the release).

Author's note…

Boy, have I got a plethora of stories to share, and between you and me, more than a dozen are already completed—rough drafts still—but completed. AND I've started over two dozen more. So hold onto your seat, because it's all coming as quick as they can get edited and time permits.

Next up is Ruth's story in the second book to Shariton Park—*A Season for Shariton Park*. Give the sneak peek a read! After that, I plan to bust out a time travel series of six (possibly more) that involves many different tropes we all love (friends to lovers, enemies to lovers, forbidden love and all that jazz). Plus, you'll get to follow characters through war-ridden Spain during the Napoleonic War and aboard Naval ships.

Now don't go thinking I only write time travel, because I don't. I've got some Regency, suspense romances, romantic comedies, and a cozy mystery with a bit of ghosts and comedy thrown in—all of which are completed and waiting for editing. If you can't wait to read all of this crazy that's been going on in my head, then follow me on Instagram and Facebook for updates on what's new.

AUTHORCHRISTINEMWALTER

A sneak peek at *A Season for Shariton Park...*

Chapter One

1812 England, Ruth

My decision to skip a meal before the night's event had not been wise of me. Nervous anticipation of the ball had prevented me from taking even a bite of our cook's delicious pastries. Now, the odors of London caused my stomach to boil like a simmering stew. The drizzle had stopped only a short time after it began, which meant it had not rained enough to rid the London streets of its daily grime and stench. Given the number of horses passing through, stepping from the carriage to the Bowers' walkway proved challenging, but I traversed it well enough.

I pressed a hand to my stomach. *Please, let my dreams come true tonight.*

I held my gloved hand over my nose and hurried inside the open door after my brother, Charles, and his wife, Celeste. Our smiling hosts stood in the foyer next to the ballroom's entry with its high ceilings, crown moldings, and arched windows lit by chandeliers and collections of wall sconces.

"Miss Elsegood!" I heard my name and turned to answer. Mrs. Bower smiled, her plump face as rosy as ever and bulbous eyes made larger by the blue of her gown.

"Mrs. Bower, I cannot tell you how delighted I am to be here," I half lied, smiling. "What a grand party it is." I took her hand in mine, and we both curtsied.

"It is always a pleasure to have you, Miss Elsegood. And you will be even more delighted, I am sure when you learn that a certain some-one is here tonight," she laughed, her large chest jiggling up and down.

"I am sure I do not know of whom you speak." I forced myself not to search the room but kept my eyes steadily upon her.

"Come now, Miss Elsegood. Do not toy with me. I know where your heart lies. He has paid you a great attention over the last few weeks. I am quite certain I will be hearing wedding bells soon." She did not give me a chance to reply before she turned to greet the guest in line behind me.

I greeted her husband, then followed Charles and Celeste into the sparsely decorated ballroom. The doors at the far side stood open, letting in the cool night air, which drifted up from the London streets and over the hundred or so guests who mingled within. However, little improvement was made, as London streets were not known for their fresh, clean air, after all.

Celeste laid her fingertips on my upper arm and whispered, "Ruth, keep clear of Mrs. Reid. It looks as though she has had too much already."

I followed her line of sight and spotted Mrs. Reid's red face. I nodded, trailing behind Celeste and Charles to an open alcove. Celeste rested her cheek against Charles's shoulder for the briefest of moments in a gesture of affection. Four years previous, I had joyfully watched my only brother wed my dearest friend, who had mysteriously entered our lives from the twenty-first century. I had rejoiced in their union every day since, not only for her welcome companionship, admirable intelligence, and wild stories of a time we could hardly comprehend but also due to her genuine sisterhood. Seeing the two of them even more in love today warmed my heart . . . and filled me with envy.

I found Captain John Hughes among the crowd, the "certain someone" Mrs. Bower had mentioned. He stood straight and tall, speaking with another gentleman, most likely about politics—his favorite topic next to horse racing. I smiled when he noticed me. He winked behind his comrade's back and made his way through the throng to join me.

I had thought of Captain John Hughes every day since our first meeting soon after I arrived in London, although he did not begin to call on me until later in the season.

Celeste gave me a pointed look, then nodded toward Charles when she noticed the Captain's trajectory. I glanced at Charles' stiff posture. My brother showed less enthusiasm than Celeste on the subject of my affection. I cannot say I blamed him. On more than one occasion, he had remarked that a young lady such as myself should seek a gentleman of good fortune who stood to inherit a title. Captain Hughes would inherit the title of Earl only if something should happen to his elder brother. Thus, his pursuit of a military career to make his way in the world.

His attention toward me came as a relief. People had begun to talk. I knew they whispered that my youth was fading and I was well on my way to spinsterhood. I nearly believed their cruel gossip. Celeste was my saving grace. I could always count on her to set them straight. After all, I was only four and twenty, though at times I felt older.

"Good evening, Ruth. You look enchanting." John bowed over my hand, keeping his eyes locked with mine.

My heart leaped at the sound of my name on his lips. I had not permitted him to use my given name, but I did not mind in the least. *Does this mean he has decided? Am I to be wed?* "I am glad you think so. It took me hours to become this enchanting."

"Now, Ruth, lying does not suit you. You are a natural beauty— anyone can see that." He glanced down, brushed his fingertips against my arm, and locked eyes with me again. "Your beauty is the envy of all

263

the *ton*."

Can he possibly love me? Does he see beyond my freckled face and full cheeks?

My face warmed at his compliment. "How would you know what the *ton* think of beauty?" My voice cracked, and the pain in my throat filled my eyes with tears. I blinked hard and resisted the urge to rub my neck.

"Are you feeling quite well, sweet Ruth?" he asked distractedly, his eyes following something across the room. "You sound a little hoarse."

I hesitated, wishing he had not noticed. It took great effort to maintain my serene expression with the mysterious and persistent pain as of late. It frightened me. Voicing my weakness and discomfort would only make it more real. Before I could reply, an acquaintance approached, wishing to speak to him.

He paused before whispering in my ear, "You will save the supper dance for me?"

"Of course." My heart fluttered in a joyful flurry, hoping it would not be our only dance of the evening.

The ensuing hours crept slowly by. Several gentlemen asked me to dance, and I obliged reluctantly, wishing to save what little energy I had for Captain Hughes. My gaze moved through the room in search of him. With a wistful heart, I watched the supper dance come and go without a sign of him. Had he left the ball on some urgent business? Had some tragedy befallen him? In my mind, I continued to make excuses for him when I overheard a lady mention some "juicy bit of news" to Charles and Celeste, standing beside me at the edge of the room.

"There must be some mistake," Celeste protested.

"No, indeed. He was found in the library with her, wrapped in an embrace. Such shocking behavior requires that a match be made." She sounded like a clucking hen gloating over a choice worm. "*Scandalous*, to be sure!"

"But are you sure the gentleman was Captain Hughes?" Charles asked, looking as if he'd love to run the man through.

My chest constricted, gripping my lungs to the point they may never fill again. *No. Not my Captain.* Celeste's hand clamped down on my arm.

"Of that, there is no doubt," the lady replied with satisfaction.

Another clucking hen, in the form of Mrs. Reid, hurried to our side and hiccupped, "Have you heard? Everyone is in an uproar. Captain Hughes is engaged to Miss Webb!"

Celeste glanced surreptitiously at me. I avoided her gaze and swallowed hard, raising my fan to my face. My eyes fell upon a young couple by the windows, speaking to one another with their heads bowed together. The lady's eyes were downcast, and her cheeks were pink with pleasure. Pain shot through my heart like a bullet hitting its mark, and I could not draw proper breath. *I hate them.*

The first clucking hen placed her hand upon my arm, bringing me back to the conversation. "I must say I am surprised, for I thought his affections were more drawn to *you*, my dear. I expected to hear of your engagement these two weeks!"

"Perhaps he thought Miss Webb's forty thousand pounds preferable to my own thirty-two," I replied, my words sharp. "If you will excuse me." I nodded curtly and hurried quickly away, needing room to breathe.

I hated this. Not just tonight. All of it. Over the last few years, I had increasingly felt as though I had a price written on my person, advertising my worth. The buyer would stop, assess the merchandise, and move on when a more valuable object stepped into view. I was tired of feeling like a banknote. I wanted someone to *love* me.

How could I have been so mistaken? He seemed genuine in his affections and was attentive and kind. He had made me blush on more than one occasion and caused my heart to flutter. Now I felt as if my heart were tied to my ankles, and I was dragging it through the room for all to see and step on.

"Would you like to return home, Ruth?" Celeste hurried to my side as I made my way out into the crowded hall.

I answered without looking at her. "I want to go home . . . to Shariton Park. I have had enough of London." Someone bumped my shoulder, and a sharp pain pierced my neck. I winced and gingerly put my hand on the spot.

Celeste gave the signal to Charles, and we quickly said farewell to our hosts. I carefully hid the turbulence in my heart during the short ride to our London home. When we arrived, I changed into my nightgown and lay safely in bed before I let myself feel the pain. My body racked with sobs, further irritating my aching neck. The unfairness made me want to break something, just as my heart shattered. I clenched the pillows, wishing I could tear them apart, but my strength was spent. I could only lie there and weep.

* * *

Present Day Denver, Colorado, Abbie

I was ready. So ready to get out of dodge. Rocking back and forth on the balls of my feet, I waited for the line in front of me to grow shorter. The cheers grew louder as my peers stepped onto the stage to receive their diplomas. I'd waited for this day for ages. The only other day I'd looked forward to with as much anticipation was my eighteenth birthday, which I had celebrated more than two months ago, on April 1st. With that and graduation all but behind me, I was finally free.

"Abbie Lambert."

I stepped forward into the spotlight from backstage. There was some applause, but no cheers. I shook hands with the principal and a few other people I didn't recognize, and was handed my diploma by the last person in line. I smiled at the camera and returned to my seat.

I didn't try to search for anyone I knew—no one would be there. My father's permanent residence was in prison, an obvious no-show—not that it mattered. I'd never met him and only thought about him when my friends' dads were around. My mother flitted in and out of my life so often that her coming and going gave me whiplash. My grandmother, who took me in each time my mother decided to split, passed away more than a year ago. At last, for the past nine months, my luck had taken a turn for the better when my friend's family opened their home to me. I owed them everything.

Kacie's name sounded over the chaos. She was one of the last to receive her diploma. I watched her wave to her cheering family, and I called out, clapping along with them. The crowd settled down the moment someone began to speak again.

Oh, come on! Not another speech!

I leaned forward with my elbows on my knees. My palms pushed my cheeks into my eyes, forcing them into a squint. *It would be much more interesting if the speaker had a guitar.* Too much energy for the anticipation of the future kept me at the edge of my seat, ready to bolt for the door. It felt like an eternity before we could finally participate in the traditional throwing of the cap. The moment it ended, I raced outside. Kacie's parents cried and kissed us both. I returned each hug and kiss, thanking them repeatedly for all they'd done for me over the years. They were wonderful to take me into their home and treat me as one of their own.

"Abbie!" Someone called from behind me. I turned and my eyes landed on the source of my greatest excitement the past few weeks. "Grace!" I threw my arms around her.

"Green?" She took a lock of my long hair in her hands and examined it closely.

I laughed and batted her hand away. "Yeah. I tried to dye it with blue Kool-Aid last night, but with my blond hair, it turned green. Figures, right? I would've used real hair color if I hadn't been saving up for our big adventure."

"Speaking of, our flight leaves in four hours, so we should get going. Traffic's only going to get worse."

I held up my hand. "Let me say goodbye to my friends first."

She nodded and waited amid the noisy crowd.

I wended through the crowd, deftly dodging a large family group, all gesturing adamantly with their arms, on my way back to Kacie. "Hey, I need to get going. My flight leaves soon."

"I'm going to miss you." Her spiky hair poked my ear when we hugged.

"I'll miss you, too."

"When you get to France, don't forget to kiss a French man for me. Maybe a Scottish one, too," she said, wiggling her eyebrows.

I gave a snarky laugh. "Yeah, like I'm going to walk up to some French guy and kiss him."

"If he was cute, I totally would."

"If I were to kiss any foreign man, it would be an Irish man. They have the best accents." I placed my hand over my heart, sighed, and fluttered my lashes.

"Seriously, though, be careful and keep your distance from Ray. You have plans to go to college, after all."

I scrunched my nose. "Why would I hook up with Ray? He's Grace's cousin, and he's *old*."

"He's only five years older than you."

My stomach twisted, as it did every time I spoke with Kacie or her mom about my trip—and my tour guide. They were right. The group wasn't ideal, but it was my only opportunity to travel before real life began. "Don't flip out. I'll keep my distance." I took hold of the bottom of my graduation gown and pulled it over my head to reveal jean shorts and a T-shirt. I pushed my many bracelets back down my arm and handed over my cap and gown. "Could you turn these back in for me?"

"Sure thing. Have fun."

After saying my goodbyes, I followed Grace to her cousin's car. Ray parked in a "No Parking" zone, kept the engine running, and slumped behind the wheel beside another guy riding shotgun. My insides felt as though they'd all switched places. I hadn't mentioned to the Zimmermans that Ray's friend was also traveling with us. If I had, they really would've put their foot down. Not that they had any say in the matter, but I liked giving them the impression that they did. Mason's numerous tattoos and piercings would've done little to ease Kacie's parents toward acceptance. Fortunately, his bad-boy reputation and rumors of the girls he'd dated remained secret. Even Kacie hadn't heard the whispers.

Well, the gossip didn't matter much. If Ray wanted a friend who'd taken French class and might help with the language barrier, it was fine and dandy with me. Coincidentally, French class had a lot to do with the rumors, and they were not about french bread or french fries. What did I care if he practiced more than the language with the girls in class? He was a good guy . . . just misunderstood.

My conclusion did little to ease my nerves as my insides still protested.

"I know you're thinking it, and yes, your backpack *is* in the trunk. I didn't forget it." Grace opened the back passenger door and climbed in. I followed.

"You got my guitar, too, right?" I asked.

"Yep."

I settled into the seat and buckled up. "Hey, Mason. Hey, Ray."

"Hey, Abbie," they said together.

"Are you ready? By tomorrow you'll be eating corned beef and cabbage," Mason said in his best Irish accent, which sucked.

269

I laughed. "Can't wait." The four of us had spent a month planning this trip, which would last the entire summer. It was going to be unforgettable.

Read the rest of Ruth's story this winter in

A Season for Shariton Park

Acknowledgments

There ain't no way in h-e-double-hocky-sticks I could have published on my own. There are so many people to thank, my head is spinning. First, I'd like to thank my children and my hunk of sugar lovin' husband for giving me time and support to write. Thank you to my editors, Alexa, Lynne, Lauri, and Shelley, for the crap load of junk you had to shift through to polish my work to what it is now. If there are any mistakes, they're all on me. Sometimes I can't see what's right in front of my face, so they are lifesavers. A huge shout out and thanks to those at Eschler Editing for the beautiful cover. Thanks to my family and friends who have encouraged me in getting my stories out there. A great big appreciation to Lynette Taylor, you were the first to push me to write, so thanks for giving me confidence to do so. Traci Hunter Abramson, thanks for the pat on the back, the kindness, and the inspiration to keep going. Thanks to my Sweet Tooth Critique group for all your feedback. Also my ANWA writer's group. You ladies rock! Thanks to all the Youtubers and other authors on social media who have shared their publishing stories and advice with the world. It's a huge support to those starting off.

And thank you to my readers!

Here's to dreams and many more stories! Cheers!

About Christine M Walter

Christine adores her husband, her three adult*ish* children, and her attention-seeking dog, Chewbacca, so much that she'll pause writing and reading just for them. Well, most of the time. When she's not drawn to writing, she often spends time in lego building, painting, drawing, hiking, rock collecting, and off-roading through saguaro cactuses near her home in Arizona. Christine's artwork has been featured in the novel *Blackmoore* by Julianne Donaldson, as well as in the movie *8 Stories*. Christine has been the recipient of multiple awards in the first chapter contests and most recently won honorable mention for a first page contest from Gutsy Great Novelist. Seeing new places and experiencing new cultures are top on her list of desires. In fact, her sense of adventure inspired her and her family to sell their home, move into a 400-square-foot RV, and travel the country simply to see and enjoy life outside of the norm. Best year ever!

You can reach Christine by following her on Instagram.

Insta- @AuthorChristineMWalter

Check out my website at authorchristinemwalter.com and sign up for my newsletter!

AUTHORCHRISTINEMWALTER

Milton Keynes UK
Ingram Content Group UK Ltd.
UKHW022234280324
440175UK00017B/1241

9 798224 610860